Praise

Blood of the White Witch

"*Of Witches and Warlocks* is a series that only gets better. *Blood of the White Witch* has passion, romance, excitement and shocks that you will never see coming - everything I could ever want in a book. Lacey Weatherford had me hooked from the very first word and I couldn't put it down. Best series I have read all year!"

~Lyndsey Rushby, Reviewer for Heaven, Hell and Purgatory

"*Blood of the White Witch* delivers plenty of thrills and excitement. You will be mesmerized by Portia and Vance's chemistry from the start, it's a true love story that compels you to hope for their togetherness and survival."

~Susan Mann, Susan K Mann Reviews

"From the hot, blood pounding, kisses in the beginning, to the climatic moments at the end, *Blood of the White Witch* is guaranteed to hold your heart hostage and keep you mesmerized in your seat. Drawn into a story of deep love and wild desperation, prepare yourself for an all-night reading marathon because this is Portia and Vance at their very finest!"

~Belinda Boring, The Bookish Snob

"Blood of the White Witch is filled with danger, romance, intrigue, trust, deception, and love. The story starts off right where we left off in book two and the plot hits the ground running. Once again Lacey has created a phenomenal story that keeps you turning the pages!"

~Beverly Sharp, The Wormhole

Of Witches and Warlocks

Blood of the White Witch

Book Three

By Lacey Weatherford

Moonstruck Media
Arizona

ISBN-13: 978-1463764265
ISBN-10: 146376426X
Published by

Moonstruck Media
Arizona

This book is also available in ebook format.
http://www.ofwitchesandwarlocks.com

DEDICATION

For my beautiful niece, Larissa Lunt. Without you, your idea, and your thirst for more, this book would have never existed.

For my muse, and gifted actor, Matt Lanter. Thank you for being you and helping Vance to come alive in my imagination!

And for "The Vance Gang". Here's to world domination!

ACKNOWLEDGEMENTS

There are so many people to thank when it comes to doing a project like this. I have had the most wonderful support team around me.

First off, I would like to thank my core group of readers who often proof read for me and let me know what does and doesn't work for them. To the Queen Bee "alpha" reader extraordinaire, Belinda. You have been more help than you will ever know. Many hugs and kisses from me! To my wonderful group of "beta" readers, Chalene, Misti, Candy, Lena, Jenny, Dayna, James, Kamery, Jake, Kysee, and of course the ones who started it all, Connie and Larissa, my love and gratitude go out to you as well.

This go around, I have to add a very special group of people to my list, a group affectionately known to the world as "The Vance Gang". These lovely ladies are spread all over the globe and they have done wonders to help with the marketing and spreading the news about these books. I don't add names, because they know who they are, and since the numbers of this group are growing daily I don't want to leave anyone out, but THANK YOU for all that you do!

Lacey Weatherford

Chapter 1

This was something very unusual— at least it was for most sixteen-year-old girls.

The fact I was even getting to experience this now had been the result of a huge compromise on behalf of my parents. They wanted it to happen at a much later date, but the circumstances changed, and the situation demanded we change with it. The discussions had been long and arduous, the pros and cons weighed heavily before any type of agreement was reached. Even then I was pretty sure my mom and dad were still having terrible misgivings, though I could see they were trying to put on a brave face and be supportive for my sake. I appreciated that.

"There," my best friend Shelly said. She finished what she was doing and stepped back to survey the result. "You look beautiful!"

I turned to look at my reflection in the ceiling-to-floor mirror. I didn't even recognize myself, but I agreed with her assessment without one ounce of conceit in my heart.

I paused to take everything in. The dress was perfect. The square-cut neckline, the tightly fitted bodice which led down into the full, bejeweled taffeta skirt with a bubble hem complete with a chapel train, looked as if they had been made specifically to enhance every turn and curve of my body.

My long black hair was piled intricately in becoming swoops and swirls on the top of my head and had tiny pearl pins running throughout the design. A simple pearl-adorned comb had been inserted in the back of my hairdo, and my straight shear veil hung softly from it.

Shelly placed a bouquet of fresh red roses, bunched together and tied with a white satin ribbon, into my hands.

"You're going to knock Vance's socks off!" she said, a soft smile spreading across her face.

"I hope so!" I laughed, and I thought of my handsome groom, who was undoubtedly doing something similar to this, elsewhere in the building.

We'd gone through so much together in the last few months. Magic, mystery, and mayhem had been a large part of our existence and continued to be so. In fact, it was the reason this wedding was taking place eight months earlier than planned, but I didn't want to think about that right now. I just wanted to savor every moment of this day.

"Oh! Portia!" my mom said, and I turned to see her enter the room, her red formal dress suit rustling slightly as she closed the door.

She stopped to look at me, and several emotions passed through her eyes. I could see love and happiness there, right before worry and doubt crept in. I noticed the moisture that began to fill them, and she reached a hand up to pat her perfectly coiffed dark hair, trying to hide her reaction.

"Mom, don't you dare start with that already!" I chastened her. "You'll get me started, and it'll ruin my makeup."

"Sorry, sweetie," she said with a slight laugh allowing a huge smile to cross her face, and she came closer so she could hug me. "You're just so beautiful!"

"Thanks, Mom," I replied, hugging her back for several long moments before leaning back to question her. "Is the photographer here yet? I want to get a picture of the three of us together."

"Yes. She's waiting outside. I wanted to make sure you were ready first." She turned back toward the door.

"I'll get her, Stacey," Shelly said to my mom, and she rustled past in her dark red satin dress that hugged her flawless form. She looked more to me like a Barbie doll than I'd ever seen her before.

The photographer came in and introduced herself politely to me before she posed us together, draping my dress out around me, so she could take a picture of the three of us in front of the giant mirror.

"Beautiful!" she breathed while her expensive camera clicked away in rapid succession. "I just grabbed a couple of shots of the groom and his best man before I came in here," she added when she paused, straightening so she could look at me. "You two are going to make a fabulous looking couple."

"I want to see the pictures! May I?" I said to her in excitement, moving toward her slightly.

"No!" Shelly said, stepping in between us. "It's bad luck to see the groom before the wedding. You know that!"

"In a picture?" I asked in a laughing tone as I stared back at her. "I don't think it applies."

"It does if he is all dressed in a tuxedo, ready for his wedding!" She folded her arms in front of her chest, giving me a hard look to signify she wasn't going to budge on the issue.

I looked over at my mom for some backup.

"I agree," she said with a shrug though she at least tried to look a little bit apologetic.

"Fine!" I waved my hand in dismissal of the subject before looking back at the photographer. "Forget I even asked."

There was a knock on the door once more, and I heard my dad's voice call from the other side.

"Is it safe to enter?"

"Come in, Sean," my mom answered him.

My dad entered the room wearing a black tuxedo with a dark red tie and a matching vest that had black pinstripes running through it.

"Pumpkin, you look great!" His eyes lit up when he saw me, and he walked over to place a light kiss upon my cheek.

"You're working that tux pretty good yourself." I smiled back at him, thinking he did indeed look very handsome.

He did an overly exaggerated pirouette for us. "I don't look too good, do I?" he asked, humor flashing in his eyes. "I wouldn't want to show up the bride."

"Whatever!" my mom said laughingly, and she playfully slapped at his shoulder. "Don't tease her at such a moment, Sean!"

"Perhaps you'd prefer for me to tease you?" my dad responded, and he sidled up against her. "I must say it's obvious where Portia gets her beauty from." He grinned wickedly.

There was another slight rap at the door, interrupting their banter, and this time the wedding coordinator stepped into the room.

"Are you all ready?" she asked with a smile, looking around at each of us. "Everything is set to go."

I nodded, suddenly feeling a wave of butterflies rush through my stomach. "I'm ready," I replied as I placed a hand over my midsection, trying to settle them.

"All right," she said, turning to my mom. "Let's go get you seated, shall we? Shelly, you go wait by the door to the chapel, and I'll give you the signal. Vance and Brad are already at the altar."

Shelly picked up her white bouquet of flowers, hurrying after them, leaving only my dad and me together in the quiet space.

"It's time," Dad said looking at me seriously now. "Are you sure you're ready for all this?"

"I've never been more ready for anything in my life," I replied, and I stepped over to take his arm. "The real question is are *you* ready for all this?" I watched his expression carefully.

"It's definitely required some adjusting to," he replied honestly. He reached out, gently touching his free hand to my face. "I certainly never imagined my daughter getting married at the age of sixteen or the fact I'd be agreeing to it. That being said, however, I do realize the two of you are mature for your age. You've proven on several occasions you're old enough to handle things on your own. I think it will work out just fine."

"Thanks for having faith in us, Dad." I smiled, squeezing his arm tenderly, knowing exactly how difficult it had been for him to do so.

"My little girl is all grown up," he said softly. He looked at me, and I felt his hand tremble against me momentarily before he dropped it back to his side.

He led me gently out of the room and into the hallway. We walked in silence together until we stopped a few feet outside the door to the chapel.

Shelly was standing there in the entrance, and as the music began, she took her cue from the director to begin her march down the aisle.

The doors to the chapel were closed behind her, and the wedding planner ushered me into place, making sure my dress was spread out perfectly behind me, and my veil was hanging just right.

I heard the music change and the wedding march begin to play on the other side of the door. I slipped my hand back through my dad's arm, resting it lightly at his elbow, wondering if he felt my slight nervous tremble as it rested there.

"I love you, Pumpkin," my dad said, and he lightly patted my hand.

"I love you too, Daddy," I replied with a smile as the butterflies reappeared and began to dance anew in my stomach.

The doors moved, swinging slowly open to reveal the flower-decorated aisle in front of me. I lifted my head, searching for the only thing I was interested in seeing at that moment.

My eyes settled on him, and I saw his breath catch when he saw me. A slow smile spread across his face, lighting the whole world in front of me.

I would've forgotten to move, I was so mesmerized by his appearance, but my dad placed his hand gently on mine and began walking me toward the glorious figure who stood there waiting. I couldn't see anything besides him—only him.

Vance Mangum. My Vance.

My heart began beating harder with every step I took. He was perfectly groomed as usual— his dark hair textured in the perfect messy style I loved, his white teeth gleaming against the dimples of his smile, and the slight cleft in his chin. His bright blue eyes fairly flashed with anticipation as he stood in his black tuxedo, complete with a white vest and tie, looking every inch the powerful man he was. He was breathtaking.

He stepped down to greet me as I approached, taking my trembling hand from my dad, and squeezing it reassuringly, before turning to lead me up in front of the minister.

"I love you," I heard him whisper softly into my head through the uncommon mental connection we shared.

"I love you, too," I replied back into his mind, broadening my smile and glancing over at him.

The minister moved closer to us and began to speak. "Dearly beloved, we are gathered here today...." I felt little shivers of joy race through my body.

I listened intently to every word, but my gaze never left Vance's face, nor did his ever leave mine.

The minister spoke to us about love, commitment, and honor, as well as always being true to each other, before he turned the time over to us to recite our vows.

I went first. "Vance," I started, and I felt as if I would never be able to keep my excited tremor out of my voice. "I give my heart to you completely at this time. My love is my gift to you, never shaking, unfailing. I promise to always stand by your side through thick and thin, to be your helper and your companion. I bind myself to you before God and man, promising to always support you in life and love, even into the next life. I love you." I squeezed his hand meaningfully.

Then he spoke. "Portia, I love you with all my heart. Words fail me in how to describe the depths of my feelings for you. You complete me in every way imaginable; you're everything about me that is good. When I eat, sleep, live, it is always with you in my thoughts. I accept your love and promises, offering mine to you in return. I promise to always love and support you in all your endeavors as we join together as husband and wife. I will love you for eternity." He smiled at me, and I could feel his emotions surging from his body into mine with great force, causing tiny prickles to run over my skin in a wave of desire.

"Do you, Portia Mullins, take Vance Mangum as your legal and lawful husband?" the minister continued. "Do you promise to love, honor, and care for him from this day forward?"

"Yes," I replied, my eyes beginning to water as I stared up into Vance's loving gaze.

He turned to Vance. "Do you, Vance Mangum, take Portia Mullins as your legal and lawful wife? Do you promise to love, honor, and care for her from this day forward?"

"Yes," he answered, and the emotion in his eyes equaled mine as small bits of moisture gathered there.

"Do you have the rings?" the minister asked.

Brad and Shelly both stepped forward to hand us our rings. I handed my bouquet off to Shelly and turned back toward Vance.

"Portia, place the ring on Vance's left ring finger and repeat after me," the minister said.

I took the white gold band and slid it gently over his long, masculine finger still unable to control the slight tremors in my hand.

"With this ring, I thee wed, if front of God and these witnesses," I repeated.

Vance took the matching ring he held and slid it tenderly into place.

"With this ring, I thee wed, in front of God and these witnesses." He lifted his gaze back to my eyes.

"Let it be known these two are now joined together in the eyes of God, the eyes of the church, and in the eyes of man. What God has joined together, let no man put asunder. I now pronounce you husband and wife."

Vance didn't wait for the minister to tell him to kiss his bride, instead grabbing me up in a giant bear hug and kissing me passionately in front of everyone as they burst into cheers and applauding.

I wrapped my arms tightly around his neck, not wanting to let go. The kiss went on a lot longer than decorum dictated it should have, but I didn't mind. Finally, he stepped back from me, leaving both of us breathless, but his eyes didn't leave me nor did the smile that was spread widely across his face.

"I present to you Mr. and Mrs. Vance Mangum," the minister said to the crowd and we turned to face them as they cheered again.

Vance took me by the hand in an iron grip and led me back down the aisle, through the chapel and out into the hallway. He didn't stop there though, and I was surprised when he pulled me quickly into the first room we came to, shutting the door behind us.

He grabbed me, pulling me flush up against his body and really kissed me, like I knew he wanted to do out there, letting all of his passion move into that moment. His mouth slanted hard over mine, demanding all, yet giving all of his in return as he ran his hands up and down over my back.

I closed my eyes and savored the feel of him, pressed as close as he could get to me, not leaving a millimeter of space between our bodies. I loved every breathless second of his heated assault. Little sparks of lightning flashed through me and over my skin as his hot breath mingled with mine, and I felt goose bumps pop out on my skin as a result.

I dropped my bouquet on the floor without a care, and wound my arms tightly around his neck. I stood on my tiptoes to reach him better, as I became all consumed by his kiss.

For several long moments, our mouths danced together in an ancient rhythm of love, speaking intimacies to one another that couldn't be shared with mere words.

"Wow! You look amazing!" he said when we broke apart, gasping for some air, and his eyes flitted over the entire length of my body. "I've never seen anything in my life that looked so good."

"I was just thinking the same thing about you," I replied with a grin while I looked at his lips which were swollen a bit from his fervent kissing of me.

"I love you," he said. He stepped back against me, this time cradling my face gently in both of his hands, running one of his thumbs tenderly over my lips as he stared.

"I love you, too." I smiled looking into his beautiful blue eyes, unable to tear my gaze away.

"Dang reception!" he muttered under his breath while he watched my face, and I understood exactly what he meant.

I laughed at his disgruntled expression. "Patience, Vance," I spoke. I placed my hand lightly against his cheek, caressing the hard, masculine planes there. "The time will come soon enough, as I am sure you know, but right now we have guests."

"They can wait," he said, and he pulled me hard against him once more, kissing me again, trapping me effectively in his iron grasp.

I willingly wound my arms back around his neck and wished we could just run off together right now. Leaning into the kiss, I felt his tongue trace the contours of my lips. I opened my mouth at his request, following him in his sensual movements until I felt his very emotions would consume me as they raced forcefully through my body, setting me aflame as if he lit a torch of fire to my skin. I never wanted him to stop, but reality stepped forward, intruding once again, and I pulled away instead, though he did not let me go willingly.

"Come on, Vance. We've been in here kissing for several minutes now. Let's go to our reception before something starts you won't want to stop." I smiled, placing my hand against his finely tailored chest.

"Too late," he said with a grin, though I could see the extreme disappointment in his eyes as he allowed me to take his hand and drag him out the door.

The wedding coordinator was standing outside with a knowing look on her face, and I briefly wondered if anyone would be at all surprised by our kiss-reddened faces and my obvious lack of makeup around my mouth. She led us back to the bride's room, so I could retouch my makeup, while she kept Vance occupied in conversation just outside the door. Then she directed us down the hall to the reception room where all our guests had been shuttled.

A man at the door stood at our approach and opened it for us, calling out to the crowd.

"Please, welcome Mr. and Mrs. Mangum!" his thunderous voice boomed into the room before us.

We stepped into the lavishly decorated space, with its fragrant red roses in large crystal vases, silk-draped tables, and sheer-fabric-lined walls with soft lighting, to greet our guests. Immediately we were wrapped in a throng of well-wishers, shaking hands, hugging, and giving kisses.

Slowly we weaved our way across the room toward the head table, which was set in fine china, crystal, and silverware, stopping to visit many times along the way. When we were finally seated, we enjoyed a lovely meal of roasted meats, fruits, salads, and many other concoctions, which a truly delightful chef had prepared for us and our company.

Afterward, when the dinner portion was complete, Vance and I headed out to the dance floor for our first dance as a wedded couple. He pulled me into his arms, and I was surprised at how well we moved together. We never really had the opportunity to dance with one another before this time in our relationship.

He held me tightly in his arms as we swayed, his eyes never leaving mine, and though we didn't speak any words to each other, many thoughts and feelings were conveyed in those precious moments between us. The rest of the room slowly melted away from my vision, and he was at that moment the only other being in my universe. It was as if time had come to a complete standstill around us as we held each other in a loving embrace. It was a magical moment, a true union of our two souls. Guiltily, I wondered if our guest were beginning to feel neglected since the two of us were so completely absorbed with each other. I didn't mean to be rude, but he was all I was interested in right now.

"They understand," he said as he moved across the floor with me, never breaking his gaze from me.

"Mmm?" I asked, continuing to look up at him with starry eyes, his words not really registering.

"Our guests. They won't be offended we can't stop looking at each other. That's what you were thinking, right?" A slight grin tipped up the corner of his mouth, barely revealing one of his beloved dimples.

I nodded with a dreamy smile, suddenly wishing I could kiss that charming little spot on his face.

"I love you," I said again, enjoying the feel of his strong, muscular body.

He bent forward and kissed my lips. I responded instantly, moving my arms up over his shoulders and slipping my fingers up into the back of his hair. It registered somewhere in the back of my mind that we had quit moving to the music, but the thought was quickly brushed aside as the heat of his tender touch suddenly intensified.

We forgot we had an audience, and he ran his hand up my back, sliding underneath my veil, over my neck. I felt a soft moan escape my lips as he pressed my head harder against his, feeling completely wrapped up in the pure bliss of the moment.

Suddenly I was yanked away unceremoniously from Vance's grasp, and we both stumbled slightly at the intrusion. I found myself wrapped in my dad's arms.

"Save it for the honeymoon, son," he whispered with a laugh, and he reached out to pat Vance on the shoulder before he spun me out onto the dance floor.

I blushed deeply at the comment, glancing back apologetically toward Vance who was standing stock still where we had left him, with a slightly amused and somewhat bewildered expression.

We spent the rest of the evening visiting and dancing with family and friends until it was time to cut our wedding cake.

Our cake was a simple, but elegant, three-tiered masterpiece, frosted in white, with red roses draped down it in a spiral. Artfully styled frosting gave the appearance of a basket weave around the sides with little edible pearls delicately placed throughout the design.

It almost seemed a shame to cut into something so beautiful, but we picked up the knife together, slicing gently into the red velvet concoction before removing a section and placing it on a china plate. I broke off a small piece of it and fed it with my fingers demurely to Vance, who made a purposeful point to lick the ends of my frosting-covered appendages as I did it. This caused little shivers to course involuntarily up and down my arm at the contact.

He was equally kind when it came to feeding me mine, carefully placing the dessert in my mouth, trying not to damage my makeup, though a tiny amount of frosting made its way onto the corner of my lips. Vance, of course, took complete advantage of the situation as he swooped in to kiss me, licking it away with his tongue in the process.

Everyone cheered loudly as the photographer moved in, snapping away with her camera, forever preserving the moment for us on film.

“Can we get out of here now ... please?” Vance pleaded under his breath with a smile, pulling back away from my face.

I nodded. “Absolutely,” I purred back at him before extending my hand out. “Lead the way.”

I was surprised when he turned instead to address our guests. “I’d like to thank all of you for making the trip here on such short notice to support us this evening,” his strong voice boomed out to the crowd around us. “But the time has arrived for us to bid you goodnight. Feel free to stay and enjoy yourselves for as long as you would like.”

He grabbed my hand in his, interlocking our fingers together, and we waved at our guests as we ran through the throng toward the door that led to the hall.

Many happy well-wishers followed us, as we made our way out of the building and to the waiting limousine which graced the entrance.

We waved once again before we climbed in, the chauffeur closing the door behind us.

As soon as we were out of sight of the venue, Vance leaned over to wrap his arms around my waist, sliding me against him and began truly kissing me in earnest.

I laughed, placing my hand against his chest and attempted to push him back a little, feeling my blush creep over my face.

"Calm down!" I said. "We don't want to scare the driver with our public display of affection."

"We have privacy glass," he mumbled, and he hardly broke stride in his pursuit of me, leaning in to place a lingering kiss against the curve of my neck.

"That may be, but we've waited this long—you can wait a few minutes longer." I shoved him away even harder. "I want it to be just right. You know ... special."

He smiled at me, sighing before he released me.

"Fine," he said drawing out the word in exasperation, reaching out to take me by the hand. "I should've known you'd make me work for it."

"Hey!" I replied, slapping him lightly on the shoulder with my rose bouquet. "What's that supposed to mean?"

"It means you're a tease." He laughed, before giving me a wink, enjoying toying with me.

"Whatever!" I turned away slightly, pretending to be annoyed with his behavior.

He let go of my hand and reached over to hook his finger under my chin, turning me back to face him.

"I love you." He smiled, looking deep into my eyes, and my heart began beating faster.

"I know." I smiled back, unable to break my gaze away. "And I love you, too."

We pulled up to the towering hotel, and the driver exited the vehicle, coming to open our door for us.

"Thank you!" Vance said with a grin, tipping the man generously after he helped me to exit the vehicle.

"Many happy wishes to you both, too, sir."

Vance pulled me quickly and anxiously through the lobby, much to the delighted stares of several people passing by. We found our way into the elevator, which was thankfully empty, because he kissed me enthusiastically again during the ride up, not stopping until the doors opened on our floor.

He pulled me out after him, and we ran together down the hall like a pair of giddy schoolchildren to the penthouse suite he booked for us.

He slipped a key card from his pocket, opening the door before he turned back to me with a grin. He picked me up, swinging me into his arms. I gave a squeal of delight, and he proceeded to carry me over the threshold, kicking the door closed behind us with his foot. He carried me through the main living space and into another dark room.

Suddenly everything was bathed in warm glow as what looked to be a million white, pillar candles of various sizes flamed magically to life, and I could see we were standing in a beautifully decorated gigantic master suite.

Soft music filled the air around us, and it was clear to me Vance had been planning ahead for this evening.

"Your room, Mrs. Mangum," he said with a sexy glint in his eye. He let go of my legs, letting me slide slowly down the length of his body, placing me gently back on my feet.

"I love the sound of that," I replied, letting a soft sigh escape from my lips.

"So do I." He leaned in to kiss me again, this time his fingers picking through my hair to pull it free of the pins and restraints, running his hands through it, until it fell around my shoulders. "There. That's better," he said, leaning back to survey it.

"I can't believe we're really married." I reached up, trailing my fingers over the side of his face.

"Believe it," he replied capturing my hand against his cheek, turning to kiss each of my fingers suspended there. He caught me off guard when he swung me off my feet and into his arms.

"You look tired," he said with a sly grin and a wink. "I think I'd better put you down for the night."

I laughed, and he carried me over to the plush bed, where he placed me gently on the soft mattress before climbing on next to me.

He leaned over me, looking at me with all the love in the world radiating from his beautiful blue eyes.

"Do you love me, Vance?" I asked seriously, reaching out to fiddle with his neck tie then pulling it free from his collar.

"More than words can tell," he replied, bending to place a gentle kiss against my lips.

"Then show me," I said, biting a little at my lower lip at the bold words that had just slipped from my mouth.

"With pleasure, baby," he whispered as he bent to place a light kiss there. "With pleasure."

Chapter 2

I was lovingly awakened first thing in the morning by sweet kisses being trailed over my face, neck, and shoulder, sending little shivers of delight racing all over me. Slowly, I opened my eyes, a smile creeping quietly across my face.

"Mmm ...," I let the soft moan roll from my lips. I tried to wrap my brain around what was going on around me, suddenly remembering where I was, who I was with, and why I was with him.

My eyes settled on the handsome face of my husband, who was leaning over me with an expression full of mischief.

"There's my beautiful wife," Vance said with a grin, continuing to feather his kisses over me, speaking in between each one. "I didn't think you were ever going to wake up."

"What time is it?" I asked, slightly groggy, and I looked around for a bedside alarm clock.

"Seven," he replied with a chuckle, without breaking his stride as his face slid down into the crook of my neck.

"Seven! And you're waking me up already?" I complained. "We just got to sleep four hours ago!" I said playfully slapping at his arm.

"I guess you didn't wear me out enough!" he replied with a cocky grin and a slight shrug of one shoulder. "You're going to have to work harder at that." He lifted an interested eyebrow at me.

"I think you're going to kill me before the honeymoon is even over," I laughed, feeling my blush at his attentions creeping over my face.

"That will never happen," he muttered, leaning in to suck at the spot he liked on my neck.

"How do you figure?" I asked turning my head to the side so I could completely enjoy his lavish treatment of me.

"Well, first off," he began, speaking against my skin, and I could feel goose bumps begin to pop up all over my body, "I'd never do anything that would kill you. And second, I don't ever plan our honeymoon being over."

"So we're just going to live in bliss like this for the rest of lives?" I asked, my breath catching in my throat as he hit an extremely sensitive spot.

"Works for me," he replied, and he began to trail his kisses farther down my neck. I reached up to thread my fingers through his hair, pulling him closer.

We finally got up around noon and went into the kitchen for "breakfast," which apparently Vance had ordered for us from room service, but we hadn't stopped to eat.

I blushed at the idea that someone had been in the penthouse delivering our food while we were locked in the bedroom together.

"I like it when you blush like that," Vance said. He picked a strawberry up off a plate, placing it against my lips so I could bite it.

I opened my mouth willingly, not breaking eye contact with him and took a big bite. It turned out to be a very ripe strawberry, and some of the juices squirted out and ran down the side of my mouth.

Vance was there before I could even move, and he licked the spot away with his tongue.

"Mmm ... tasty," he said with a smile, and I knew he wasn't talking about the strawberry.

I blushed even harder. "So what are our plans today?" I asked, trying to direct his attention away from my complete inability to control my own physical reaction to him.

"I'm thinking more of the same, until it's time to catch our flight," he replied, biting into a strawberry of his own.

The mention of our flight brought everything crashing back in upon me, and the reality of our current situation made its way back into my thoughts.

We recently found out Vance's mom, Krista, might still be alive somewhere, being held prisoner by a demon coven.

The information we had been given was she was overseas, somewhere in Scotland, though it hadn't come from the most reliable of sources.

Vance had been about to kill a demon witch from his father's coven by the name of Darcy. Darcy begged for her life and in return imparted this information to us about Krista.

Vance wanted to leave to go search for her immediately. Of course he insisted on me going with him. We had made a pact, after the previous incidents we had been through, not to leave each other behind ever again. It was a vow neither of us was willing to break—for any reason.

My mom and dad were not too keen on the idea of sending their daughter off on a trip halfway around the world with her boyfriend, however. Even though Vance was a legal adult, my fiancé, and he had sworn to protect me, they felt it would be too tempting for us, since we would be alone so much.

The entire coven had just spent a lot of time helping us out in Mexico, so it made things difficult for any of them to follow after us, especially since we were unsure if we were being led on a wild goose chase.

My memories flitted back over the discussion that had taken place just a few days ago.

"Vance," my dad said. "Calm down, son. Why don't you stay here and finish the rest of your senior year? I'll try to gather some more information for you through my connections and see if we can find some more things out. Who even knows if this Darcy girl was being honest? She's a demon after all. There's no sense in running off halfway around the world without getting all the facts."

"You have to be kidding!" Vance replied a bit angrily. "There's no way I'm going to sit here and do nothing while there's a chance she's over there suffering! I'm going as soon as I can make the arrangements."

"And what about Portia?" my dad demanded. "Are you really going to leave her behind again? Even after the way the two of you suffered before?"

"No," Vance said firmly. "She's coming with me. I'll not leave her."

My dad sat up straighter in his chair, leaning forward aggressively while my mom shifted uncomfortably beside him.

"Oh, no she's not!" my dad replied in a low menacing tone. "She's my daughter, and I'll say what she does Vance, not you! I'm not going to have the two of you running off together doing who only knows what. Portia stays here."

I could see this situation was quickly getting out of control and decided to step in.

"Dad," I said softly. "You're misunderstanding what we're asking."

"Which is what?" he asked, his gaze flickering over to me.

"We know how you feel about us being alone, but Vance is very worried about his mom. And you're right. It's extremely hard for us to be apart. We don't want to be separated. So we thought in order to appease you, and help ourselves out as well, we'd ask your permission to let us get married now."

I waited with baited breath for his reaction.

My mom gasped, a hand going to cover her mouth.

My dad jumped to his feet, towering over the top of us.

"What?" he demanded.

"Think about it, Sean," Vance replied, slowly rising to his feet so he could face him. "It makes sense. I know Portia is young, but you have to admit she's also very mature for her age. You know we're going to get married anyway, eventually. It's inevitable with the magical connection between us. I'm trying to respect your wishes here as well in regard to your daughter and her reputation. This seemed to us like the wisest course of action. Why put off something that's going to happen anyway?"

My dad stared hotly at him for a second before turning to walk away a few steps in frustration.

"Absolutely not!" he said, but in a softer voice this time. He turned his head to look at Vance. "Look, son. I know you're worried about your mom, but Portia still has a year and a half of school left. I'm not going to let her throw away her education to go away with you. It's too risky. I think you need to stay here and finish the half year you have left as well."

"We've already discussed this together," Vance replied glancing down at me. "I've contacted a tutoring agency and researched all the particulars. The tutor will help me with testing out so I can get my diploma and will get Portia caught up on everything so she can pick up right where she left off. Both of us have excellent grades, so catching up shouldn't even be an issue. I've done my research, Sean. We aren't running into this like a couple of stupid lovesick kids." He reached down to grab my hand, pulling me to stand up beside him. "We want to respect your opinions, and we'll abide by whatever you decide. We just want you to hear us out and have an honest, open-minded discussion with us."

My dad was quiet for several moments before he finally moved to sit back next to my mom.

"All right then, let's hear it."

The four of us had a very frank and open talk together which lasted over the next several hours. My parents finally decided to begrudgingly give in and see things from our point of view. They gave us their permission to get married.

Vance had to promise my parents repeatedly we would finish school as soon as we returned and we would come back at the earliest possible time.

Technically, Vance should have already been graduated at this point in his life. However, when he had fled from his father, he got behind in school so he had to play catch up after that. So, while he was a little more two years older than I was, we were only a year apart in school.

I had the distinct impression Vance was not at all brokenhearted about finishing school with a tutor and getting married before he graduated. In fact, I'd have ventured to say everything was moving exactly on his preferred timetable. In the past, he made no bones about his desire to marry me as soon possible. He got his wish, and now we were headed to Scotland as husband and wife, something I would have never dreamed possible at this point and time in my existence.

Thankfully, we were still in Las Vegas when all this was decided, which made planning a wedding super easy once we found a chapel we liked.

After the decision was made, we married in just two days' time and were now getting ready to head out on the Scotland part of our honeymoon.

Vance booked our stay at the beautiful Inverlochy Castle in Inverness-shire. Our flight was scheduled to leave this evening from Las Vegas, nonstop to New York, where we would switch planes at JFK and fly to London overnight.

"Hey!" Vance said, calling me back to reality. "No sad faces today." He leaned over to place a kiss under my chin.

"Sorry," I replied, trying to let go of all the worries about what might lie ahead. "I'm just wondering what the future may hold for us."

"We'll think about that later," he said, continuing to nuzzle against me. "Right now, in this moment, everything is just about you and me."

His distraction tactics worked. He kissed my worried thoughts into oblivion, and we finally ended up getting around to finishing breakfast sometime around four o'clock in the afternoon.

After we had eaten, we packed up our belongings, stopped to ship our wedding attire back to Sedona so we wouldn't have to haul it with us, and headed off to the airport to catch our flight. We made it through all the checkpoints just fine and soon were boarded on the plane, and on our way to New York.

"This is much better than the last flight I was on," I said, as I snuggled against Vance's shoulder, remembering back to my flight with his father, Damien, after he kidnapped me.

"I'm sorry you had to go through that," he replied, reaching his arm around so he could pat me gently on the head.

"It's over," I sighed, enjoying the safety I felt in his arms. "Let's not even talk about it."

"Fine by me," he whispered, moving to place a gentle kiss on the top of my head, before resting his head against mine.

Our earlier activities of the day finally caught up with us, and soon we were both fast asleep.

I assumed the rest of the flight was completely uneventful since we both slept deeply until we were awakened several hours later when the pilot's voice came over the loudspeaker, announcing our decent into New York.

I slowly stretched my limbs out, trying to get the blood flowing once again.

"Hi," I said softly, when I looked over to find Vance staring at me with a tender smile on his face.

"Did you sleep well?" He let his eyes travel over me.

I nodded. "I always sleep better when I'm with you."

"Well, it's good we're married then," he replied in a lowered voice, "Because I plan on spending every single night of my life at your side."

I smiled, reaching over to squeeze his hand as the wheels of the plane touched down on the runway.

We disembarked and hurried through the airport to catch our connecting flight to London. We made it easily and settled into the comfy chairs of our first class seats to await take-off. There were definitely going to be perks to having married a multi-millionaire.

Thankfully, though, the money hadn't seemed to change Vance's demeanor, except for the fact he seemed happy to share it with everyone he possibly could.

"How are you feeling?" he asked me with a smile as we waited for departure. "Tired?"

"Actually I'm feeling pretty rested right now after our last flight. Why?" I was suddenly suspicious of the secretive grin on his face.

He leaned in close to my ear so he could whisper. "I thought you might have some interest in joining the mile-high club between here and London," he said seductively, his warm breath caressing my skin near my earlobe, causing tiny goose bumps to break out on my skin.

I pulled back in shock at his comment and slapped his shoulder. "You're going to get us kicked off the plane!" I laughed, flushing crimson from head to toe.

"That color really does look beautiful on you." He laughed, grabbing my chin in his hand, pulling me back before leaning over to kiss me, not caring about who was looking.

When he moved away, he caught the eye of an elderly woman seated across the aisle who was staring at us with a frown over our public display of affection.

"Sorry," he apologized to her with a wink. "We're on our honeymoon."

Her frown changed to a smile, and a knowing light reached her eyes. I could see he had instantly won her over with his charm.

"Congratulations," she said. "I hope you'll have a very happy life together."

"Thank you," we both replied, smiling, before turning to look at each other once again.

We began taxiing down the runway a short time later, and the two of us leaned back against our seats. Vance reached over and took my hand in his, interlocking our fingers together. I looked at them as he absently rubbed his thumb back and forth over mine.

It amazed me how even the smallest gesture of his could convey so many messages to me. It was almost as if I could feel his feelings for me pulsating through his very skin into mine, leaving no doubt in my mind that he loved me with every fiber of his being.

I turned my head so I could look at him as he rested against his seat with his eyes closed. I didn't think I'd ever tire of staring at him—his purposely messed up hair, the strong perfect features, and that wonderful physique, all wrapped up nicely in the humble t-shirt and jeans.

His eyes opened slightly and he looked over at me briefly, with a slight question in his gaze.

"What?" he asked softly as he repositioned his head, closing his eyes once again in relaxed comfort.

"I was just thinking about how I'm never going to get tired of looking at you. You're beautiful," I replied, honestly.

He smiled, as if amused at my comment, but didn't open his eyes.

"You have it all wrong. You're the beautiful one in this relationship."

"No, I'm not," I said shaking my head and I placed a kiss against his cheek.

He turned his head right then, catching me, and the kiss landed full on his mouth. I heard him chuckle slightly and he reached a hand up behind my head, locking my lips in place against his own.

"I love you," he said into my head, his tongue flitting briefly over mine.

"I love you, too," I replied, enjoying his stolen kiss and the pin-prickling waves it was causing to rush madly through my body.

I heard him sigh, and he pulled away from me shaking his head. I realized he was experiencing the same feelings I was.

"Stupid seven hour flight," he grumbled settling back into his seat, his eyes never leaving me as they trailed a hot path over my body.

I laughed at the lustful look in his eyes.

"What are you laughing about?" he asked with a slightly frustrated tone.

"No matter how much you get it's never going to be enough, is it?" I asked more than a little in awe of him and the power of his ardent desires.

"Not bloody likely," he replied with a grin, throwing a little English slang into his accent.

I watched as his gaze traveled up and down me once again, not hiding any of his intentions. My own desires jumped to life as he looked at me like that. Suddenly I felt the same frustration he did.

"It *is* going to be a long flight," I agreed, returning the same come hither look he was flashing at me.

"Well, I did offer a suggestion to help with that," he teased, his eyes sparkling with mischief, and I knew in that moment he would totally follow through with that suggestion if I were to let him.

"As tempting as your offer is, it isn't going to happen," I whispered back.

He sighed heavily at the comment and trailed his gaze over me once more. "I was afraid of that." He grinned. "The proper wife in you is already coming to the surface."

"Sorry to disappoint you." I laughed, and he pulled me into his arms, cuddling me against him.

"Portia, nothing you do is ever a disappointment to me," he said and hugged me tightly.

Chapter 3

We landed at London Heathrow Airport around eight in the morning. After getting off the plane we boarded another small flight to Inverness, Scotland, arriving about an hour and a half later.

We gathered our luggage and met the driver from Inverlochy Castle. He was very friendly and collected our bags from us before leading us out to a beautiful Rolls-Royce Phantom. Vance helped him load our things inside, despite the man's protests he shouldn't worry himself over such things. When they were done, Vance climbed into the car beside me, and the smiling man closed the door behind him.

"Great car," Vance said while he looked around with an appreciative eye at the custom interior.

I nodded, smiling at his male attributes coming to the surface. He rubbed his hand almost reverently over the leather interior, before he sidled up closer to me, lifting my hand and placing it in his lap as he held it.

Our chauffeur's name was Connell. He was a very friendly man, short and stocky in his build with graying hair that looked as though it may have been a flaming shade of red during his younger years. He was dressed informally in sportsman styled tweeds. He pointed out the sites and facts of interest along the trip through the countryside, on our way to the castle. I had to listen to him carefully so I could understand him, since he spoke in a thick Scottish brogue, but it was a delightful tribute to the authenticity of our current experience.

The drive was breathtaking, and we could see the snowcapped mountains around us as well as the icy loch off to our right for most of the way.

When we approached the castle I had to hold my breath for a second just to enjoy the view, my eyes widening in wonder.

Inverlochy Castle was a large granite stone facility that sat at the bottom of some of Scotland's highest mountains. The famous peak of Ben Nevis shadowed overhead, while the castle itself sat on perfectly maintained grounds. The massive structure was framed in by tall trees on the property, which sloped down a gentle decline until it overlooked the gorgeous waters of the loch.

"It's beautiful." I smiled at Vance, unable to think of a grander way to describe the scene.

"Fit for a queen," he replied and squeezed my hand while placing a tender kiss against my neck which gave me a little shiver of excitement down my spine.

The car pulled to a stop, and we exited the vehicle. Vance led me up to the great gothic looking doors while Connell got our luggage, and we went inside to the front desk which was located in the great hall.

After we were checked in and given our room key, Vance followed the bellhop to our room, towing me behind him.

I looked around, taking everything in as we passed by, the beautiful old oak staircase, the grand fireplace invitingly ablaze, and the fine furnishings that held quietly mingling guests here and there in comfortable looking nooks and crannies. The décor was amazing.

The room Vance reserved was called The Queen's Suite, aptly named after a visit from Queen Victoria who had apparently spent a week there at some point during her lifetime, becoming quite enchanted with the place.

We entered the plush room, and I could see why she might have found it so charming. I wandered around looking at the pale colored furnishings with its canopy bed, silk drapes, and other fine fabrics, before venturing to the windows to take in the view. The bellhop put our luggage up, after which Vance tipped him generously, closing the door behind him.

"The Queen's Suite?" I asked when he turned to face me, feeling a little overwhelmed by his extravagant treatment of me.

"I thought it was appropriate for the guest I was bringing here," he replied, walking up to place his hands on the sides of my face. "After all, you deserve only the best."

He kissed me, gently taking my mouth at first, before moving to rain over the rest of my face with tiny, tenderly placed affections. I loved getting to know the romantic side of him even more, as my heart leapt up in tempo at his soft touch. He surprised me when he pulled away a few moments later and walked over to the suitcases.

"Do you want to take a shower?" he asked casually, unzipping our luggage. "We've been traveling for a long time. I thought it would be nice to freshen up from our trip and relax some of those tight muscles."

"That sounds lovely," I replied, and I joined him to help unpack our things, thinking a shower sounded exactly like the perfect thing. I gathered up some items and followed him into the adjoining bathroom.

After we were refreshed and relaxed we crawled into the luxurious looking bed, deciding to spend the rest of the day there recovering from our jet lag.

Our room had all of the latest modern technology in it, despite the age of the castle. Vance picked up the remote, clicking on the television as I lay snuggled lethargically in the crook of his other arm.

"So why did you choose this place to stay?" I asked him while he flipped randomly through the channels looking for something to watch.

"Well, it's near to the town of Fort William," he said after a pause, though he seemed slightly hesitant.

"What's in Fort William that you would want to be close to it?" I asked, suddenly getting the impression he was keeping something from me, and I lifted my head so I could see his face.

A minor irritated expression flitted briefly over his features, which he quickly composed once again.

"There's a coven there your dad was able to get in contact with. Someone is supposed to meet with us in a couple of days," he replied, but before I could ask him anything else he rolled on his side to face me better. "But this is our honeymoon, and for the next two days that's all I want to concentrate on, okay? I want this to be *us* time. No mysteries, magic, or missing persons, just us."

"All right," I said, nodding in understanding, relieved he wasn't upset with me, only the situation.

"I'm sorry our wedding had to be tangled up in all this mess," he spoke softly, reaching to brush my damp hair away from my face.

"I'm not. We wouldn't be married right now if that weren't the case," I reminded him.

"True," he replied as his eyes flitted over my face, and I could see some regret there. "But I would've loved to sweep you off somewhere for a couple of months where we didn't have a care in the world, and everything could just revolve around me being with you."

"That does sound lovely," I agreed as my mind paused on the thought of being sequestered away with him somewhere. "Maybe we can do that someday soon. Don't worry about me, though. I'm fine with everything." I smiled and looked into his eyes. "The view here is very nice too."

"It is, isn't it?" he replied not missing a beat, knowing I was talking about looking at him, while he looked at me.

He wrapped both of his arms around me and pulled me up close to him, looking deeply into my eyes.

I waited for the kiss I knew was coming, moistening my lips in anticipation as he tilted his head, moving toward me. I was completely taken off guard when he stopped short and pulled back from me a little.

"Are you hungry?" he asked suddenly, looking at me with concern.

I nodded and laughed, his quick change of subject throwing me off as I struggled to catch up.

"Yes. But not for food," I replied and nudged the end of his nose with mine, knowing he would get my message.

That was all the encouragement he needed to proceed with his previous thought. He rolled me over onto my back, not allowing anything to distract him from his intended target this time.

We ended up deciding to stay in the room and ordered room service for dinner that evening.

I watched from behind the crack afforded by the partially open bathroom door, where I was hiding, when it arrived on a beautiful tray that was wheeled into our room by a young male waiter. There was a vase of flowers on the cart along with linen napkins and polished silver cutlery with pretty china.

"You can come out now, baby," Vance called to me when he closed the door behind the exiting man.

I blushed a bit and couldn't help the girlish giggle that escaped my lips when I walked back into the bedroom.

"I can't believe you just answered the door in a bathrobe!" I exclaimed while I tightened the belt on my own robe, which was identical to his, only smaller. "I would've died of embarrassment!"

"What could I possibly have to be embarrassed about?" Vance grinned. "I'm here on my honeymoon with the prettiest girl in existence, having a romantic dinner with her in matching bathrobes. Every guy in this place would be absolutely jealous of me right now and my extreme good fortune."

I blushed again at his appraisal of me. I'd always felt inferior to Vance when it came to looks. He had a way of making women of all ages stop dead in their tracks just so they could stare at him, me included. I never saw any boys or men stop to stare at me the way women looked at him. Well, that wasn't entirely true. Vance looked at me that way all the time.

"Earth to Portia," Vance's voice broke into my thoughts, and I suddenly realized he was holding a chair out for me to sit in.

"Oh, thank you," I said, feeling a bit flustered for a moment.

"What are you thinking about?" he asked which I found funny since he could have just ruffled through my thoughts on his own and found out for himself. It meant a lot to me that he respected my privacy enough to not do something like that.

"It's nothing," I said, dismissing my previous thoughts with a wave of my hand as he moved to sit in his chair.

"Really?" he probed. "Because I can almost see those wheels turning in your head."

I laughed. "I was just thinking about how incredibly handsome you are and how lucky I am to have you ... again." I smiled at him—sure I was stroking his ego to a flame by this point.

He surprised me once again, when he shook his head.

"Someday I hope I'll really be able to make you understand I'm the lucky one in this relationship, Portia. I'm almost afraid to take my eyes off you sometimes ... for fear I'll wake up and this will have all been a wonderful dream." He looked at me, his eyes overflowing with love.

"I'm not going anywhere, Vance," I replied and reached out to lay my hand over the top of his.

"Good," he answered with a smile, and he turned his hand slightly so he could squeeze mine. "Now eat up before your dad comes bursting through the door complaining that I'm keeping you too occupied with ... other pursuits and not feeding you enough."

"Yes sir!" I said laughing at the wicked grin and wink he sent my way.

The smells lifting from the delicious dinner in front us soon had our mouths watering in delight. We enjoyed the crispy duck in a lovely sauce, something I'd never tried before, with baby carrots and asparagus. Vance also ordered us the hot rhubarb soufflé for dessert, which was perfection in and of itself.

After we were done with dinner and our tray was picked up by the waiter, we opted to snuggle together for the rest of the evening until we both fell asleep in each other's arms.

The next morning, though it dawned bright and clear, was going to be another chilly one outside. The weather didn't affect us, though, because we still opted to stay in our room for most of the day. I soon began to realize that going off on a honeymoon to an exotic location was absolutely pointless, since we never wanted to leave our little hideaway to do anything else.

"Do you feel like you're ready to venture out into the world yet? Maybe explore the place a little?" Vance asked me in the middle of the afternoon after a pretty heated couple of hours.

"I guess we can ... if you want to," I said. I was lying in his arms, letting my hair spill across his chest like he liked.

"I'm perfectly content right where I am," he said, drawing his fingers through the dark strands, which was giving me a very relaxed feeling. "I just thought you might be getting bored with me by now."

I snorted at that comment. "Not likely." I smiled a very satisfied smile, and I lifted my head to look at him. "I've been having a marvelous time thanks to you." I had a thought which worried me then. "Unless you've grown bored with me, that is."

"I thought my feelings where you're concerned have been rather obvious," he commented with a chuckle.

"I just want to make sure you're enjoying yourself." I settled my head back down on his arm.

"Well, apparently I'm not doing a good enough job at showing you my intense pleasure at this whole situation if you actually have to ask," he replied, and he suddenly rolled me over onto my back and began kissing me again.

"I believe you!" I said with a little squeal, laughing, and he moved to trail his kisses down my neck to where the slightly purpled scar still showed where he had bitten me before.

"Too late," he mumbled against my skin before he licked and sucked at the spot. "I have to prove myself now."

I greatly enjoyed it as he proved himself to me once again.

When evening arrived, we decided to go down to one of the three restaurants on the premises.

We got dressed up nice, he in a suit and tie, and me in a cocktail dress. After debating what we were in the mood for, we finally decided to dine in The Red Room where we enjoyed beef Wellington and a marmalade soufflé.

The atmosphere was wonderful as we listened to the live music that was being played by a very accomplished pianist on the large grand piano. After dinner, we strolled around the castle taking in the sights and history offered there. We ended our little tour in the Great Hall next to the crackling fireplace, where we enjoyed a glass of wine together as we continued to listen to the lovely music floating in the air.

We socialized a little bit with other guests, making friendly conversation with some who were local and others who were visiting from around the world. Everyone seemed so infatuated with the idea we were there on our honeymoon, and I was surprised by how many people gravitated to us throughout the evening. We received a lot of well wishes from the people we met, though I was amazed all through the night as I watched the unveiled appreciative glances the women threw constantly in Vance's direction. I suppressed a slightly nervous giggle of discomfort for him, wondering if he felt like a prime serving of meat set up on an auction block.

After much visiting, we eventually made our way back to our room at a very late hour.

"Well, I'm glad that's over with!" Vance grumbled as he closed the door behind us. "I didn't think it would ever end."

I let the laughter out I had been holding back. "I wondered if you were feeling nervous at all. Those ladies were eyeing you up and down all night."

He looked at me like I had lost my mind. "What *are* you talking about?" Suddenly I wasn't sure we were speaking about the same thing.

"What were you referring to?" I asked him back, feeling completely confused at the moment.

"Those men out there!" he exclaimed while he shrugged out of his suit coat. "I understand how easy it was for them to be completely captivated by your charms, but did they have to look like they were undressing you with their eyes every single second? I was beginning to think I might need to knock a couple of heads off or at least poke somebody's eyes out!"

I looked at him, dumbfounded. Surely he was just toying with me.

"Quit teasing me," I finally said, mostly for lack of anything else to say.

"Seriously? You didn't notice anything at all? I felt certain that was what was making you so uncomfortable out there."

"If I was uncomfortable, it was because of all the women that were ogling you," I replied. "I'm certain you must've misread the men. As I've said before, you're the beautiful one in this relationship."

He walked over to me, grabbing my hand, pulling me over to a mirror on the wall and forcing me to stand square in front of it.

"I want you to look at yourself, Portia. Really look. It's time for you to see yourself the way I see you," he said, his voice gruff with some emotion I couldn't read.

I stared into my reflection, feeling very self-conscious about what he was asking me to do, but then he started speaking again.

"Look at your beautiful black hair," he said, and he pulled the few pins I had in it out so it was lying in a thick curtain around my shoulders. He ran his fingers through it. "I can't stop touching it. It's one of the most luxurious sights I've ever seen, and it feels just like spun silk." He lifted a large strand, bringing it to his lips so he could kiss it.

I watched him, my eyes wide in amazement.

"I can't stop with your hair, though, because your eyes have me completely mesmerized," he continued, stepping behind me to place his hands on either side of my head before he turned it slightly back and forth. "Look at them, Portia. They're like black onyx jewels that flash in the light. I've never seen eyes the color of yours, and I constantly feel like I'm drowning in the depths of them."

I felt my skin heat up, blushing at his words.

"Yes. That's right, baby. Don't let me forget this beautiful porcelain skin of yours. Perfectly alabaster in one moment and then flushed pink with desire in the next. You have no idea what it does to me to see your skin react like that."

I figured this was a good thing since my skin was currently flaming from the picture he was painting for me.

"And then there are those ripe, full delicious lips of yours. They're like a plump fruit, just waiting to be picked and promising to offer up the nectar of the gods to whoever is partaking of it. I want to be the *only* one ever partaking."

My mouth was salivating at his comments now, and I wished he would just kiss me already.

He slid my hair away from my neck and kissed the scar he had created there.

"This should be even further proof of my desires for you. You fill me with a need and longing so great that it's been almost disastrous for you," he whispered softly. He sucked at the spot as his large hands slid down over my bare arms, sending shivers over my body. "I want to touch, hold, and caress every part of you until you understand completely what I feel for you. I won't be whole until your entire soul, which is the most beautiful part of you, is a part of me. You're so amazing...inside and out. Truly you're the most breathtaking, bewitching creature I've ever seen."

My eyes watered at his sweet words, and I felt overwhelmed by this glorious figure standing beside me as he declared his love and desire for me. In that moment, I really saw myself in his eyes, and it was a revelation to me.

I turned around in his arms, but was interrupted when we both noticed the flashing light in front of us on the telephone. There was a message waiting.

He paused to look at me, neither of us wanting to break the special moment we were experiencing.

"You should check it," I encouraged him after a few seconds. "It could be something important."

Vance gave a disappointed sigh before he answered it, listening intently to whoever was speaking.

"Who was it?" I asked, after he placed the receiver down.

"It was your dad," he replied, and he scooted the phone back toward the rear of the dresser. "He says he hopes we're having a good time together. He also said our contact will meet us in the morning at a restaurant called Crannog at the Waterfront, in Fort Williams at ten o'clock. He said the man's name is Brian."

"How will we know him?"

"He said he'd be waiting for us outside the front door."

"Sounds cold," I said thinking of the brisk weather we had been having since our arrival in Scotland. "We'd better dress warm in case we have to wait on him."

He nodded, before changing the subject back to the previous topic. "How did you enjoy your evening though, really?" he asked, wrapping his arms around me.

"It was wonderful, thank you," I replied with a smile. "Did you have a good time?"

"Of course." he answered. "At least I did when I wasn't frustrated with every other man in the room. But then again, any time I'm with you constitutes a good time."

"I can think of a few times when we've been together that don't make it very high on my list of good times," I reminded him, and several memories of the past flashed through my head.

“Let’s not think about those anymore. We’ll just make new happy memories, okay?” he suggested, bending to kiss my lips.

I was just getting warmed up with his kiss when he pulled back, staring at me with a puzzled look on his face.

“What is it?” I asked a little concerned.

He looked me over for a moment, as if weighing his words before he spoke.

“I don’t know. It’s just I always thought when I’d finally be able to be with you, in the physical sense, it would ease some of the desire, the ever-constant drive I have to be with you.”

“And now that we’re together that way?” I asked him, truly curious about his answer.

“It’s a million times worse.” He laughed, seeming pretty amazed at his own statement. “I hope you don’t think I’m crazy, Portia, but I just can’t get enough of you. You drive me to complete distraction.”

“Well, if I’m being honest, then I must admit I’m enjoying your affections greatly,” I replied as I wound my arms around his neck. “And if it helps you at all, I feel the exactly the same way.”

“Do you?” he asked, holding me tight in his iron grip. “Because you seem to be controlling it a lot better than I am.”

“Not really. I just enjoy watching you be the aggressor in this relationship. You do it so well.” I smiled seductively and could actually feel the wave of passion as it rolled off him, lighting us both on fire.

“Now that’s a role I can definitely handle,” he said. He scooped me off my feet and carried me over to the bed.

He tossed me onto the soft surface, before reaching down to my feet and removing my black strapped heels, kicking his own shoes off before coming to lie next to me.

I reached over to grab his necktie, working it loose until I could pull it over his head. I began working on the buttons on his shirt as he searched out the side zipper of my dress.

"I love you," he said, and he placed a kiss against my exposed collarbone.

"I love you, too," I whispered back. I slipped my hands into his shirt, pushing it back over his muscular shoulders, and the two of us spent the rest of the night wrapped together creating our own blissful haven.

CHAPTER 4

The morning did indeed turn out to be very cool as we stood bundled up in front of the restaurant, waiting to meet our contact, Brian. We were a little bit early though, so Vance currently had me tucked up against a nook in the wall, shielding me with his body from a bone-chilling breeze.

"I wish this place were open so you could go inside," he said with a concerned look, and he wrapped his arms around me in a giant bear hug, laying his head down against mine. "I don't want you to get sick."

He occasionally reached down to pull my hands up to his mouth where he would blow long puffs of his warm breath onto them, after which he would rub them briskly between both of his warm hands, heating them slightly with his magic for my benefit.

"I'm fine, really," I said with a smile, loving every second of his careful treatment of me, watching his hands as they heated mine. "How do you always know to do stuff like that?" I asked, looking up into his eyes.

"What do you mean?" he replied, meeting my glance with a bit of a confused look.

"I mean how do you know how to use your magic? Everyone is always telling me how gifted I am and that my powers are so strong for how new they are, but the fact of the matter is I have no idea what I'm doing or how to use them even. You respond so naturally to things, like you know exactly what your powers can and can't be used for."

He chuckled slightly. "Portia, you do have an unnatural ability to control your powers when you use them, but no one expects you to know what you're doing or to even feel comfortable with them at this level. My powers manifested at the age of five. I've had years to learn to manage and master them effectively. It'll probably take the same amount of time for you to come into your own as well. Don't sweat it. Just take your time, play around with your powers, and feel out what you can do. You've reacted to situations as a normal human being your whole life. It's going to take time to change that mentality."

"You just make everything look so easy." I smiled at him. "How are things for you now that you've assimilated more powers?" I asked, referring to the powers he had taken from his father during their fight to the death.

He sighed heavily. "That's the perfect example of what I'm trying to tell you. I have powers I'm not even aware of. At some point in my life I may discover them and learn how to properly use them to the point they'll begin to feel comfortable to me. It really is a trial and error process, and not having any knowledge of the people my dad performed a demon kiss on, I really don't know what kind of magic is there." He laughed a little. "See, we're kind of in the same boat."

"True," I replied seeing his point. "But you're already very accomplished in your magic. What if I never reach the level people expect of me? I don't want to be a disappointment."

He lifted my hands to his lips and kissed them. "You'll never be a disappointment to anyone, baby. Just keep doing what you're doing and try to figure things out for yourself. If it'll help you feel any better, maybe we can find some time to work on our magic together."

"I think I'd like that," I replied with a smile, and he kissed me lightly on the lips.

After several long minutes of standing there together, we noticed a black car pull up alongside the restaurant. A young man, who looked to be in his early twenties, stepped out and began to walk over.

"Mr. and Mrs. Mangum?" he asked as he approached.

"Yes," Vance replied, turning to stand in front of me.

"I'm Brian Fitzgerald," he said, extending his hand politely.

Vance reached out and shook it. "Vance," he replied with a nod before turning to me. "And this is my wife, Portia."

I laughed internally at the notable emphasis he put on the "my wife" part. The Alpha male in him was obviously racing to the surface. He was definitely more determined to put his stamp on me of late.

"It's a pleasure to meet you," I said with a smile. I reached out and shook his hand also.

"Likewise," he replied with a bright smile, his green eyes flashing as his sandy hair ruffled gently in the breeze.

He's a nice looking guy, I thought to myself, only to feel the tiniest surge of jealousy run through Vance's head as he picked up on that particular thought. I squeezed his hand in reassurance. No one in the world would ever be better looking to me than Vance.

"I spoke with your father then?" Brian asked, and he looked at me with a congenial expression.

"Yes." I nodded.

"He was inquiring about some information that would lead you to find your family," he said, turning to Vance. "I'm happy to say I have that information right here for you."

He reached a gloved hand into his pocket, pulled out a slip of paper and handed it to Vance.

"The Cummings family is very respected around here," he added. "I'm pleased to meet another relative of theirs. They're great people."

"Really?" Vance replied, quirking an eyebrow.

I knew he was more than a little confused. We were expecting his grandparents were possibly holding his mother prisoner and not to be a good sort of people.

"Yes. Their humanitarian work is quite well known throughout the area," Brian continued, still smiling. "In fact, I took the liberty of contacting and letting them know you were inquiring about them. They were thrilled to hear of your arrival and extended an invitation for me to drive you to their place, if you so desire. They seemed very excited to meet you."

Vance turned back to look at me in question, surprise written clearly on his features.

"What do you think?" he asked, and I could hear the caution threaded through his voice.

"I'll do whatever you think is appropriate," I replied, not really knowing what I thought about the situation, but I was happy he valued my opinion on the matter enough to consult it.

Vance turned back to Brian. "I'm sorry about the hesitation," he explained. "This wasn't exactly the news we were expecting."

"No worries," Brian responded with a grin, in his thick Scottish accent. "I'd be happy to take you there and even wait for you if you'd like."

Vance looked at me once more before making a decision. I could almost see the wheels turning in his head while he tried to quickly weigh out the pros and cons in this turn of events. He finally glanced back toward Brian.

"Okay then. I guess we'll accept your offer," he agreed, and I had to admit I was a little surprised to hear it.

"Wonderful," Brian said, gesturing toward his waiting sedan. "Shall we?"

Vance told our driver he could head back to the castle without us, then he took my hand, and we followed Brian over to his vehicle. Both of us climbed into the back seat together, while Brian entered the front.

"How far away is this place?" Vance asked.

"Just a few miles over River Lochy and toward Torcastle," he replied. "We should be there in about thirty minutes. It's a beautiful drive through the countryside to your grandparents' estate. I think you'll really enjoy it."

"They live on an estate?" I asked more than a little intrigued to learn about the place we were heading to.

"Yes. It's a beautiful old manor house, made from granite. Douglas and Fiona have always taken special care to see that the grounds are kept immaculate, and the out buildings are maintained in perfect condition."

"Douglas and Fiona?" I asked in confusion at the unfamiliar names.

"Oh! I'm sorry," he apologized, looking back at us through the rearview mirror as he drove. "I assumed you might know their names. Douglas and Fiona Cummings are your grandparents," he said looking specifically at Vance. "They're truly wonderful people."

I looked over at Vance who turned my direction and was now arching an eyebrow at me. I could see he wasn't entirely comfortable with this situation as doubt filled his gaze.

"How do you know them? If you don't mind my asking," he said, determined to probe a little deeper.

Brian laughed lightly. "My mother heads up one of the local charities in the area. Fiona has donated her time to the cause on many occasions. I met them mostly through the several charity functions we've attended together."

"I see," Vance said, sitting silent for a moment. "So they knew about me when you contacted them?"

"Yes. They said something about you having disappeared as a child before they ever had the opportunity to meet you. They said you've changed your last name, though. I spoke directly to your grandmother. She was quite overcome with emotion at the thought of finally getting to meet you. Apparently she and your grandfather had some type of falling out with your father in the past and he refused to introduce you to them," he explained.

Vance leaned back into the seat, taking in everything Brian had just revealed to us.

"He seems legit," I said into his head.

"He definitely knows what he's talking about," he agreed mentally. "This sudden turn of events has thrown me off my game," he added. "I don't know what to think."

I reached over and squeezed his hand.

"Are you nervous?" I asked, and he stared into my eyes.

I saw a lot of conflicting emotions there.

I knew having a real family was a dream of his. It was something he always longed for. He hoped to someday reunite with his mother and have some type of family life together. As it was, he believed he was the one who killed his mother, only to find out it was possibly an imposter he destroyed instead. Of course, there was no question he had been the one who killed his father. Now he was getting ready to walk right into the unknown, meeting relatives he'd previously known nothing about.

"I have no idea what I'm feeling," he replied honestly, giving my hand a gentle squeeze.

I linked my arm through his and leaned my head over onto his shoulder, snuggling up against him.

He placed a gentle kiss against my hair.

"How long have the two of you been married?" Brian asked, watching us through the rearview mirror.

"Four days," Vance answered with a smile and looked down at me. I was amazed at the fascinating way his face suddenly transformed from worry to a look of complete rapture.

"Wow! Newlyweds! That must be exciting. So are you here on your honeymoon?" Brian continued.

"Yes," Vance replied without taking his gaze away from me. "We figured we could come enjoy the beauty of Scotland and see if we could look up some of my family while we were here. I have to admit, I wasn't expecting things to be this easy, though."

"Well, I'm glad I could help out," Brian said with a grin.

We drove on for several more miles before we finally turned off the main road to travel down a well-maintained private driveway.

The narrow, tree-lined road continued probably another quarter of a mile into the property before it widened out into a circle drive that ended up in front of a very large manor house.

I stared out the window, up at the beautiful architecture. It was two stories tall with many high-pitched peaks in the roof. Small wrought iron crosses decorated the tips of each point in the structure.

There were leaded glass panes in all of the windows, and several wide stone steps led up from the driveway to the massive wooden doors that graced the entrance.

Vance opened the car door, lifting his head to eye the imposing dwelling with a curious look before stepping out, then turning to offer me a hand out of the vehicle.

Brian joined us, leading the way up the steps to the door, knocking boldly with a metal knocker that hung from the heavy wood.

We waited for a few moments before the door swung slowly open to reveal a somber looking man in uniform.

The gentleman was quite tall and thin, with dark hair that was slicked backward. He had a narrow gaunt face, with a slightly hooked patrician nose. He looked down that nose at us slightly as if we were less than equal to him.

"May I help you?" he asked in a quiet, yet no-nonsense, baritone voice which clearly signified he wasn't to be trifled with.

"Good morning," Brian said with a smile as if nothing seemed amiss. "This is Mr. and Mrs. Mangum, here to meet with Mr. and Mrs. Cummings this morning. I believe they're expecting them."

The man, whom I aptly assumed was the butler, looked us over carefully before giving a nod and stepping to the side, allowing us to enter into the small vestibule just inside.

"Welcome to Bell Tower. May I take your coats?" he offered in a measured voice, and we shrugged out of them and draped them over his arm. "Wait here, please," he added and disappeared into the house.

Vance held my hand tightly, and I could tell he was a bit nervous by the firm set of his mouth.

We waited together in silence for the butler to announce us. He returned a short time later.

"Madame requested to greet you in the Grand Salon," he said looking mainly at Vance. "This way, please."

We followed him out of the entrance and into a large foyer complete with a sweeping marble staircase that led up to the second floor. A large crystal chandelier dangled above, filling the cavernous space overhead.

We turned into a large hallway with beautifully sculpted ceilings. My eyes drifted curiously over the amazing artwork, along with mirrors and moldings that perfectly framed the accent furniture lining the walls.

We turned left and were led through a door into an equally impressive room, with meticulously maintained antique furniture grouped around a large stone fireplace that was crackling brightly.

"Mr. and Mrs. Vance Mangum," the butler said from the entrance as he ushered us farther into the room.

A tall distinguished looking man with silver hair stood and offered his hand to a petite woman whose dark hair had many gray streaks running through it.

Both of their faces had a hard-looking edge to them, as if life might have been harsh for them to endure somehow.

They were dressed in light morning attire, the man in a cream-colored suit, and the woman in a smartly tailored dress of the same shade.

I suddenly felt completely underdressed for such an occasion since Vance and I had dressed for the cold, both of us wearing jeans and t-shirts covered by pullover sweaters, and sneakers.

The couple paused for a second, taking us in. "Vance?" the woman, Fiona, spoke in a whisper, as her hand slid up over her chest resting against her heart.

"Yes, ma'am," he answered politely as he watched her, his face completely devoid of any emotion.

She opened her arms and hurried over, grabbing him with both arms around the shoulders, hugging him down to her small frame.

"We're so glad to meet you," she said with a smile, before reaching up to place a kiss on either side of his face.

"Welcome to our home, son," the man, Douglas, spoke as he joined us, standing near Vance's side.

I could feel the heady yearning that rushed through Vance in that moment ... hope. It sprung up in his chest though he tried immediately to tamp it back down.

"Thank you, sir," he replied offering a hand in greeting, and a very small hint of a smile appeared on his face.

Douglas shook his hand warmly, covering Vance's hand affectionately with both of his.

"This is my wife, Portia," Vance said and slipped one of his arms around my waist, pulling me up next to him.

"Welcome, dear," Douglas added looking at me.

"Thank you for having us," I replied, not really knowing what the proper etiquette was for meeting a spouse's long-lost family.

"Where are our manners?" Fiona said as she reached up to pat her perfectly coiffed hairdo. "Do come in and sit down."

We followed them over to the sofa in front of the roaring fire and sat down across from them.

"I couldn't believe it when Brian called and said you were looking for us," Fiona said, and she reached over to pat Brian affectionately on the knee. "We were so happy to hear that you were in Scotland."

"Well, we were coming here for our honeymoon and thought maybe we could try to look up some relatives while we were here," Vance said, offering a partially truthful explanation.

"We're so glad you did. We haven't known where you were since you were born," Fiona replied, with a sad shake of her head. "I'm afraid we had a bad falling out with your father. He was doing some things we didn't approve of. As punishment for our disapproval he took you and your mom away. We never heard from him again."

"I'm sorry for that," Vance said, as he squeezed my hand slightly, working his thumb in circles over my skin.

"Are you still in touch with him?" Douglas asked, clearly searching out some news of his wayward son.

Vance nodded. "I've seen him ... recently," he added, and I could tell he was loathe to volunteer more information than he felt he needed to.

"How's he doing?" Fiona asked, leaning forward, pressing the issue directly to the place Vance had been trying to avoid.

"Not well, I'm afraid," Vance hedged before continuing. "He, uh ... passed away about a week ago."

"What? No!" Fiona raised her hands to cover her mouth in horror, and her husband wrapped his arms around her.

I could feel the turmoil in Vance as he wrestled with the direction the conversation had taken.

"What happened?" Douglas asked with a stricken look upon his face as he tried to comfort a clearly distraught Fiona.

Vance sighed heavily, reaching up to rub at his temple with one hand, closing his eyes for a moment.

When he opened them again he looked straight at them, and I knew he had chosen to take the direct route.

"You should know Damien was a very bad man," he began as he looked back and forth between the two of them. "My mother ran away from him and took me with her. I hadn't seen him for years. As it happened, he found us and kidnapped Portia, threatening to kill her if I didn't do what he wanted. I found Portia and tried to help her escape, but we didn't get away in time. My dad and I fought each other and," he paused before plunging ahead, "I killed him in the heat of that argument."

He leaned back into the sofa, waiting for them to absorb the things he had told them, watching them carefully.

They sat for several shocked seconds just looking at him, perhaps with both a little fear and awe mixed on their faces as Fiona slowly lifted her hand to cover her gaping mouth. I thought I could see tears glistening in their eyes as they stared at Vance.

"He did it to save me," I popped up trying to ease the situation, not wanting him to lose the love of his newly found family so quickly.

Their eyes turned to me, and Douglas released his breath. "No doubt," Douglas replied, waving his hand in dismissal. "Forgive us please for our rudeness, but he was our son, and we'd hoped he had changed."

"No," Vance said quietly. "It's me who should be asking for your forgiveness. It's a horrible thing to drop on you unexpectedly."

"There's never an easy way to break news like this," Douglas replied. "I'm sorry for everything the two of you have had to go through at his hand. He wasn't always this way, you know."

I couldn't imagine Damien any other way personally, but I tried to appear caring over their situation even though I couldn't have been happier Damien was dead.

"He was always very driven," Douglas continued. "He pursued his education relentlessly, building on his successes, learning from his failures. He was always so positive. He eventually became the leader of his own coven. We were very proud of him and his accomplishments. But then something changed. He became consumed with studying all aspects of magic, often trying things out just see what he could do or discover. He was always pushing the limits, going past the boundaries of propriety as he tried to build his magical powers. It got to the point that we confronted him on it, calling him out, so to speak. But he wouldn't listen to reason. Instead he turned on us, and we never heard from him again. Your mother was pregnant with you the last time we heard from him."

Douglas cast his eyes down toward his lap, and Fiona reached out to briefly grasp his hand.

"It's obvious that you're magical also," Fiona said and she placed her hand back into her lap, twisting it with the other which rested there. "Otherwise you would've never been able to defeat him. He was a very powerful warlock."

Vance gave a slight nod of his head, acknowledging they were correct in that assumption.

"Is your mother with you then?" Douglas asked.

"No," Vance replied with a shake of his head. "I'd received a tip from one of Damien's previous staff members that she might actually be here."

"Here? At Bell Tower?" Fiona asked with a puzzled look.

"That was what the woman said."

"What would've possessed her to say something as ridiculous as that? We haven't seen Krista since before you were born," Fiona stated flatly.

I felt the heavy disappointment sweep over Vance at this news.

"Darcy was afraid you were going to kill her. She probably lied so she could get away," I said softly to Vance, wishing I could help ease his disappointment somehow.

He just nodded and clenched his jaw, and I could see that he was working to get his emotions in check.

"This staff member was a demon witch perhaps?" Douglas asked.

Vance nodded again.

"Enough of this talk," Fiona said, standing suddenly. "It's clear the boy is completely distraught."

She came to sit by Vance's side, placing her hand lightly against his forearm, patting him in a motherly fashion.

"Would the two of you be willing to honor us by coming to spend the rest of your vacation here with us? We have a lovely suite on the second floor which overlooks the grounds. I'm certain you'd just adore it. It would mean so much to us to have you here with us."

Vance looked over at me with question in his eyes.

"It's fine with me," I whispered.

He paused for another moment before he turned back to Fiona.

"We'd be happy to. Thank you for the invitation," he said with a small smile, even though his heart was breaking.

Brian hopped up. "Why don't the two of you just stay here, and I'll see to it your things are transferred from Inverlochy Castle," he offered.

"What a wonderful idea!" Fiona said, brightening at the thought. "Then the two of you can join us for lunch."

Vance agreed to let Brian help us out, and Douglas led him to a telephone so he could call the concierge at the Castle to let them know we would be sending someone to check us out early.

Fiona slid closer to me while Douglas continued to visit with Vance and Brian.

"I'm so excited you're staying, dear. It'll be such fun!" She smiled happily at me.

I smiled back. "You've very sweet to offer us such nice accommodations," I replied sincerely.

She reached out and patted my hand, changing the subject completely then, catching me a little off guard.

"If you wouldn't think it too rude, may I ask how old you are? You seem so young," she said her eyes boring into mine.

"I'm sixteen," I replied honestly.

"Oh!" Her eyes quickly traveled down to my stomach area with a probing glance.

I chuckled at her reaction, though I had completely expected it.

"I'm not pregnant," I said firmly, letting her know I knew exactly what she was thinking. "Vance and I were just madly in love."

"I'm sorry," she said as she patted my knee. "Forgive my lack of manners. You're a very pretty girl, and that grandson of ours is quite a looker, too. The attraction seems obvious."

"Yes, but I do love him," I stressed again, wanting her to understand this relationship was about a lot more than just attraction.

"Of course you do!" She smiled with a wink.

I had the feeling she wasn't really hearing me. Whether it was because she didn't understand, or she didn't want to, I wasn't sure.

Vance returned to my side, with Douglas following close behind him. He reached out a hand and pulled me to my feet.

Fiona stood next to us, smiling at each of us.

"Let's go show you your room, shall we?"

CHAPTER 5

Vance and I followed Fiona up the large staircase to the second floor. We went to the left when we reached the top, passing several closed doors as we walked down the tastefully decorated hall.

Fiona led us to a large set of double doors at the end and opened one side for us to enter.

To say the suite which lay beyond was plush was a complete understatement. The furniture was made of wood and painted white. In fact all of the décor in the room was white. There was an extremely large king-sized bed with thick pillars that twisted up into the wooden canopy overhead. It was covered in a luxurious silk duvet, with pillows of every size and variety strategically placed all over, starting at the head and trailing out to nearly the middle of the mattress. The foot of the bed had a bench covered in a soft chenille material tufted with buttons.

At one end of the room there was a sitting area with beautifully carved chairs in the Queen Anne style, next to a slightly distressed white coffee table.

The windows had sheers hanging over them, filtering the light, while heavier drapes hung over the top that could be closed to keep the light out completely if the occupants so desired.

The walls of the room were in sharp contrast to the furnishings, covered in a dark, richly paneled wood. The richness of the walls helped to set off all the white-on-white décor in the space.

"Will this room do for you?" Fiona asked as she rubbed an imaginary wrinkle out of the duvet with her hand.

"It's perfect," I said, feeling a bit like a fairy princess in a magical tower.

"Yes, I agree," Vance added with a nod, still seeming formal as he addressed her. "Thank you again for your hospitality."

Fiona walked over and placed a hand on the side of Vance's face, stroking it gently.

"You have no idea how excited we are to have you here, my dear boy," she said, with a longing look at him. "I look forward to getting to know you better."

"Likewise," he replied, giving her a slight smile.

"Well, I'll leave the two of you here to get acquainted with the place," she said, and she walked over to the door. "Get comfortable and make yourselves at home. I'll send Colin up to tell you when lunch is served."

"Colin?" I didn't recognize the unfamiliar name.

"The butler, dear," she replied. "If there's anything else you find yourselves in need of, just ask Colin and he'll be sure to get it for you."

"Thank you," Vance said as she stepped through the door, her hand on the knob.

"Oh!" she said, almost as an afterthought. "Feel free to explore any part of the house you wish, except for the east wing. We're currently under renovations there, and my allergies act up if people keep coming in and out with all the dust and everything."

"No problem," Vance said.

"Hopefully the work will be finished while you're here and you'll be able to get the complete tour. Feel free to explore the grounds of the estate as well," she added with a smile, before she walked out and closed the door behind her.

Vance immediately turned to me, and I walked up to wrap my arms around his waist, leaning my head against his muscled shoulder.

"How are you holding up?" I asked, and he wrapped his arms around me, resting his chin on the top of my head.

"I'm not sure," he said, letting out a large sigh as if he were releasing the weight of the world off his shoulders. "This is a bizarre and unexpected turn of events."

"Well, they seem genuinely happy to have you here with them," I countered, trying to give something positive to look at.

"That's true," he replied before pulling back to look at me. "What about you? Do you feel comfortable about staying here?"

"As long as I'm where you are, I'll be fine," I smiled up at him as I squeezed his waist a little tighter.

"You're too good to me. You know that, right?" he said, and he lifted a hand to the side of my mouth, reaching out to stroke my lips with his thumb.

"Not possible. You deserve the best of everything life has to offer. I know how much you've always wanted family to share that with. Maybe this is your chance."

"Speaking of family, what are your thoughts on my mom?" he asked, pulling me over to sit in the chairs by the coffee table.

"I think Darcy was probably lying," I answered him honestly, though I knew it would be the last thing he would want to hear.

"I'm afraid of that, too," he said with a sigh. "I was so hopeful she was right. I wanted to know the person I destroyed was not my mom."

"Don't give up yet." I tried to encourage him, not wanting to see the crestfallen look on his face. "Maybe Darcy was only misleading us about your grandparents. We'll keep looking around while we're here, just to make sure."

"That sounds good."

I got up, feeling the urge to explore, and walked through one of the adjoining doors in the room. I found myself in a very large walk-in closet, which was bigger than my whole bedroom back in Sedona. I was surprised to find several articles of women's clothing hanging inside.

"It looks like someone has stayed here at some point," I called out the door to Vance. "There are a lot of things in here."

I wandered out of the closet and through another door finding it led to an extravagantly large bathroom.

"Vance, come look at this!" I said, taking in the sight before me.

"Wow," he replied when he entered, coming up behind me to look at the giant custom-tiled bathing area that was set into the floor. It looked more like a small swimming pool than bathtub. A slow grin spread across his face. "I think we're going to need to try that out."

"It sounds like the perfect thing to relax an overwrought husband," I said stepping around behind him, lifting my hands to his shoulders to massage the tense knots I could feel in them.

"That feels wonderful," he replied, hanging his head, allowing my fingers better access.

"So how about we have the bath after dinner this evening? I'll finish massaging you, and you'll sleep better," I suggested, wanting to help him somehow.

"There's only one reason I haven't been sleeping well lately and I have no intention of changing any of that." He grinned, turning to face me, giving me a sultry look I couldn't possibly miss the meaning of.

He reached out and grabbed me by the shoulders, and I thought he was going to kiss me. He surprised me though when he turned me around so he could massage my neck.

"You're right," I responded with a soft groan at the touch. "That does feel good. I can't wait until this evening."

He reached down, taking my hand and pulled me out of the bathroom, heading over toward the massive bed.

"We have about an hour before lunch. Do you want to take a quick nap with me? All of our ... umm ... eventful nights are starting to catch up with me," he said with a wide smile.

"A nap sounds divine," I replied, thinking we had indeed been pushing our physical limits lately.

He pulled the bedding back, lifting me gently so I was sitting on the edge. Then he removed my shoes followed by his, before he crawled up to join me, pulling the covers over both of us, as I cuddled up into the crook of his arm.

"This is nice," I said draping my arm over his waist.

"Yes, it is."

I closed my eyes and let the rhythm of his strong, beating heart, along with his steady breathing, lull me to sleep.

When we awoke sometime later, it was clear we slept through lunch and well into the evening. I instantly felt regret, wondering if we might've offended our gracious hosts.

When I sat up I noticed a silver tray, loaded with food, had been placed just inside the door.

A note had been left from Fiona that said she couldn't bear to wake us when we were sleeping so peacefully. She also said she and Douglas had an appointment for the rest of the evening that they couldn't back out of, so to please make ourselves at home and they would see us tomorrow.

It was then I noticed our luggage had also been brought into the room.

It was official. We were now residents of Bell Tower Hall.

Vance helped me as we magically unpacked our suitcases, before we sat down to enjoy the wonderful meal that was left for us.

After we had eaten, I went into the bathroom and began to fill the massive tub, while Vance lit a fire in the grate.

I looked through some of the cabinets and found a bottle of bubble bath, and soon the tub was filled with a steaming, sweet-scented aroma.

Vance and I both sank into the tub with the foamy water up to our chins. He leaned against one end, pulled me up against him and continued the massage of my shoulders he had begun earlier.

"You have magic fingers," I moaned, and he laughed.

"Yes, I do, as a matter of fact," he replied, and he lifted his hand from my neck and twirled his fingers around.

Bubbles from the bath suddenly swirled up into the air creating an amusing environment of colorful reflections dancing about us.

I playfully splashed him with some water.

"You know what I meant!"

"Hey, watch it! You're going to start something you can't possibly win," he chided me.

"Oh, I could win," I responded, fully confident in my own water sport skills.

He laughed at my remark. "Maybe you could, but we aren't going to find out tonight. This bath is about relaxation, so behave," he ordered me.

"Yes, sir!" I replied, finding I was more than willing to give in to his demands at the moment.

He worked out my kinks and knots for several minutes, after which I traded places with him and returned the favor.

"Mmm ... that does feel good," he agreed as I moved my hands over the sinewy muscles around his neck and shoulders.

When I had finished massaging his back, he turned to pick up a bottle of shampoo, loading his hands up with soap and began to wash my hair.

That in itself was probably my favorite massage as he rubbed the shampoo through my thick strands and down to my scalp.

"I love your hair," he said while he moved his fingers through it.

"I hadn't noticed," I said facetiously, closing my eyes at the wonderful sensations he was creating.

When he was done, I returned the favor and washed his, although I had a bit of fun using the soap to shape his into funny hairstyles and laughed childishly over them.

When we were finished, we pulled the plug on the tub and headed over to the shower to rinse off before wrapping ourselves into two luxurious bathrobes and heading out to sit by the fire.

I was completely surprised to find a bottle of champagne chilling in a bucket on the coffee table.

"Where did that come from?" I asked looking at it and the two glasses that accompanied it.

"I'm guessing Colin must have brought it in," he replied with a shrug as he stared at the bottle.

"Didn't you lock the door?" I asked, feeling a little exposed over the fact someone had been so near to us without our knowledge.

He shook his head. "I didn't even think about it," he said, glancing up at the door and pointing finger at it.

The lock in the door turned easily.

"There. Is that better?" he asked with a wink.

I nodded. "Sometimes privacy is a good thing," I laughed quietly, "Especially when I'm with you."

"I understand completely," he replied. He popped the cork out of the bottle and proceeded to pour each of us a glass.

I didn't know if I really cared for the champagne or not. The bubbles did tickle my nose, and I kept hiccupping every time I would try to drink a swallow. Finally, I just gave up and set the glass on the table.

There was a plush white rug on the floor in front of the fireplace. I got up and went over to sit on it, relishing the heat there.

Staring into the flames, I enjoyed watching them dance around. I became mesmerized by the movements, and I lifted my hands to mimic the motion I saw, moving them from side to side. Centering my thoughts, I let my energies flow out of me, until the fire started to follow me in the same motion as my hands.

I was completely absorbed in my little game when Vance came to join me on the rug, setting his empty glass on the table behind me.

He lifted my damp hair away from my neck, leaning in to kiss me there.

"You look enchanting sitting here in the firelight," he whispered, and he nibbled and licked at my skin.

As usual, I tipped my head back to give him better access to the spot.

"So beautiful," he said while he ran his fingers through the wet strands of my hair.

I closed my eyes, just enjoying his touch and the magical moment he was weaving around us.

He turned my face toward his and kissed me gently on the lips, parting them with his tongue, before he wrapped an arm around my waist and carefully laid me back onto the rug.

He kissed me like that for several long minutes, holding me softly, looking into my eyes. The rest of the room began to melt away until all I could see was him.

I reached one hand up to thread it through his hair, and placed the other on his sculpted cheek allowing my fingers to trail lightly over the surface.

"I love you so much, Vance," I whispered, completely wrapped up in his spell, always his willing captive.

"I'm glad. Loving you makes me happier than I could've ever imagined," he replied as his eyes traveled over my face. "You cannot possibly know what it means to me to have you as my wife."

“Then why don’t you show me,” I suggested, moving my fingers up to trace over his brow.

I felt the pull almost instantly as his mind opened up wide and linked with mine. All of his thoughts and emotions poured into my head, causing a rush of vibrations to move throughout my body. The feelings he gave me were so intense I gasped out loud.

He chuckled softly at my reaction. “You asked for it,” he said, a seductive grin lighting up the masculine dimples on his face.

“Yes, I did,” I replied, my breath quickening as sensations I never felt before danced through me. “Whatever you’re doing, please don’t stop!”

“We’re doing this, Portia, both of us,” he explained. He sucked at my neck and my breath caught in my throat again with the intense emotions he caused by adding that physical touch. “This is my passion reacting to yours, each of us echoing back and forth off one another.”

“But I have no idea what I’m doing! Why hasn’t it been like this before?” I asked. I threw my head back, as he licked up the side of my throat.

“I guess because we were never mentally linked during our previous times together,” he mumbled against my skin.

“For heaven’s sake, why not?” I exclaimed in exasperation, wondering if he had been holding out on me on purpose.

“Too preoccupied ... didn’t think of it ... didn’t want to rush you,” he spoke in between kisses. “And I’m learning, too,” he whispered in my ear right before he nibbled at my earlobe, sending little waves of pleasure over me.

“Teach me everything you know. Don’t leave out a thing,” I begged, wanting to make him feel exactly as I did.

“That could take a while,” he laughed softly.

"I don't care," I replied, right before he took my mouth with his.

We ended up spending the whole night right there on the floor in front of the fireplace.

Chapter 6

We awoke in the morning to a soft knock on the door to the suite.

Vance quickly jumped up, pulling me with him, swinging me off my feet and carrying me over to the bed. When I was safely tucked in with the covers up to my chin, he donned his robe from the night before and opened the door.

Colin was standing outside with a tray of food.

Vance stepped aside to let him enter. “Thank you, Colin,” he said while Colin carried the tray over to the area we just vacated. “We would’ve come down for breakfast, though.”

Colin gave a small smile. “Madame has ordered breakfast for your room during your stay here. She said that was most appropriate for honeymooners.”

“Ah, I see,” Vance said with a knowing grin as he winked at me. “Please tell her I said thank you.”

“Is there anything else I can get for you this morning, sir?”

"No. I think we're good," Vance replied, as he followed Colin back over to the door, closing it behind him.

I blushed a thousand shades of red at the thought of us nearly being caught sleeping together on the rug.

Vance laughed and he retrieved my robe for me, bringing it over to the bed. "I must say I'm thrilled to see I still have a blushing bride this morning—especially after her wonderful displays of affection last night." He grinned, and I knew he was baiting me.

Having him call attention to last night certainly did nothing to ease the state of my flushed skin, and I blushed even harder.

"Don't be embarrassed," he said and he kissed my flaming cheek. "Last night was amazing, and I loved every second of it."

"Me too," I admitted softly.

"Glad to hear it, because I'm greatly anticipating a repeat performance sometime in the near future," he replied with a wink, and I wondered if my skin would forever carry the stain of this color.

"Would you care for a drink?" Vance asked, and I looked to see a carafe filled with orange juice on the tray as well as another bottle of chilled champagne.

"They sent champagne for breakfast? Isn't it a little early in the day for such a beverage?"

Vance laughed slightly while he poured a glass of orange juice, turning to hand it to me.

"I think Fiona is enjoying celebrating our nuptials with us," he said with a slight shrug, and he turned back to pop the cork on the bottle before proceeding to pour himself a glass. "And I can't think of anything else in the world I'd rather celebrate!" he added with a grin and a wink before he clinked his glass with mine then quickly downed the contents.

Smiling at him, I took a swallow of my fresh-squeezed orange juice, happy he was so content with me and wanting to celebrate.

After we had eaten breakfast, we got ready for the day and ventured back out into the long hallway.

Vance had previously discussed the possibility of touring the grounds of Bell Tower today and perhaps finding a place where we could work on practicing our magic together.

I thought that sounded like fun things to do, and we set out to find Fiona to see if we could make the arrangements.

Vance reached over and grabbed my hand, linking our fingers together as we made our way down the stairs.

Colin met us at the bottom and led us into the morning room where Fiona sat at a table, drinking a cup of tea.

Her head popped up at our arrival, and she closed the planner she was working on.

"Good morning!" she said with a happy smile as she stood to greet us. "Come join me!"

We sat at the table with her, while Colin poured us two cups of tea.

"Thanks for the wonderful breakfast this morning," I said, tipping my cup to take a sip of the steaming liquid.

"My pleasure," she said, looking back and forth between the two of us. "I actually had a proposition for the two of you."

"Okay," Vance said, "tell us about it."

"I was wondering if you'd allow your grandfather and me to throw a reception for you here. We'd love to introduce you to our friends and family, plus it would give us the opportunity to celebrate your nuptials with you." She held her breath in anticipation of the answer.

Vance looked over at me with a smile, reaching out for my hand.

"Well, I always love an opportunity to show off my beautiful wife, but you don't have feel obligated to do something like that for us," he said, giving my hand a quick squeeze.

"Nonsense, I want to do it. We are family after all." I could see she wasn't going to give up on the idea easily.

"What do you think about it, baby?" he asked turning to look at me.

"I think it sounds kind of fun actually," I replied with a smile.

"Wonderful!" Fiona said, clasping her hands together in delight. "I'll have it set up for tomorrow night, if that's all right."

Vance nodded. "That should be fine."

"Is there somewhere we could go shopping for some new clothes, though?" I asked. "I don't know that we brought any proper evening attire with us."

"Absolutely!" she exclaimed and stood up. "I can have a car brought around right now to take you to Inverness this morning, unless you have other plans?"

"Nothing we can't put off until later," Vance smiled at her before turning to squeeze my hand again. "We can go now."

"I need to grab my bag, though," I said. I stood removing my hand from his. "You visit with Fiona. I'll be right back."

I left Vance with his grandmother as I slipped back out into the hall, hurrying up the stairs. When I entered our room, I heard a sound and turned to find Colin coming out of the closet. I stopped in surprise.

He looked at me with only a second of shock registering in his eyes before his artful mask slipped back into place.

"Pardon me, Madame," he said standing straighter. "Mrs. Cummings wanted me to check on the possibility of having the clothes in this closet removed for your convenience."

"Oh. I noticed the items in there."

"Mrs. Cummings has a dear friend who comes for frequent visits. She has become accustomed to leaving her things here as a matter of convenience," he explained to me.

"We can move to a different room," I suggested to him. "I wouldn't want our stay here to put anyone out."

"You're not causing any problems. Mrs. Cummings is quite partial to this suite, which is why she put you here."

"Oh, okay. Well, unless you're expecting Fiona's friend soon, you really don't need to trouble yourself about the items on our account. Vance and I don't need much space."

He smiled and gave a curt nod before he headed toward the door.

I went into the closet, grabbed my bag and both of our coats before heading back down the stairs.

Vance met me in the foyer, taking his coat from me before helping me into mine, and we stepped outside just as the car pulled up front. A smartly tailored driver stepped out and opened the door to the black luxury sedan with its dark-tinted windows, and we climbed inside.

The drive through the countryside was relaxing. When we arrived in Inverness, the driver maneuvered with ease through the traffic, safely delivering us to the store Vance's grandmother had recommended to us.

The sales people met us at the door, apparently having been informed of our impending arrival.

We were shuttled to a private viewing room, and our every need was catered to as we looked over several outfits the staff had already pulled for us before we arrived. I realized Fiona must have called ahead to describe us in detail to the efficient staff.

After trying on several different things, Vance settled on a lovely black tuxedo, with a white tie and vest, while I chose a long black satin dress, with a scooped neck and a dropped back that hugged every curve of my form. There was a slit up the back that went up to my mid-thigh, and the edges of the dress were lined in silver threads.

I picked a pretty pair of black heels with a tiny silver buckle to match.

Vance paid for our purchases and walked with me out to the waiting car while our things were put in the trunk by the driver.

Vance spoke briefly with him outside the door before sliding into the seat next to me.

"What was that about?" I asked, curious.

"You'll find out." He smiled mischievously.

A few minutes later we pulled up in front of a fine jewelry store.

"What's this?" I asked suspiciously, when the driver got out, coming to hold our door open for us.

"You need something pretty to wear around your neck with that dress," he said, and his gaze glanced down to my throat.

"But I already have something," I said and I fingered the chains that held the silver locket containing the clippings from his hair, as well as the one to my beautiful purple amulet.

"I love those on you," he said reaching out to run his own fingers over them lightly. "But I want to give you something special for tomorrow. Is that okay?" he asked while he continued tracing a finger down toward my chest. "Would you mind taking them off for the evening? I'll be right by your side, so you won't need the silver locket, and as far as the amulet ... well, I'll do my best to protect you should the need arise."

I nodded and kissed him lightly on the lips. He quickly threaded his hand behind my neck, pulling me closer and deepening the kiss, not caring the chauffeur was standing right there.

When he stopped, I was breathless once again, and I blushed when I realized the driver was purposely occupying his gaze elsewhere to give us some privacy.

Vance chuckled at my reaction and turned to look at the driver.

"Give us a minute, will you?" he said, glancing out at him.

"No problem, sir," the well-mannered man replied, and he shut the door.

"What are you doing?" I asked when Vance turned back to face me with a wicked glint gleaming in his eye.

"Finishing what I started," he smiled, and he pulled me back to his lips.

I laughed and pushed against him, feeling my flaming skin rising in temperature.

"People will see!" I said, nervously turning to glance over my shoulder toward the sidewalk outside.

He shook his head with a grin.

"Not with the tint on the windows of this car," he said, his lips mere millimeters away from mine, his eyes flashing with desire. "Now, are you going to kiss your husband, or are you going to make him beg?"

"I think ... beg," I replied, and a playful grin spread across my face.

"Wrong answer," he said, and he crushed his lips to mine, holding my head tightly to his as he slipped his tongue into my partially open mouth.

I leaned into his embrace eagerly and brought my hands up to his chiseled face, touching his cheeks gently with the tips of my fingers. He twisted his mouth slowly and heatedly back and forth over mine, tasting me from every angle he could until I was practically smoldering with desire.

He broke away suddenly and stared into my eyes, his breathing ragged as he looked at me.

"What are you doing to me?" he accused, and I was completely perplexed by his meaning.

"Doing?" I replied.

"You're intoxicating. I can't get enough of you. How can you seem so innocently unaware of your effect on me? Surely you know what a seductress you are?" He pulled me up against him again.

I would've laughed at his words had his emotions not been overpowering me. I could feel his need as it washed through him. He was very serious.

Wrapping my arms around his neck, I sighed, and he suddenly leaned my body back against the seat, resuming his intense kissing of me.

He pinned me there effectively, though I was a willing prisoner, letting his hands caress down my arms, over my face and through my hair.

After enjoying his attentions for several moments, I pushed him away from me.

"Vance, we're on a street out in front of a store. This is totally inappropriate," I said, with a slightly nervous giggle.

"Since when have I ever cared about propriety?" he asked, and he pulled me back to him, this time kissing down the side of my neck.

"Never," I responded, and I tipped my head to the side while closing my eyes, enjoying the pleasurable sensations he was creating. "But I can't in good conscience do this with that poor nice man standing right there against the door while cars are rushing by on the street!"

Vance let out a deep sigh, resting his head in the crook of my neck.

"Fine," he said quietly, and I could clearly hear the disappointment in his voice. "You're right, as usual."

He lifted his head and smiled softly at me.

"I'm sorry," I replied.

He shook his head, grinning seductively at me. "I'm not," he said. "And don't think you're getting out of this that easily. I fully intend to pick up right where I left off!"

He turned and knocked on the window of the car, and I hurried to straighten my disheveled hair while the driver opened the door. I blushed furiously, unable to look at the man while Vance helped me out of the car and walked me into the store.

Vance had several gorgeous items brought out of the cases for me to consider, from the very simple to the extremely extravagant. I had a hard time deciding what to purchase, mostly because he insisted on me trying everything. He would put the jewelry on me, and every time his fingertips slipped over my skin I would recall our heated moments in the car, causing me to blush once again and become distracted.

While I felt like a bumbling fool, I could tell he was enjoying the display very much, so well in fact, I became convinced he was distracting me on purpose. He was constantly in contact with my overheated skin, until I was sure the storekeepers must've assumed I had some sort of prickly rash moving over my body.

After all was said and done, I ended up choosing a tasteful teardrop diamond necklace on a sparkling platinum chain. Vance insisted I get the matching earrings also.

He paid for the items, and we headed out to the car.

"Thank you for the gift," I said after we were settled back into the vehicle.

"I like spoiling you," he replied with a grin, tracing one finger up my throat.

"So I've noticed. But you don't have to. I'm completely happy with everything just the way it is."

"I know. I feel the same way, but I hope you won't mind if I indulge you once in a while. I can't seem to help myself."

"Well, I guess that would be all right," I replied, smiling, and I could see the laughter dancing I his eyes.

He hooked his finger under my chin, lifting it higher and bringing it toward him.

"Now, where were we?" he whispered against my lips before he wrapped his arms around me, kissing me hotly for many miles as we sped back toward Bell Tower Hall.

CHAPTER 7

The next morning I woke to find myself alone in the massive bed of our suite.

"Vance?" I called out softly, glancing around the empty space.

There was no answer.

I swung my legs over the edge of the bed, pulled on my robe and walked toward the bathroom.

"Vance? Are you in here?"

My heart leapt up in tempo when I realized he wasn't here either. I turned to go back into the other room, and there was a soft knock on the door.

I tightened the knot on my robe and went to answer it. I found Colin standing on the other side.

"Good morning, Colin," I said with a small smile.

"Good morning to you, Madame," he replied with a slight bow. "Mr. Mangum requested that I please remind you he is fencing with Mr. Cummings this morning. He said to invite you to take your breakfast with him in the gymnasium unless you would prefer to have it here in your room instead."

I suddenly recalled our after-dinner conversation with Douglas and Fiona from the evening prior. Douglas had asked Vance if he knew how to fence. When Vance replied in the negative, he offered to give Vance a lesson in the morning.

"Thank you, Colin," I said, my thoughts returning to the present. "Would you please tell Vance I'll be down soon and I'll eat my breakfast there with him?"

"As you wish," Colin said with a curt nod before turning to walk away.

I closed the door and meandered over to the closet. I pulled out a pair of comfortable black jeans and a teal-colored shirt before heading into the bathroom.

After I was done showering and getting dressed, I opted to go casual for the day, knowing we would be getting fixed up for our reception this evening. I pulled my hair back in a ponytail and lightly used some mascara and a pale lip gloss to give some shine before I headed down to the gymnasium.

Colin appeared magically, as usual, at the bottom of the stairs and led me through the massive house and into the gigantic room.

I tried to keep my jaw closed when I cast my gaze around the ornate space. Large white pillars graced each corner, twisting up to a domed ceiling with a grand mural that depicted ancient dueling scenes from eras gone by. My eyes flitted back down over mirrored walls to the outer wall which was covered in closed French doors that led out to a beautiful fountain area and to the rolling grounds beyond. It was breathtaking.

Colin cleared his throat slightly, catching my attention once again and gesturing for me to follow him over to where Fiona was sitting at a round white table with a delicious looking breakfast spread in front of her.

I sat down in one of the three vacant chairs at the table, next to her.

"Good morning, dear." She smiled while Colin placed a plate in front of me and poured me a glass of orange juice.

"Good morning to you," I replied smiling back before turning to follow her gaze out into the middle of the floor, where Vance was standing on a mat with his grandfather. Douglas was explaining something to him. "What's going on?" I asked, thinking how good Vance looked dressed up in the white protective clothing.

"Douglas just finished showing Vance the three main weapons used in fencing—the foil, the epee, and the saber," she explained. "They're going to use the foil for their match."

Another man approached Vance and Douglas, dressed in similar attire though he was all in black.

"Who's that?" I asked Fiona.

"That is Armell, Douglas's fencing instructor. He's here to teach Vance some of the moves and rules," she replied.

"That's good." My heart leaping up as Vance picked a foil and stepped into the center of the mat. I was suddenly concerned for him. "This is a safe sport, right?"

Fiona laughed gently and reached over to pat my hand.

"Don't worry, dear. The suits are electronic. The end of the sword is actually a push button which will register the official hits each opponent makes on one another. The vest, or jacket as it is called, has sensors in it which are triggered when the tip of the foil presses against it, thus registering the point and sending it to the electronic scoring apparatus."

"That's interesting," I said while I watched the instructor coach Vance on the proper way to hold his foil before he proceeded to show him some moves, like advancing forward, lunging and so on.

It was amazing for me to observe Vance, watching the ease and speed he seemed to be learning with. He should have been a dancer; he was so graceful in his movements. If it had been me out there, I would've looked like a bumbling fool.

When Vance looked fairly comfortable with the footwork, the instructor moved on to blade work, showing him several different moves with his weapon.

"Are you going to eat, Portia?" Fiona's voice broke into my thoughts, and I looked down at my empty plate.

"Sorry. I completely forgot about the food, this is all so interesting." I reached over to pull some warm muffins and fresh fruit off the tray in front of me. "Do you watch Douglas often?"

"Goodness no!" she replied with a laugh. "I'd be down here all the time! Douglas is very fond of the sport and has become quite the master of it. He often competes."

"Really?" I said, feeling surprised at this revelation, though I wasn't sure why. It was clear that the Cummings men had a natural ability toward athleticism. "How long has he been competing?"

"Oh for several years," she answered with a wave of her hand. "We've even hosted some events here."

I could believe that easily as I took in the size of the massive room once again while I bit into a muffin.

"I hope Douglas will take it easy on Vance then," I said when I finished chewing. "He can't possibly learn enough to be good competition to Douglas in one day."

Fiona laughed. "That's true, but they decided earlier to teach him a few basic moves, and Douglas will be restricted to those same moves as well. That should help even the playing field a little."

This was an interesting scenario for me to consider. I never considered Vance to be a weak opponent in any type of situation. He always seemed strong and formidable in situations that required aggression in the past. I found it was hard for me to envision him as the underdog here, and it was making me feel slightly nervous.

I was done with eating my breakfast when the instructor finally finished warming up with Vance and he stepped to face Douglas on the mat. Suddenly, I wished I hadn't eaten at all as a case of the nervous butterflies attacked my stomach.

Vance dropped his protective mask into place, lifted his foil and waited. Douglas stepped forward and began the attack, thrusting in a forward motion. Vance moved backward in reaction, parrying against Douglas's foil at the appropriate times.

I found myself biting at my lower lip, and I could hear Fiona chuckle lightly beside me when Douglas continued to force Vance farther backward down the long mat. I began to wonder if Vance was too overwhelmed to even remember what he was supposed to do. Suddenly Vance lunged forward, catching Douglas off guard, landing the tip of his foil squarely against Douglas's chest, registering a point.

Douglas lifted his mask and looked down at his chest in complete shock, and I couldn't help the grin that spread across my face as I watched.

"Point to Mr. Mangum," the instructor called out.

The two men walked back to the center of the mat and began once again. It soon became clear Vance was allowing Douglas to beat him back while he studied his moves when he landed another point in similar fashion.

Douglas didn't remove his mask this time, but I could tell he was not very happy by the way he strode back to the center of the mat, abruptly lifting his foil as he waited for Vance to join him.

This time, however, Vance was the one who attacked, and he successfully forced Douglas backward. Their weapons clashed loudly together, sending the sound of clinking metal throughout the room.

"I've never seen anything like this," Fiona said, her eyes dancing as she watched with her hands clasped in delight. "The boy is a natural."

It was clear Vance's extreme speed was giving him a definite advantage. Douglas fought desperately to keep up with him, and in the end they both thrust at the same time, landing equal blows on each other's chests.

They lifted their helmets, laughing together, and the instructor said it appeared that Douglas landed the point first, barely.

Douglas clapped Vance on the back before pulling his mask off his sweat-drenched head. Vance followed suit, and the two of them made their way over to the table while the instructor gathered up the weapons.

"What do you think of our grandson this morning?" Douglas asked Fiona as he sat down at the table. Vance came to kiss me on the cheek before he sat down as well.

"I think you'd better be careful or you may find yourself run through," she replied with a laugh. "I've never seen anything like it."

"Me either," Douglas replied. "I was really sweating it out there!"

"So I can see," Fiona replied wryly as she waved her hand back and forth in front of her face lightly, scrunching her nose up slightly. "You're a mess!"

"Blame it all on this one," Douglas replied, reaching over to squeeze Vance's shoulder.

Vance was beaming, thoroughly enjoying himself. "You're giving me too much credit," he replied modestly with a slight shake of his head. "I'm just as sweaty as you are, and you landed the last point."

"True, but there were three points, remember? That means you're the currently the victor," Douglas replied. "Now let's enjoy some breakfast with our lovely company, and then we'll hit the mat again."

"That sounds like a good plan," Vance agreed with a grin, and he reached to fill his plate.

I watched him as he moved, thinking he looked like a gorgeous mess with his flushed face and sweaty hair, clothed in the white garment. If he worked out like this every day, he would certainly have me as a captive audience for every minute of it. My eyes practically devoured every inch of him.

"Portia," his voice suddenly penetrated into the thoughts in my head. "You've got to quit staring at me like that. You're making my grandmother blush."

My eyes quickly flickered over toward Fiona who was indeed watching me with avid interest, and I quickly cast my gaze down into my lap, feeling the flush creep into my own skin.

Vance chuckled out loud at this, and I kicked him under the table, mortified at his reaction. He leaned over and kissed my cheek once more.

"Don't worry, baby," he whispered into my ear. "It's all good." He winked as he pulled away from me, and I could tell he was totally enjoying my reaction to him ... again.

After they were done eating, Douglas and Vance returned to the mat. This time the instructor explained things in much greater detail to Vance, and the two worked slowly together on moves.

"Well, I think I'm done here." Fiona sighed as she stood. "I have some correspondence to take care of this morning."

"I'll walk with you," I said, standing also.

Vance flicked me a smile as I left the room. "See you in a little while, baby," he said into my head, and I smiled widely back at him.

"I'll send Colin up for your dress shortly," Fiona said, capturing my attention again. "He'll have the maid get it properly pressed for this evening."

"Thank you," I replied. "Is there anything I can do to help out with the preparations for tonight?"

"No, not at all. The catering staff and the decorators will be here shortly after noon. They should have things well in hand. Just get rested up and be ready to enjoy yourself."

She paused when we reached the grand staircase.

"Okay. I'll go pull mine and Vance's clothes out for Colin now."

"Thank you," she said. "And I enjoyed your company at breakfast this morning."

I turned to smile back at her. "Thanks, it was fun for me, too," I replied with a smile.

Vance walked back into the bedroom a couple of hours later, still dressed in his protective fencing gear, thoroughly sweaty and flushed.

"Hey, baby," he said, walking toward where I was sitting in front of the roaring fire.

"Don't you even touch me!" I protested, and I lifted a finger in warning when I saw the wicked glint in his eye.

He laughed seductively. "Aw, you're no fun," he mumbled, leaning his head in toward me and I shied away from him.

"You're all sweaty!" I exclaimed.

"Come on, baby. Just one little kiss on the cheek for me then," he begged, and he tapped his index finger on his face, his eyes sparkling.

I couldn't resist him. His power of persuasion over me would be my complete undoing. He knew I would do whatever he asked, following him to the ends of the earth and beyond.

I leaned in to lightly to place a peck against him, but before my lips landed, he turned his head and kissed me full on the mouth, wrapping his fingers around my chin and holding me there.

Sighing, I made up my mind right then and there that if kissing were a sport, Vance would win in every category every time. He could turn my insides to complete mush with even the slightest touch.

He pulled away from me with a chuckle, his face mere millimeters from mine.

"See, that wasn't so bad now, was it?" he asked with a dimpled grin, his eyes searching mine.

"Go take a shower," I said, smiling, refusing to give in to his charmingly manly display.

"I want to show you something first," he said straightening, and that was when I noticed he had something draped over his arm. He lifted it, revealing a red and green plaid kilt. "What do you think?" he asked with a grin, lifting an eyebrow.

"A kilt?" I asked with a slight snicker at the idea of Vance wearing such an article of clothing, completely unable to wrap my mind around the thought. "Where did you get it?"

"Douglas gave it to me. This is the Cummingses' tartan, I guess. He said I was part of the family, and I should have one."

I knew this was a huge thing for him, to actually be treated like family by his family, and I tried to tone down my humorous reaction.

"Does he want you to wear it to the reception?" I asked, not really sure if I would care for that or not.

He shrugged. "He said I could if I wanted to, but it was up to me since I already bought the other suit."

"So what're you going to do?"

"I don't know." He chuckled. "I told him I'd think about it. Honestly though, I don't know if it's my cup of tea. I have a hard time even wearing the tuxedo."

"Well, it was a very nice gesture for him to make."

"I agree," he replied, leaning down to kiss my cheek. "I'm going to get in the shower now," he added.

My eyes followed him as he left before turning to look back at the fire while I contemplated recent events.

I was very happy Vance seemed to be finding his niche with his family and that they seemed to be genuinely receiving him with open arms. Family was something he'd always wanted a connection with.

The fire danced in the grate before me, and I soon became caught up in my thoughts, so much so I didn't hear him approach until he spoke.

"So what do you think?" he asked and I looked up to see him standing just outside the doorway.

My mouth went slack, and I thought my teeth might fall out onto the floor.

He was standing there dressed only in the kilt with the length of plaid thrown up over his shoulder. His wet towel-dried hair stood up messily off his head, and I could smell the scent of his aftershave wafting through the air toward me. He looked down to make an adjustment on the belt at his waist, and all the muscles in his body rippled in response.

My gaze traveled from his head to his toes, and I was afraid to blink for fear this luscious apparition would disappear. He looked like an ancient highlander straight out of a romance novel.

"Well?" he asked me again, when he was done with the adjustment.

I got out of the chair and walked boldly toward him, grabbing his face in both of my hands and kissing him with every ounce of my being.

I caught him off guard, but he chuckled against my lips before his arms came tightly around me and he really kissed me back. Threading one hand through his hair, I let the other drift down his muscled shoulder and over his bulging bicep, squeezing it slightly as I passed.

This evoked a low growl from him, and he moved forward aggressively several steps until I was pressed up against the wall.

He ravaged my mouth until I felt faint from lack of air before he broke the kiss, staring at me as we both gasped for breath.

"So I take it you like the kilt?"

"On you, Vance ... definitely," I answered with a nod, breathing heavily, and he pushed into me again, picking right up where he had left off.

The place was aglow that evening. I stood at one of the windows in our room watching the cars pull into the circle driveway one after another to drop their richly attired guests off at the door.

I was all dressed in my new clothes and had pulled some of my hair up into a knot at the back of my head, letting the rest drape in a long curl down the side of my neck, which helped to hide the scar there with a little artfully applied makeup.

The jewelry Vance had given me went perfectly with everything, and I felt quite sparkly, despite the nervous butterflies in my stomach at meeting a bunch of people I had absolutely nothing in common with.

Vance stepped out of the dressing room, and I turned to look at him in the formal cut tuxedo he purchased, while he fastened his tie in the mirror over the mantle.

He was magnificent, and I couldn't even blink, let alone look away from him. For someone who was a self-proclaimed t-shirt and jeans kind of guy, he sure could pull off the formal attire well.

After finishing with his tie, he finally turned, letting his hands drop to his side while he stopped to stare at me.

"Stunning," was all he said, his gaze raking over me, not once but twice, his blue eyes sparking to life as if I lit a match in them.

He was over to my side in two seconds, reaching out for me, and I backed away laughing, holding him at arm's length.

"Don't touch me. You'll mess me all up again," I said, knowing he wouldn't care in the least.

He grabbed me easily and pulled me to him up against his chest, his fresh breath floating over me as he spoke.

"I'll be gentle. I promise," he said, and he placed a soft kiss on my lips.

I relented under his masterful touch, wrapping my arms around his neck and really kissing him back, letting my emotion flow into him, and he did the same to me. It was a breathless, yet tender, moment.

In the end, when the kiss was over, he kept his word. I only had to retouch some makeup around my mouth.

"I guess we've kept the guests waiting long enough," I said with a sigh while he watched me reapply my lip gloss in the bathroom mirror.

"We don't know any of them," he replied with a smile. "If it weren't so rude to my grandparents, I'd be much more inclined to stay in here tonight with you."

"Me too," I added with a nod, and I turned to place my hand against the side of his handsome face.

His eyes flitted down over my features and to my neck. "I guess I should let you have the opportunity to show off your new jewelry, though," he teased.

My hand flitted up to where the new necklace lay at my neck, and I fingered it as several thoughts ran through my head.

"What's the matter?"

"I was just thinking about how my amulet protected me when the roof fell in at the school, but it didn't do anything when you or Damien bit me. Why is that?" I asked him.

He let out a soft sigh and pondered this for a moment before he answered. "Things like talismans are very selective in the way they activate. It's a magic that's helpful, but not to be relied on heavily." He held up the hand which had the ring my grandma sent to him. "I wear this because it's a gift of good magic from the coven. Maybe it'll help me someday, maybe it won't, but what does it hurt?"

I nodded. "I remember Grandma telling me it might not do you any good since your dad's coven had already figured out ways around charms in the past," I replied.

"It's very difficult for something like a charm to ward off live magic," he said while he fingered the diamond at my neck. "Your amulet protected you from something non-magical when the explosion happened, and it may have very well played a part in you being unharmed when you were almost hit by the car.

Neither of those instances had a magical force directly behind it."

"Oh, I see," I said, suddenly understanding the difference in the situations I had been placed in.

"Why all the questions tonight, baby? Are you feeling nervous, under protected?" he asked while he looked at me carefully.

I laughed nervously. "No. I just feel a little naked without the amulet. I've worn it for so long. And I'm a little nervous about meeting a bunch of people I don't know," I admitted truthfully.

He reached out and stroked my face with his hand. "Portia, you have nothing to worry about tonight," he began. "You'll be the most beautiful thing in the room, and the guests are sure to be mesmerized by you as much as I am. And I promise you, I won't let any harm come to you."

"I know you won't," I said, trusting him completely, staring into his blue eyes.

I held my arm out to him, and he took it, leading me out of the door and to the grand staircase. We walked carefully down, turning into one of the massive hallways, walking until we reached the doorway to the ballroom.

A uniformed man, holding a large rod in one hand, looked at us before banging the rod three times on the floor.

"Mr. and Mrs. Vance Mangum," he announced loudly with a booming voice into the room, and I was surprised he knew who we were since I'd never laid eyes on him before in my life.

Every single person in the room stopped whatever they were doing and looked over at us standing at the entrance.

Vance led me into the room, and Fiona quickly weaved her way through the throng of people to come give him a kiss on both sides of his face.

Douglas stepped up to his side, placing a hand on his shoulder.

"Ladies and Gentlemen, may I present you with our grandson, Vance," Douglas spoke proudly to the crowd.

People immediately began lining up to come meet him, and suddenly I found myself pushed back behind the three of them in the shuffle of the crowd.

I smiled, though, as I watched him standing there with his family, feeling very happy for him in this moment.

Only a few seconds passed before I saw him turn to look for me in the crowd. He stepped away from his grandparents, effectively shunning those who were milling around him vying for his attention, reaching out to pull me firmly up next to his side.

He didn't let go of me for the rest of the evening, politely introducing me to every person who came to meet him. If anyone called his attention or threatened to separate us, he would make them wait until I could join him.

After meeting so many people we couldn't have possibly remembered any of their names, he finally led me out onto the dance floor.

He swept me up, moving to a romantic waltz while the string quartet played away, but I could tell he was upset about something.

"Don't you ever let people push you to the side like that again," he chastened me with a serious look.

"It didn't bother me. I'm no one to these people. They were all excited to meet you, and rightly so," I said softly.

"I don't like it when you talk like that, Portia," he said gruffly, though his voice softened a little. "You're the most beautiful person in this room, inside and out.

They may not know what they're missing, but I do when you aren't there."

He had a point he was trying to make, and he chose to do it here. He stopped dancing with me as the other couples in the room swirled around us, and pulled me into his embrace. He lifted both hands to my face, tilting it to his, placing a gentle kiss on my lips.

I stood there rooted to the spot while he tenderly moved over my mouth for everyone in attendance to see. I could almost feel the heat from the stares we were getting as people began to notice us in this sweet embrace.

He took his time, not caring what anyone was thinking, or what protocols he was breaking, sending his message to me and everyone else in the room. I was part of him, and he was part of me.

A quiet cough interrupted our interlude, and we pulled away from each other slowly to look at the intruder.

Brian Fitzgerald was standing next to us. "May I cut in?" he asked politely, extending a hand to me in invitation as was customary.

"No," Vance said, clearly irritated, and he sized Brian up, refusing to let go of me.

"I'm sorry?" Brian asked, taken aback at the refusal, and I thought I saw anger flash briefly in his eyes.

I spoke up quickly, trying to ease the tension in the situation. "My husband and I were having what should have been a private moment, Brian. I'm sorry if we weren't being discreet enough." I lightly reached out to rest my hand on Brian's forearm.

I felt the anger seethe through Vance at this, though, and I quickly removed my hand, worrying I had somehow made the situation worse.

"Don't apologize for us, Portia," Vance said, and he took a step closer to Brian, so he was standing in between us.

This time I put my arm on Vance in an attempt to restrain him from doing something stupid.

"Could I speak with you for a moment, Vance?" I said with slightly clenched teeth while I forced a smile.

Vance looked at me for a long moment before giving me a nod and allowing me to tow him out of the room.

I walked with him into a sitting area in the next room, closing the door behind us.

"What was that all about?" I asked him curiously, my eyes wide.

He gave a sigh before he turned to walk away from me. "I don't know," he said, running a frustrated hand through his hair. "I was upset by everyone shutting you out in the beginning. I just want to be alone with you instead of at this stupid party. Then this Brian joker walks up and wants to dance with you." He looked up at me seriously. "I don't like that guy."

"Why not? He's been nothing but kind and helpful to us," I replied, surprised at his sudden declaration against the man.

"I just get this vibe every time he looks at you. It's like you're something he wants for himself. He doesn't care that you're my wife, and it's driving me crazy with the need to rearrange his face," he said angrily.

I laughed in spite of his anger. "I think you're jealous, and there's nothing to be jealous of. I certainly have no feelings for him," I replied, watching him. "You're the only person I can even see, Vance. There's no one else for me but you. Nothing will ever change that."

"I know," he said coming back over and placed his hands on my arms, running them over me. "But so help me, you belong to me, and if that punk gets any idea in his head otherwise, he won't live to regret it!"

I felt a shudder move over my body, thinking Brian would indeed be a complete fool to cross him. I had absolutely no doubt in my mind Vance was completely serious.

Chapter 8

I finally managed to coax Vance back to the party, where he put on a pretty good show of proper manners for the rest of the night.

The only thing people found curious, including myself, was that he turned down every request anyone made to dance with me.

He would laughingly explain he was still such a newlywed it was impossible to let me go anywhere without him. He stuck to me like glue the entire evening, breaking all the rules of propriety. By the end of the night, though, I think everyone thought he was charming in his devotion and affections toward me.

I, however, began to watch him a little closer, noticing his behavior became ever more possessive. He seemed nervous to me, grabbing a glass of champagne every time a waiter passed, and quickly downing the contents. I could see something was really eating at him—I just didn't know what it was.

I was happy when the last of the guests departed well after midnight. After thanking Douglas and Fiona for the wonderful evening, I led Vance gently by the hand up the stairs to our room.

"What is going on?" I asked once we were safely inside with the door locked behind us.

"Portia, I'm losing my mind," he said sinking to sit on the tufted bench at the foot of the bed, looking completely dejected.

I went over to kneel in front of him, placing my hands gently on his knees.

"Can I help you somehow?" I asked, truly concerned at his attitude.

He looked at me for several long moments, not replying, his gaze never wavering as he stared deep into my eyes.

I waited, not pressuring him or trying to read the thoughts in his head, letting him decide when he was ready to speak.

"Something is wrong. I've felt funny ever since we stayed the first night here. Temperamentally, I get irritated by the smallest things, and I just have this constant itch to be with you. Physically, I mean. I'm not saying that's a bad thing, but something is different. It's almost an overwhelming need to be with you ... all the time." He rubbed his hand through his hair in frustration. "I know I'm not making any sense. I always want to be with you, but this is something really intense. It's almost like the desires I had when I was going through the demon conversion."

That did scare me.

"You aren't having some type of relapse are you?" I asked in alarm, looking him over closely, searching for any of the telltale signs. "We did just assume you'd been cured of everything. Could we have missed something?"

"I don't know," he said shaking his head, reaching a hand out to draw it lovingly over my cheek. "I'm not really noticing anything like withdrawal, and I haven't noticed any red eyes or anything."

He stood up and walked around me to go to the table where a new bottle of champagne was chilling in the room. He popped the cork and poured himself a large glass before turning to me.

"Do you want some?"

"No, thank you," I replied. "It doesn't settle well with me."

He quickly downed the entire contents of the glass and poured himself another one.

I watched him with concern. I'd never seen him drink like this. We both stayed pretty far away from alcohol in our lives, except for the small sip of wine here and there when performing rituals.

I didn't say anything about it, though, figuring he needed it to calm his nerves.

He drank in silence, and I noticed after a few minutes he did seem a bit less antsy. I went and wrapped my arms around him.

"Do you feel better now?" I asked while I hugged him.

"Yes, thank you." He sighed, placing his glass down on the table so he could pick the pins out of my hair, bringing it down from its up-do. "I'm sorry for scaring you with all this."

"Don't be sorry. I'm your wife. This is what I'm here for." I smiled up at him, and he fanned his fingers through my hair, bringing it around my shoulders.

He didn't reply, instead bending to kiss me. The kiss was soft at first but quickly deepened into more.

Our previous thoughts were soon well distracted, and the first morning light was creeping into the room when he finally pulled me into his embrace so we could both fall asleep.

It was late in the afternoon when I woke up. I noticed right away he wasn't in bed with me anymore. I turned to search the large room, finding him standing next to the fireplace in his robe, leaning over the mantle while he watched the fire burn. I saw he had a bottle of champagne in one hand and an almost empty glass in the other.

He lifted the flute to swallow the rest of the contents and immediately raised the bottle to pour another refill.

Something was really wrong here. I didn't know what it was, but I began to feel a bit of fear creep into my chest. This was not the way Vance acted. He wasn't a drinker at all. This behavior was completely out of character for him.

He sensed my feelings instantly, lifting his head to look at me. He downed the rest of the champagne quickly and placed the glass down, coming to crawl on the bed next to me.

"Vance? What's going on?" I asked scooting myself up against the mountains of pillows to look at him.

"Don't be scared," he said, and he caressed my face with his hand. "I'm fine."

"I've never seen you drink like this before." I looked over to the nearly empty bottle still sitting above the fireplace.

"I'm sorry. It just helps take the edge off."

"The edge of what?" I asked, completely confused.

"I don't know how to explain it," he said, his eyes raking over me. "Just trust me, okay?"

"Maybe we should go tell your grandparents how you're feeling. They might be able to help," I suggested.

"I'm fine. Really," he said before he grabbed my face with one of his hands, kissing me roughly this time. He became a little too aggressive, and I finally pushed him away. I actually felt like he was bruising my face with his strong fingers.

He looked at me intensely, almost angrily.

"Is the breakfast tray still here?" I asked, shooting the first words I could think of out of my mouth, feigning hunger.

I didn't think I would really be able to eat as my insides were shaking horribly.

"Oh, I'm sorry. I forgot you haven't eaten yet," he said as he climbed off the bed and went over to get the cart and wheel it to the bedside.

I watched him carefully.

He still seemed like himself, yet there was this edge that hadn't been there before. I wondered lamely if he just wasn't getting enough sleep. Surely that, combined with stress, could cause some strange behavior.

He sat down on the edge of the bed and began feeding the food to me. I watched him intently while forcing myself to chew what he was giving me, even though it tasted like sawdust in my mouth. I soon noticed how every now and then he would raise his hand to his temple like he was getting a headache or something,

"I'm really tired today," I said in between bites of food.

"Well, I did keep you up quite late." He smiled, feeding me another mouthful, and I saw a flash of the lusty look from last night pop back into his eyes.

I nodded. "Do you think maybe we could sleep some more this afternoon? I think all this honeymooning is catching up with me." I tried to add a little laughter.

He lifted his hand to his head again, this time closing his eyes as he held the bridge of his nose. "I think that sounds great," he answered a few moments later, his voice sounding slightly pinched.

When the moment passed he continued to feed me until I told him I couldn't eat another bite. He took the tray and placed it by the door, before returning to climb in next to me.

He actually fell asleep quickly, and I felt a little more at ease. Maybe he was just really tired.

I watched over him for a long while before I finally relaxed enough to go to sleep, too.

A couple of hours passed by the time I ventured back out into reality, and I awoke to find him gone from the bed again.

This time he was fully dressed and pacing the floor at the end of the bed, holding both of his hands against the sides of his head as if he were in agony.

"What is it?" I asked, watching him, my eyes wide in concern.

He whipped his head over to look at me while I spoke, as if I caught him totally unaware, dropping his hands instantly back to his sides, though his fists remained clenched.

"You're awake," he said, coming over to the side of the bed. "Do you want to go for a walk with me?"

"Right now?" I asked. I looked over at the fading light in the window. "It'll be getting pretty cold outside."

"I need some air," he said, standing to resume his pacing at the end of the bed. "I think I'm getting cabin fever."

I could see he did indeed need to get out and do something. He was acting very strange.

"Just let me get dressed real quick," I replied, swinging my legs over the edge of the massive bed.

I walked into the closet and pulled on a heavy sweater and jeans, as well as some good walking shoes before brushing through my hair and adding a knit hat over the top for warmth.

He had his coat and hat on when I came back out. He helped me into my coat and picked up my red scarf, wrapping it around my neck.

We went down the stairs, passing Colin on our way to the front door.

"We're going on a walk," he said brusquely when we passed, pulling me behind him.

"Please tell Douglas and Fiona we're sorry we haven't had the chance to visit with them yet today," I called over my shoulder, since Vance didn't pause in his stride for the door.

It wasn't like Vance to not be polite.

We stepped out into the brisk evening air, and I immediately hunched my shoulders up in protection against it.

Vance didn't let go of my hand as he moved along and I had to step up my pace to keep up with him. He turned out of the driveway and headed off across the immaculate property.

"Where are we going?" I asked.

"I have no idea," he replied shortly.

We walked for about a mile at the rapid pace he set before he finally slowed a little, though he still didn't speak to me. We wandered on until the land opened up into a very large pasture, and I noticed a herd of sheep out in the middle of the field.

"Do you care if we go to see the sheep?" I asked him.

He shrugged indifferently. "Go ahead."

Letting go of his hand, I turned to walk out into the field. I noticed he was hanging behind, watching me.

Slowly, I made my way up to the small group of sheep nearest to me, trying not to startle them.

I always loved sheep as a child. My parents had a touch-and-feel book they used to read to me. The sheep in it always looked and felt so soft and fluffy. I wanted to see if they really were as soft as they looked.

A few of them made some gentle bleating sounds as I approached, and some shifted nervously the closer I got. I stretched my hand out and spoke in soft soothing tones, allowing my magic to flow through me in an attempt to communicate with them.

As it turned out, they allowed me to walk right into the center of them. I petted one on the head, and several others came over to nudge at me, awaiting their turn for attention.

I laughed softly, crooning over them.

The texture of their coats was much rougher than I expected it to be, but they were very thick.

I played with them for several minutes before turning to look at Vance, who was leaning up against a fence post with his arms crossed over his chest, watching me in the rising moonlight.

"Why don't you come and join me?" I called out while I scratched one of the bigger sheep behind the ear. "They're very friendly."

He didn't say anything for a moment, but he finally pushed away from the post and began walking toward me. He had only gone a few steps when the sheep suddenly started bleating and running.

I stood and watched in amazement while they scattered in every direction.

"What's happening? Why did they all run away like that?"

"I guess they don't like me." He laughed in a slightly uncomfortable voice.

"That's not possible," I replied watching him. "I remember how the dolphins responded to you. You're a natural with animals."

He shrugged nonchalantly. "Don't know what to tell you."

I marched over and grabbed his hand, turning back toward the herd, determined to prove him wrong, but every time I tried to approach one of the sheep, it would run away.

I turned to him in frustration. "This is weird," I said, biting at my lower lip as I pondered this. I let go of his hand and tried walking back into the group by myself. The sheep easily let me approach.

"Why won't you let Vance touch you?" I said squatting down in front of the largest one. "He's a nice guy."

I reached out to rub the sheep around the neck with both of my hands.

"Now come over," I said, not willing to let this go. "Only this time call out to them with your magic like you did with the dolphins."

He gave a sigh, shaking his head, as he started toward me again.

The instant he began to walk forward the sheep ran off again, even though I tried to hang on to the one I was petting. The big male bucked against me until I fell over onto my rump, and he took off to join the others.

I threw my hands up in frustration.

"Just forget about it," Vance said coming up next to me. "They just don't like me."

"But why?" I said asked, feeling completely perplexed. "It doesn't make any sense."

He laughed at me then, reaching out to turn my face to his. "They're sheep, Portia. It really isn't a big deal. Everything in the world is not attracted to me the way you are. That's perfectly normal," he said, and I could see the light dancing in his eyes.

"Well, they should be, because you're wonderful," I replied with a little pout and a scowl.

He really laughed then, and wrapped his arms around me in a giant bear hug, leaning his head against mine.

"You're too good to me," he said with a grin that warmed my heart, and I snuggled in closer to him.

This was the Vance I knew and loved.

"Are you feeling better now?" I asked, and I nuzzled my cold nose in against his warm neck.

"Yes, much better," he said. "You always know how to cheer me up."

"Good," I replied, feeling relieved at his words. "Then do you want to continue on, or can we please get out of this freezing air?"

He nodded in the general direction of the manor house. "Let's go," he said, taking me by the hand once again.

Chapter 9

Colin met us at the door, almost as if he had been expecting us, taking our coats and hats for us.

I followed as Vance led me by the hand down the hall into the grand salon, where Douglas and Fiona were sitting in front of the fireplace.

"Well, there they are!" Fiona said when she spotted us in the doorway, waving us over to join them.

"Sorry we've been such horrible guests," I spoke up, feeling guilty we hadn't socialized with them before now. "Last night really wore us out!"

"Not a problem!" Fiona replied. "I slept in, too." She smiled softly, as if she were telling us some dreadful secret. "Douglas, however, was up and at the offices early this morning managing the estate."

"The party was wonderful, by the way," Vance added with a politely, looking between both of them.

"Everyone was so excited to meet our long-lost grandson," Douglas replied. "And of course you too, Portia," he added cordially, almost as an afterthought.

"I was just the side show," I laughed, shaking my head slightly. "Vance was the main event."

"Whatever," Vance said, squeezing my hand tighter as he looked over at me.

Fiona changed the subject. "I told Colin to serve dinner in here tonight. I thought we'd all enjoy a more relaxed environment after last evening's formal affair."

"That sounds nice," Vance agreed, and I saw he was being truthful when he allowed his posture to relax and lean back into the furniture a little.

"So let's visit," Fiona said brightly, watching him.

"All right. What do you want to know?" he replied with a small smile.

"Well, for starters, how long are you planning on staying in Scotland?" she asked.

"Actually, we'd been thinking of leaving in a day or two," Vance said, surprising me since we had never discussed any such thing. "We came here specifically on the hope of finding my mother, but it seems that's no longer an option. Portia and I are still in the middle of a school year, so it would probably better for both of us if we were to hurry and get back to that."

"So soon?" Douglas replied looking a bit downtrodden at the idea. "We hoped you'd stay much longer."

"What if we had a tutor come here for both of you?" Fiona piped up. "That way you could both finish your studies on time, and we could enjoy having you here for a while."

"We don't want to be an imposition," he said, and he turned to look at me, slightly raising an eyebrow.

"That wouldn't be the case at all," Douglas spoke up. "We want you to stay. We want to get to know you. In fact, I'd be willing to teach you about running the estate if you'd stay. Why not even make Bell Tower your permanent home? It'll be yours someday anyway."

Vance seemed very surprised at this comment, and he faltered, searching for the right words.

"Thank you for your offer, but I'd definitely have to discuss a decision this big with Portia and her family first."

"Whatever you need, son," Douglas said kindly. "Feel free to use the house phone for any calls you might want to make."

Vance nodded, the surprised look still on his face.

Colin arrived in the room rolling a large cart with dinner on it. He served each of us our food on small trays for our laps.

The meal was simple, crusty bread bowls filled with steaming hot potato soup. After the cold walk we had been on this evening, it was the perfect thing, warming us from the inside out.

We enjoyed small talk, mostly about the running of the estate and the charities the Cummingses were involved in, just getting to know them a little better.

When we were finished with our meal, Colin magically reappeared to clean up after us and then returned with a fresh bottle of chilled champagne.

I refused any when he came to pour my glass, and Fiona looked at me with a questioning gaze.

"It doesn't agree with me," I explained at her look.

"Would you care for something else?" she asked me.

"No. I'm fine, thank you." I smiled.

Vance had several glasses throughout the night, and Colin seemed to magically reappear every time a bottle ran dry. Vance seemed fine, though, so I tried to put it at the back of my mind and enjoy the rest of the evening getting to know his family.

When we finally retired to our bedroom, Vance turned to me immediately.

"So what do you think about the offer they placed on the table this evening?" he asked.

"About staying here?" He nodded.

"I don't know," I answered honestly, going over to sit cross-legged on the bed. "I was kind of looking forward to getting that cozy little place in Flagstaff we'd talked about."

"Me too," he said with a smile, coming over and flopping backward onto the bed next to me, resting his head on arms. "I just never imagined this as a possibility."

"Would you like to stay here? I know how much you've wanted a family connection in your life. How do you feel about all this?" I prodded.

"I truly don't know how I feel about it. I've never really had a place to call home before I met you. I think Sedona has been more my home than anywhere else in the world. Even when I was a child with both of my parents, we traveled a lot. Now, I find out I have this whole history and heritage I was never aware of. The idea is intriguing to me, I guess." He looked at me, trying to gauge my reaction.

I reached over to place one of my hands on his chest, and he covered it with his own.

"I just want you to be happy. As long as I'm with you, I'll be fine."

He looked at me seriously. "I don't want you to do something because you think it'll make me happy. I want to make a decision based on both of our needs and desires. You know, whatever is best for us."

I nodded in understanding.

"So would you like living here or not?" he asked me again.

I sat back for a moment and really thought about it for a minute before I answered him. "I don't know. I've been having a wonderful time here on our honeymoon, but I'm really missing Sedona."

"That's our answer then," he replied. "Both of us mentioned going back to Sedona. I think that's where we should be."

"Are you sure?' I asked him, knowing he was giving up a lot.

"I'm positive," he replied, pulling me down so he could kiss me.

I enjoyed that for a moment before I pulled away with a sigh. "I guess we should break the news to Douglas and Fiona tomorrow then. They're going to be really disappointed," I said sadly.

"It'll be fine. They have a lot of money, and so do we. That's what vacations are for. We'll come to visit and have them to our place as well." He shrugged, dismissing the subject quite easily, I thought.

He hopped up off the bed then and walked towards the fireplace. I felt my heart sink when I realized there was another freshly chilled bottle of champagne on the coffee table. I breathed a little sigh of relief when he walked right by it, without even noticing it, entering the closet.

"What are you doing?"

"Just taking my shoes off," he called out, before reappearing in the doorway. "Thanks for letting me drag you out on that walk earlier."

"I hope it helped," I replied, watching him.

"It really did," he said. "I think I just needed to clear my head." He laughed then. "We need to get back to Arizona. I miss riding my motorcycle. A good ride always helped me straighten out the kinks."

I smiled, remembering the first time I saw him on his motorcycle, thinking he was the most devastatingly handsome thing I'd ever seen. Never in a million years would I have guessed I would've ended up married to him, and definitely not at this age.

Lucky me, I thought.

"I'm all excited to go home now," he continued smiling. "When do you want to leave?"

I shrugged. "Whenever you're ready, I guess."

"How about the day after tomorrow?" he suggested. "That'll give me enough time to call the airport and give us one more day to spend with my grandparents before we have to leave."

"Sounds wonderful," I replied, catching his enthusiasm.

He surprised me when he came over and picked me up off the bed, twirling me around in a circle.

"We're going home!" he said with a grin. "Home. I really like the sound of that."

He leaned in to kiss me, but stopped suddenly, getting a strange look on his face.

"What is it?" I asked as he let me gently slide down the full length of his body back to my feet.

"I don't know," he said, looking at me.

"Are you feeling okay?" I asked, watching the turmoil that moved over his face.

"I don't think so," he replied. He quickly turned and headed for the bathroom. "I think I'm going to be sick."

He started running.

I stood there stunned for a moment, until I heard him begin to heave. I ran after him and found him kneeling at the edge of the toilet.

He was vomiting hard, unable to stop.

I knelt next to him, wrapping my arms around his waist not knowing what to do. I just held him while it went on and on, until I began to feel a little sick myself. He wasn't even throwing anything up now—he was just racked with uncontrollable dry heaves.

I felt him struggle for control, and finally things slowed down. He sat back from the toilet with his eyes closed and he wiped at his mouth with the back of his hand.

"What caused all that?" I asked, concerned.

"I have no idea," he replied, turning to glance at me.

I jumped up and backed away from him, placing my hand over my mouth.

"What is it?" he asked.

"Look in the mirror," I replied, my heart sinking.

He stood and turned to look into the glass at the red streaks that were filling his eyes.

I looked down at his arms and reached over to lift one of them.

"Look!" I said, and I pointed at the telltale gray streaks that were beginning there.

He followed my gaze, eyes widening in horror. "But how?" He stepped away from me, shaking his head in denial. "The only way for this to happen is if I'm drinking blood."

The horrible truth suddenly clicked into place for me. "You have been," I said.

I ran out of the room, grabbed up the champagne bottle out of the bucket and ran back into the bathroom throwing it into the giant bathtub. It smashed into a million pieces, spraying everywhere.

"What the ...," he trailed off, looking at me like I had lost my mind.

"They're poisoning you!" I screamed, trying to make him understand what was plainly obvious to me.

"No!" he said, reaching over to grab the sink to steady himself. "It can't be." He shook his head at me.

"Don't you get it?" I yelled at him. "Your attitude changes! Always wanting to pick a fight! The headaches. The sex. Everything! It all makes sense!"

"No," he said again, his face blanching to a pale white.

"They aren't who they say they are," I said, suddenly paranoid, and I looked around. "We've walked right into the lion's den!"

The full realization hit him then as he sank to his knees on the floor, grabbing his hair with his hands, and he started rocking back and forth.

"I'm sorry, Portia. I'm so sorry. I didn't see it. I allowed myself to be fooled by these stupid dreams of mine." He looked over at me with tear-rimmed eyes, and I realized how deeply he was feeling this loss.

I wrapped my arms around him trying to comfort him. "It's not your fault, Vance," I said. "I was completely snowed by them, too. We need to figure out how we're going to get out of here, though. We're sitting ducks."

He nodded, gazing up at me with his red-streaked eyes, and my heart felt like it was going to bleed for him.

I reached out to touch his temples, letting my healing magic flow through him, removing the gray veins and the colored eyes.

"Thanks," he said, looking tenderly at me.

I kissed his forehead. "Brush your teeth," I told him, trying to take charge of the situation. "I'm going to start packing our things."

"No," he said reaching out to stop me. "Leave them. We can't haul them with us if we're on foot, and it'll alert them to the fact we know something is going on if we try to leave with luggage."

"You're right." I watched him splash several handfuls of cold water over his face.

I just sat there in a stupor, staring while he brushed his teeth, wondering what to do now.

He stepped over to me when he was done. "Ready to get out of this place?" He rubbed both of my arms.

"Yes," I said. He grabbed my hand, leading me out of the bathroom and over to the closet.

We quickly changed into the warmest clothing we had with us, donning coats, hats, gloves, and scarves.

When we were both finished, he grabbed me to him and kissed me hard. He wound his arms tightly around my body, pulling me as close as he could through our layered clothing.

The kiss was one of desperation and longing, with pure passion and sorrow all wrapped into one. He kissed me as if he might never have the opportunity in his life to do it again, and it scared me because it was almost like he was saying goodbye to me.

I wrapped my arms tightly around his neck, not willing to break this moment while I opened my mouth to his. I found myself suddenly pinned by his body up against the wall as he ravaged my mouth over and over again with a ferociousness I'd never felt from him before.

With ragged breaths he finally tore himself away from me. "No matter what happens from this point on, I need you to remember I love you," he said, and I could see the hurt in his eyes.

"I love you, too." I placed my gloved hand on his face. "I'm sorry ... about everything."

"Let's get out of here," he replied determinedly, taking my hand in his and leading me toward the door.

He slowly opened it, glancing down the hallway and making sure it was empty before we stepped out.

"If anyone sees us or asks, we're just going for another walk," he whispered.

I nodded.

We hurried down the hall to the large marble staircase and tiptoed down as quietly as possible. We crossed the foyer and made our way into the vestibule, reaching for the doorknob.

"Going somewhere?" Douglas's voice spoke in the darkness, coming from behind us.

We turned to look at him, knowing it was too late. We hadn't made it.

Douglas was standing there, frowning at us in his full demon glory.

CHAPTER 10

Vance quickly raised his arm, and a ball of flame began to form. It danced in the center of his palm. Throwing it out at Douglas, he yelled, "Run, Portia!"

Douglas effectively deflected the fireball, smashing it into the wall, and charged toward us.

Vance stepped protectively in front of me, pushing me behind him as he did so, and I stumbled slightly, falling against the wall and then to the floor. He lifted his hand to attack again.

Douglas reached out and grabbed him by the wrist, lifting Vance's hand further away from his body.

"I wouldn't do that if I were you," he said flatly, punctuating his words with a piercing stare that promised instant repercussions.

"Yeah? Well, I'm not you," Vance replied hotly, defiantly letting the fireball go anyway.

Douglas jerked his head away to avoid being hit by it. The ball of flame soared across the room and crashed into the table at the foot of the stairs, shattering it into a million pieces.

I lifted my hand from the floor and shot several ice shards at Douglas. Using the hand he wasn't restraining Vance with, he quickly directed them back toward me. I lifted my hand just in time to wave them off to the side of me, and they slammed hard into the wall, sticking out like spikes.

Vance tackled Douglas with a roar, and the two of them went sprawling across the marble floor.

Colin came running into the room, followed by Fiona, both looking around wildly for the source of the noise.

"Get him!" Fiona commanded Colin when she saw the two men struggling together.

I lifted my hand to fire at Colin, determined to protect Vance, but suddenly found myself slammed up against the wall and held there by a force field of some sort. I glanced in surprise toward Fiona who had her hand outstretched toward me.

Colin grabbed Vance by his arms, hauling him up from behind with a strength that belied his thin frame. Vance yanked his arm free and turned around to punch Colin square in the face, knocking him backward, before turning to fire toward Douglas once more, who had just scrambled to his feet.

Douglas dodged the fireball by lowering his head and jumping toward Vance, knocking him firmly into Colin, who grabbed both of his arms up behind him again.

Vance continued to struggle against Colin. Douglas straightened and backhanded him across the face.

Vance's face reddened, and he pulled an arm free once more, lifting his hand to fire again, but Douglas quickly reached out and grabbed it, lifting it high into the air.

That was when Vance noticed me pinned against the wall, and he stopped his struggles instantly.

"Release him," Douglas said to Colin, and he did so, though Douglas kept his firm grip on Vance's arm.

"What is going on?" Fiona screamed. Colin quickly moved to douse the small flames that were devouring the wooden splinters on the floor.

"Our grandson was trying to leave us," Douglas said while he continued to hold Vance's arm into the air.

"Is that true?" Fiona said, as she walked toward us with a look of disbelief on her face, and I suddenly felt the force field around me release.

Vance nodded and wrenched his arm roughly out of Douglas's grasp.

"But why?" she asked stepping closer, reaching out to place a hand on the side of his face.

Vance jerked his head away from her before she could touch him.

"Because I didn't feel too keen on staying here so you could continue to poison me," he replied glaring at her.

"Is that what you think?" she asked in complete innocence. "That we were poisoning you?"

Vance nodded. "That was the general impression I had when I started vomiting, my eyes turned red, and black started to creep up my veins. Of course, all this happening after spending another evening enjoying your fine champagne," he accused, his eyes staring, daring her to refute it.

"We would never poison you," she said, shaking her head in denial. "We were giving you a gift, something which would allow you to see your true heritage."

Vance took a menacing step closer to her, and Douglas put a hand out on his chest to restrain him.

"Let me make this clear to you," Vance said, leaning over her, speaking through clenched teeth. "I have no desire whatsoever to become a demon or anything like it. I don't care what you say or what you do, it will never happen."

A sad look passed through her eyes, and she sighed. "As you wish," she said, stepping away from him and turning to the butler. "Colin, take them to the dungeon."

Colin stepped forward, and immediately Vance went back into fighter mode, his arm shooting into the air, the fire hot in his palm as he readied for another attack.

This time, however, Douglas was ready for him. I saw him reach deftly into his pocket and produce a syringe which he jabbed hard into Vance's neck.

Vance only had time to register a look of shock before he slumped over into Colin's arms, the fireball dropping harmlessly to the floor and dissipating.

"No!" I yelled, racing forward, reaching out for him.

Fiona stepped in front of me and grabbed my arm in an amazingly strong grip, holding me back, not letting me touch him.

"Calm down," she ordered, shaking me. Her thin fingers bit into my skin even harder, causing me to wince slightly. "We aren't going to hurt him. Now, if you'll be a good girl and come with us willingly, we'll let you stay together."

I nodded, tears welling in my eyes and streaking down my face, not even trying to fight her. I would do anything she asked as long as they wouldn't separate us. I knew he would've told me to try and get away, but there was no way I was leaving him behind.

Fiona never let go of me, dragging me as we followed behind Douglas and Colin, manipulating my body at every turn.

The two men were dragging Vance's limp form effortlessly between their bodies, each of them holding him by one of his strong upper arms. He was facing the floor, his head drooping without any control, and his legs were stretched out behind him. He looked like he was dead, and it gave me the shivers.

We entered the previously forbidden east wing, seeing no signs of construction at all, though I wasn't surprised at this point, and we were led down the hall to a large bedroom.

"So this is the dungeon? Nice," I said sarcastically, looking around.

"Not quite," Fiona smiled, yanking my arm in another direction, and I almost tripped. "This way, please," she added, her calm tone belying the calculating demeanor which lay beneath.

To my surprise, we entered the large walk-in closet where we stopped at the back wall. Colin reached out and activated a hidden spring mechanism, and a section of the wall slid open to reveal several stone steps in front of us, leading down into darkness.

"The dungeon is original to the property," Fiona began speaking, as if she were leading me through the house on a casual tour. "Of course, we've upgraded it with electricity and several modern conveniences."

We reached the bottom of the curved stone stairwell, and she continued on with her informational lecture.

"We have several...um...guest suites here, as well as a lovely ritual room where our coven meets together."

"Sounds great," I said facetiously.

"It really is, isn't it?" She smiled and patted my arm in a friendly gesture, as if I were being totally serious.

We stopped outside a large metal door which Colin opened magically, then he turned back to drag Vance through it with Douglas. Fiona shuttle me through right behind them.

I was surprised to find the small room was actually quite nicely furnished. A soft looking full-sized bed covered in floral bedding was in one corner, pressed up against the wall. Pushed up on the opposite wall was a small oak drop-leaf table with three sturdy chairs that matched it.

A door open in the corner revealed a very small bathroom space complete with a shower, fresh towels, and soaps on the counter.

Douglas and Colin tossed Vance unceremoniously on the bed, and I wrenched my arm from Fiona's grasp, rushing over to his side.

"I'm sorry things won't be quite as comfortable for you as they were upstairs," Fiona said. "If Vance decides to have a change of heart, however, maybe we can readdress that issue."

I ignored the three of them completely, not even looking at them, until they finally backed out of the room. I heard the steel door slide shut and lock into place, but a plate on the outside of the door opened, revealing a windowed area with bars.

Douglas stood on the other side. "Let me reassure you this door has been magically reinforced to the extreme, so you don't need to waste your energies on it. It can only be opened from the outside," he said with a smile, before sliding the plate closed again.

I stretched my body out, lying next to Vance on the bed, wrapping both of my arms tightly around him, cradling his head with one and wrapped my other around his waist.

"What are we going to do now?" I whispered to myself, feeling an overwhelming sense of dread creep through me.

Placing the palms of my hands against his body, I let my healing powers flow through him. I could feel the powerful sedative he had been given running thickly through his veins. While I tried to push through the medication, I could quickly see there wasn't going to be much more I could do for him. There was some type of magical component added to the substance which I couldn't seem to overcome. His body would need to work the foreign material from his system. He was going to be asleep for a while.

Sighing, I stayed there for several minutes before I got up and began trying to give myself something useful to do, checking out the room, looking for air ducts, possible weapons, anything that could be used in a spell, but there was nothing to aid in our possible escape.

I tried using my magic to test out the locks and different surfaces for weak points, finding that things did seem to be greatly reinforced just as Douglas warned.

Feeling completely discouraged, I lifted my hands and shot out several ice shards at the door. They bounced harmlessly off the surface, shattering against the concrete floor.

Giving up for the moment, since I didn't know what else to try, I went back to the bed, sliding my back up against Vance's stomach and wrapping his unconscious arms around me.

I comforted myself with one thought. Being trapped with him was better than being without him. I lay there in his unknowing embrace until I finally drifted off to sleep.

Vance's jerking movements against me woke me sometime later. I rolled over to look at him, and he groggily opened his eyes, blinking several time trying to focus.

"How are you doing?" I asked with concern.

He looked at me, concentrating on my face for a few seconds, before he gathered himself together enough to reply.

"Okay, I guess. Where are we?" He swallowed thickly before his tongue darted out to lick his dry lips,

"In the dungeon suite, courtesy of your grandparents," I answered, watching for his reaction.

He rolled over onto his back and took a look around the room, before turning to me.

"Are you all right? They didn't hurt you, did they?" His eyes flitted over me with a worried glance, and he ran a hand softly down my arm, assessing my physical well-being himself.

"No, they didn't hurt me. I'm fine," I replied, hurrying to reassure him. "Fiona advised me that if I came along nicely, they'd let me stay with you. I'm sorry if I caved in too easily, but I wasn't about to do anything that would risk us being separated from each other."

"I'm glad you're here," he said, sort of smiling while he sat up. He reached out to pat my leg gently in the process, before turning his attention away. "Now how do we get out of this place?"

He got up and paced around the room himself, looking things over much as I had earlier.

"I've already checked it out," I said, feeling more than a little discouraged about our predicament. I watched him use some of his powers to test the door and the walls, his gaze moving over every surface.

He turned to look at me, the hope fleeing from his face, and he nodded in understanding and came to sit back on the edge of the bed with a dejected sigh.

"I think there's some type of containment field around all the interior surfaces of the room. Our magic will be unable to affect it, I'm afraid," he said, pausing to stare off into space for a moment. "Portia, baby, I'm sorry I've dragged you into all this again. I should've known from the beginning something wasn't adding up."

"None of this is your fault," I said, and I sat up, crawling over to kneel behind him, wrapping my arms around his shoulders. "We were just tricked, plain and simple."

"I'm such an idiot!" he growled, and he pulled away from me, standing to pace the small spot of open floor in the room.

I followed him off the bed and grabbed him by the shoulders with both of my hands, forcing him to look at me.

"There's nothing we can do about this right now. Hopefully someone will notice we're missing," I said, and I popped up on my toes to give him a peck on the lips. "Until then, just try to think of this as our honeymoon in a different location while we try to come up with a new plan." I forced myself to smile at him, in an attempt to cheer him up and relieve some of his stress.

He pulled me into his embrace, wrapping his arms tightly around my waist now, smiling slightly down at me.

"My sweet Portia, ever the optimist, aren't you? You're literally having the vacation from hell, yet all you concentrate on is the honeymoon part." He looked at me with wonder and amazement in his eyes.

"I've actually been greatly enjoying my honeymoon, thank you," I replied, sliding my hands up over his shoulders toward his neck. "This is a little bump in our plans, but we'll figure it out somehow. At least we're still together."

"Yes. That is a plus," he agreed, and his gaze flitted over my features, suddenly sparking to life with a fire I instantly recognized. "So what do you think we can do to fill the hours while we're stuck in this place?"

"I have no idea," I replied with a smile, and he bent to kiss me.

Our fear at the situation we were in tangled up in heated our exchange quickly. He kissed me hard and heatedly before he scooped me up and carried me over to the bed, gently depositing me on its surface. He lay down next to me, leaning over me, just as we heard the lock scrape in the door.

Both of us sat up abruptly.

The metal door opened, and Fiona stepped into the room.

"I thought the two of you might enjoy a little company now that Vance is awake," she said, and she smiled with her hands folded primly in front of her.

The door opened a bit wider, and Douglas appeared, thrusting a woman into the room in front of him.

She stumbled, a couple of feet into the space, before she caught herself, standing to push her hair back away from her face.

Vance was off the bed in an instant. "Mom?" he asked, though he appeared a little leery as he took a step toward her.

Krista Mangum's eyes moved to his, and a thousand expressions washed over her face as she looked at him.

"Vance?" she whispered, and her hand feathered up to her throat, tears springing into her eyes. She reached him in two strides, grabbing him up into her arms, kissing his face, laughing and hugging him.

Vance grabbed her hard to him, wrapping his arms around her, and he buried his face in her soft curly hair.

I felt my hand tremble, and I covered my own mouth, watching the two of them together, my own eyes beginning to water at the sight before me.

When they pulled apart, tears were streaming down both of their faces.

"Vance, I just wanted to prove to you that life here isn't all bad," Fiona said with a smile, and she stepped back through the door. "Enjoy your reunion."

"She's wrong," Krista said after the door closed behind Fiona, her eyes never leaving Vance's face. "Life here is horrible. Don't ever let her make you think otherwise." She paused to reach out and touch his face again, as if she were afraid he wasn't real. "Now how did you end up here? Right in the very place I tried all these years to keep you from?"

"It's a long story," Vance began, turning back toward me, pulling Krista in my direction. "Before I tell you about it, I want to introduce you to someone, Mom. This is my wife, Portia."

Krista turned to look at me with widened eyes. "Your wife?" she exclaimed, looking back and forth between the two of us with a shocked expression. "Aren't the two of you a little young for that?"

Vance laughed with a slightly nervous sound. "It's all part of the long story," he said, and he smiled reassuringly at me. "But rest assured, Mom, it isn't something I did lightly, and I truly love her with all my heart."

"Well, it's a pleasure to meet you, Portia." Krista smiled and stepped forward to give me a somewhat awkward hug. "Forgive me for being a bit overwhelmed. I can't believe this handsome young man in front of me is my long-lost son, let alone that he's married."

"I'm very happy to meet you," I said when she pulled away. "Vance has missed you in his life so much."

"Why don't we sit over here?" Vance suggested, gesturing to the small spot on the opposite wall of the room.

The three of us moved together to sit at the small dining table.

"So tell me what's happened since I last saw you," Krista said to Vance, her eyes drinking in every detail of his face, like she was drowning with joy just looking at him.

Vance launched into his life story, while I occasionally added things here and there, bringing things up to the present.

"Wow," Krista said, slumping a little in her chair. "You've certainly been through a lot, son." She turned to look at me. "Portia, thank you so much for all you've done for him."

"It was my pleasure. No problem at all," I responded, casting my gaze toward Vance. "I love him."

Vance reached over to pat my leg affectionately, leaving his hand there, before turning back to his mom.

"Your turn," he said with an encouraging smile, prodding his mom to tell her side of the past.

Krista gave a big sigh before she began. "Well, long story short, Damien caught up with me soon after I'd given you to Marsha. He was very angry with me, threatening to kill me if I didn't tell him where you were. He even tortured me with his powers to try and get it out of me. I kept my mouth shut, though. By the time he was able to force me to speak, it didn't matter anymore. I had no idea where you and Marsha had gone. That had been part of the deal to protect you. He kept me prisoner for a long time before he finally ended up bringing me here. I've been here ever since."

"How did you survive being here this long and not have them not do an exchange on you?" I asked, amazed that she appeared to be unharmed.

Krista gave a short laugh. "That's where the story starts getting kind of sick," she replied with a small shake of her head.

"What do you mean?" Vance asked.

"I happened to have something they wanted. You see, I'm a descendant from the sacred line of white witches."

"What's a white witch?" I asked, curious since I'd never heard the term used before.

She continued on. "A long time ago, many centuries in fact, there was a coven that called themselves white witches. They practiced only the purest forms of magic, fine tuning and improving on spells until they were completely perfect, without flaw. These witches were good in every way possible. They were, in fact, the beginning of healer witches. Witches today cannot be healers unless the blood of a white witch flows through them."

Vance turned to look at me and his eyes widened. "That means Portia is a white witch," he said.

"Yes. And apparently the power runs through her very strong if she was able to heal you in the middle of a demon conversion," Krista agreed. "That's unheard of."

"But my dad and grandma aren't healer witches. Doesn't the same blood run through them?" I asked, thinking this didn't make sense.

"They would be carriers, yes. But the power doesn't manifest in every single witch that carries the blood. The power of a white witch can skip several generations at a time. That's why it's so rare to find someone with the gift. It could also be the reason you seem to have more control over your powers than an early novice should," Krista explained.

"So continue on with your story," Vance said, totally interested in what she was saying.

"The Cummings family has stumbled on an ancient prophecy called The Awakening. It's a special thing that happens every few centuries. A ritual is performed, and the witch or warlock in the circle who contains the highest purity of blood from the white witch ancestry is gifted with this amazing force of power. Douglas and Fiona found out about this power and decided they wanted this magic for themselves.

"They searched for someone with a strong strain of the white witch blood and found me. Then they sent Damien for me. I had no idea he was evil. He wooed me and courted me, winning my heart almost instantly."

I cringed inside at the thought. I couldn't imagine anyone loving Damien Cummings. The nightmare moment of the kiss he had given me suddenly rose unbidden into my mind, and I found myself reaching up to wipe my mouth with the back of my hand, trying to remove the feeling with it.

"He married me with the specific intent of having a child," she continued, and she looked specifically at Vance. "You. Douglas and Fiona wanted to mix their blood with that of a white witch. Damien was to turn you over to them so they could drink your blood, thus mingling your powers with theirs."

I closed my eyes, feeling very nauseous all of a sudden.

"Why didn't they just drink your blood?" Vance asked. "Wouldn't it have been more pure coming straight from you?"

"It has to be mingled with their own blood in order for their bodies to accept it properly. The Awakening won't bind to blood cells which have only been drunk from another. It's the DNA it bonds to," she explained before she moved on. "Damien got greedy, however, and decided he wanted the power for himself. He never handed you over to his parents. He made sure you stayed hidden from them. Then I found out he was drinking your blood, and I ran with you, upsetting everyone's plans.

"After your dad found me and brought me back here, they were all determined to produce another heir. Damien came to visit me often, but thankfully it seems as if I'm unable to conceive again, though they've always held out hope I would."

I really was going to be sick now, thinking of Krista and what she must have gone through at Damien's hands.

"So now they want Vance because they can drink his blood to gain this power?" I asked.

To my surprise she shook her head. "No. Now that I've heard your story, I believe they have a different plan for you," she said.

"Which is what exactly?" Vance asked, leaning forward.

"Think, son," she replied, and her eyes locked with his. "You have the white witch blood running through your veins, and Portia has it stronger than anyone has seen in a great while."

She let the words sink in for a few seconds, and I suddenly saw Vance's face blanch completely white.

"No!" he said loudly, and he stood abruptly, knocking his chair over behind him. "No!"

"What is it?" I asked, afraid because of his reaction.

He looked at me, and I could see the dead fright in his eyes.

"They want us to have a baby," he replied.

CHAPTER 11

"What?" I said reaching out for the table, the room suddenly starting to reel in front of me.

Vance knelt in front of me, grabbing my arms, shaking me slightly with the force of his grip.

"Don't you get it?" he replied, looking into my eyes. "Combining my blood with yours will make the white witch blood even stronger than mine. The awakening goes to the white witch with the purest blood. That would be our child."

"No," I said, shaking my head. My hand went protectively over my stomach.

He noticed my reaction and reached in, placing his hand over mine where it rested maternally.

"You realize there's a chance you could be pregnant already, right?" he added, searching my eyes frantically. "Unless you've been doing something to prevent it from happening that I'm not aware of, that is."

"I haven't," I replied, and the tears began to slowly roll down my face. "There wasn't time. We didn't know we were going to get married when we did. I didn't think about it." I felt stupid.

He stood and turned away from me, running both of his hands through his hair before clenching it into fistfuls.

"And stupid me, I had to jump right in there, not even giving a thought about any real protection. I mean I've been trying to be careful but ...," his voice trailed off, and he ran his hands down over his face. "How could I be so childish? Arrrgh! It all makes sense now! They were feeding me the stupid champagne to bring up the demon lust. Just a little at a time. Not enough to turn me where I'd hurt you, but just enough to drive me insane with desire."

"They'll keep doing it, too," Krista added, and he turned to look at her. "I can guarantee you they'll put it in your food and drink. That's why they have you in this cell together. They want to manipulate you into being with her."

Vance started rubbing at his temples as if he were suffering from a horrible headache.

"As if they had to manipulate me! I haven't been able to keep my hands off her, even without the bloodlust," he said, and he looked sadly at me. I knew the conclusion he had come to in that very moment. "We have to stop. We can't be intimate at all, just in case you aren't pregnant now. Hopefully it hasn't happened, but we have to find out."

I nodded, even though my heart was breaking at the thought of not being able to be with him in that way.

He came over and knelt in front of me, laying his head in my lap, and he wrapped his arms around my waist.

"I'm so sorry, Portia," he said, and I could feel the angst coming from him envelope me, too. "I'm so sorry."

I reached down to run my fingers gently through his hair as he lay there, trying to think of a way to calm him.

"It isn't your fault," I responded softly, though my voice was shaking. "We just need to try and find a way out of this situation."

He lifted his head and looked over at Krista. "Mom, is there anything you can think of? Some way we can combine the strength of all three of our powers?" he pleaded. "We have to escape this awful place! Together!"

A sad look passed over her face as she shook her head. "I can't help you. I don't have any powers anymore Vance," she spoke, her voice laced with regret.

"What?" he asked with a surprised look.

"Damien performed a demon kiss on me," she said, casting her eyes downward. "It was his way of punishing me for not telling him where you were."

Vance left me and was at her side in an instant. "Oh, Mom ... I'm so sorry. I didn't realize." He gave her a hug. I could see his despair over her situation in the very way he held his body.

"It's fine," she said, and she hugged him back. "I've learned to cope with my humanness."

We all sat in silence for several long minutes, contemplating the predicament we now found ourselves in.

"You can use your powers to cleanse the food," I said thinking out loud, grasping at anything I could think of to help.

"Yes, and I will," he replied with a short nod.

"They'll catch on eventually," I added.

"I know," he agreed, and he turned to capture my gaze.

"When they find out you aren't sleeping with her, they'll try everything in their power to force your hand," Krista warned him.

Vance nodded again, and he continued to look at me. I could feel the emotions churning inside him. He was extremely upset.

"We have to figure out a way to escape. It's our only option. Once they get what they want from us, we're dead, unless they decide to turn us," he said frankly, not hiding from the truth.

"I don't know how we could possibly do it without help from the outside," Krista replied with a defeated sigh. "I'll keep thinking on things. Hopefully they'll let us visit together again. I'm no threat to them in my current state."

"Where are they keeping you?" Vance asked her.

"I actually have a small, but comfortable, apartment at the end of the hall. They rarely let me out, but it's cozy enough to be a home of sorts," she replied.

There was a scraping sound once more, and the lock slid aside, the door swinging open.

Colin appeared, with a well-tailored maid carrying a tray. The maid looked up when she passed us.

It was Darcy!

Vance was instantly on his feet grabbing her around the neck with one of his strong hands.

"I should've killed you when I had the chance!" he growled at her ferociously. "You led us into this trap!"

Darcy just smiled at him. "Unless you want another needle in your neck, Mr. Vance, I suggest you let me go," she said, and she nodded over at Colin.

Colin was advancing toward Vance with a large syringe.

I hurriedly stepped between the two men.

"Let her go, Vance," I said softly, and with much frustration he finally did what I asked.

"Enjoy your dinner," Darcy said with a grin and danced back out the door as if she didn't have a care in the world.

"Mrs. Cummings, it's time to go now," Colin said formally to Krista.

"You can call me Ms. Mangum now, Colin," Krista said, correcting him, and she stood to follow. "I keep telling you I'll never be a Cummings again."

She turned and threw her arms around her son one more time, pulling him tightly toward her.

"Keep the faith," she whispered into his ear as they parted, turning to follow Colin out.

After the door was closed, Vance turned back to me, coming to wrap me in his embrace.

"I won't let them hurt you," he whispered into my hair, his voice full of a strained emotion. "Ever."

"You won't let them hurt *us*," I amended while I held him. "You and I are in this together, and if there is a baby, I need to know all of us are going to get out of here unharmed."

"I agree," he said before bending to kiss me.

I kissed him back, just savoring the feel of him, pulling him even closer. After a minute, though, he stepped away.

"This is going to be very difficult for me," he said, dropping his hands back to his sides.

"For me, too," I replied, casting my gaze down to the floor, feeling an awful wave of despair wash over me.

"We have to make a pact, right here, right now, that we won't let things get out of hand, no matter what," he said firmly.

I nodded unable to bring my gaze back up to him, feeling like I was losing him all over again.

"What does that entail, though?" I asked softly, and a tear slipped from one of my eyes to trail down my face. "Can I still kiss you—or touch you even? How far away do I need to stay?"

"Portia, you're my wife. You can do all those things. I want you to. We just have to make sure things don't progress to the next level." He lifted my chin and looked into my eyes.

I looked at him mournfully for a moment, and then suddenly I had a thought pop into my head.

"Hey! Can't you just use your healer's magic to check me and see if I'm pregnant? I mean if I am, then there's no point in being abstinent, right? What's done is done."

He pondered about this for a moment. "I could try, I guess," he said with a slight shrug of his shoulders. "I don't know if it'll work that way since being pregnant isn't something that needs to be healed, but I could give it a shot."

He knelt down in front of me, placing his hands over my stomach, and I felt the warmth as the white light flowed from him and into me. He moved his hands, slowly and gently over my body as he listened carefully.

Finally, he stood, grabbing both of my hands. "I don't feel anything out of the ordinary, Portia," he said, staring deeply into my eyes. "Either you aren't pregnant, or I can't detect it. It would be extremely early right now, so I don't know."

I hung my head in defeat. "So abstinence it is," I said flatly, even though I knew not being pregnant was the best thing for us right now.

"Yes," he replied.

He held me tightly for a long time as we both contemplated our future. We probably would've stood that way forever, not wanting to let go, but my stomach chose that moment to begin growling loudly.

He laughed a little, and the sound broke the tension of the moment we had been sharing.

"Shall we eat this food we have?" he asked me while he looked over at it questioningly.

"I'm afraid to," I answered honestly, eyeing it distastefully as well. "I don't know if it's safe."

"Let's see what we can do about that," he said, leading me over to the table.

He waved both of his hands over the tray slowly, back and forth. I noticed little droplets lifted up off the food, floating into the air until he could actually catch them with his hand.

He carried the vile liquid into the bathroom sink, dropping it in the basin and washing his hands.

"Now I think you should try it as well," he suggested to me. "Just to make sure we got everything."

I followed his instructions and did the same as he had. Nothing else came to the surface.

"Let's eat," he said with a smile, reverting to his ever impeccable manners and holding out a chair politely for me to sit down in.

"I'm still afraid," I said nervously, sliding into the seat.

"Well, if we don't eat, we'll die, and I'm not ready to go that route just yet. Are you?" he replied, and he scooted his chair over next to me so he could hold my hand.

I shook my head. He was right.

He picked up a fork and dug right in, and I forced myself to do the same, not wanting him to think I was a coward.

The food was actually delicious, and I found myself even wanting seconds after my first helping. I hadn't realized how hungry I was.

When we were finished, we both went over to lie on the bed together. I placed my head in the crook of his arm with one arm draped lazily over his waist.

"So what do you want to do tonight?" he asked with a soft laugh while he ran his hand up and down my arm.

"Talk?" I responded, feeling sure it was probably the safest venue for us to take right now.

"That's exactly what I was thinking!" He smiled, albeit jokingly, but I could still hear the hint of sadness in his voice. "What do you want to talk about?

"Whatever you want is fine with me," I said, wanting only to hear his voice floating comfortably beside me.

He thought about this for a moment. "How about you tell me what you were thinking the first time you ever laid eyes on me," he finally said.

"That's easy," I said, smiling at the memories while they graced my mind once again. "My first thought was I had just seen the most handsome person who'd ever stepped foot on this planet."

"And the second?" he asked, laughing.

"The next thought was pure depression, because I knew he would never even notice I existed," I replied, remembering how crestfallen I had been.

"Look how wrong you were." He smiled widely.

Chapter 12

Vance paced the small room like a caged animal, and I could feel the tension rolling off him in waves.

We had been here for a very long time. Days, weeks, months, I didn't really know. We had no way to gauge the time or whether it was day or night. Occasionally, meals would arrive for us on what we assumed was a somewhat regular schedule.

Vance tried to attack when the door was opened again, but it activated the shield, bouncing his magic harmfully around the room before it dissipated. He never tried again after that.

We hadn't seen Krista anymore, though Vance asked if he could see her regularly. No one would ever respond to his inquiry. In fact, no one spoke to us at all if possible. We hadn't even seen Douglas and Fiona again. Our only contact was with Colin and Darcy when they delivered the things we needed.

Vance used our spare time to coach me in learning to channel some of my powers more efficiently which helped the flow seem a little easier to me though I still didn't feel like it was a natural thing. Try as I might, magic was just not the first thing I fell back on in any given situation. I often became discouraged when he would set up little tests for me to magically respond to. More often than not I responded with a completely human reaction, being momentarily stunned or dumbfounded until I realized he was trying to elicit a magical response from me. To his credit, he never lost patience and always encouraged me.

He also used the opportunity to try to test out some of his new powers. Even though he knew he had acquired all of Damien's magic, he didn't necessarily know what those powers were since they weren't natural to him. He had to try things and see if he could do them. He discovered there was now an electrical element to his magic that hadn't been there before. He could send out sharp bursts and shocks of electricity. He began practicing things with it. This course of action occasionally led to disastrous situations, though, since he wasn't well in control of these new-found abilities yet.

On one occasion, when experimenting with some new energy forces, he accidentally blew up our bed while I was sitting on it. I wasn't hurt, thankfully, since only the bed frame and not the mattress was destroyed, but he determined in that moment there would no longer be testing of powers until we were safely escaped from this place.

By this time we resorted almost exclusively to talking. We talked to each other until we had nothing left to talk about. That proved to be a dangerous thing for us, as our long-term, self-proclaimed abstinence would become unbearable and we would resort to kissing.

This is what led to our current situation. We had been involved in a pretty heated exchange that was very hard for either of us to stop. With an amazing bout of restraint, Vance sprung up from the bed and I could feel the emotions about to boil over inside him.

I stayed where I was, not interrupting. I knew he needed to vent some steam somehow, and if pacing the floor was helping him, then so be it. I also knew if I went to comfort him it would be disastrous for us both. One touch would send us spiraling over the edge of the cliff we were so precariously dangling from now.

Leaning up against the wall, I pulled my knees up under my chin, laying my head on them and wrapping my arms around my legs. I let my eyes drift over Vance's anxiously moving form.

He worked out every day we had been stuck in here. Push-ups, sit ups, and any other exercise he could invent by using objects in the room. I knew it was one of the main ways he burned off his frustrations. The side effect of it, however, were that his already perfectly sleek body had become even more so.

This, of course, made my mouth water for him even more. I couldn't resist gliding my hands over those perfectly sculpted muscles, touching that wonderful physique over and over again. Even now, just watching him move was making my heart race even faster with desire for him.

"Portia!" he growled sharply under his breath. "You have got to start thinking about something else! This isn't helping!"

"Sorry," I muttered quietly, and I shut my eyes to his image in front of me, trying desperately to move my thoughts on to a different subject.

My attention was instantly averted when we both heard the lock in the door slide, signaling someone was about to enter.

Vance was over to the door in two strides, waiting for the unsuspecting person. He lifted his hand, ready to attack whoever was about to enter.

To our surprise, Fiona stepped into the room, causing him to hesitate a second.

"I wouldn't do it," she said when she looked at his raised hand. "It would result in Portia getting hurt."

He glared at her violently before he lowered his hand, just as Douglas stepped in behind her.

Fiona turned toward me. "Hello, Portia. How are you feeling?" she asked, almost sounding like she really cared.

I didn't say anything, but did feel a moment of surprise since she had never seemed too concerned about me before.

Fiona walked over to where I was sitting on the bed and thrust her hand up against my stomach. She started pushing around in a hard deep motion.

"What are you doing?" I asked angrily, trying to push her hand away from my body.

"Don't touch her!" Vance spoke, and he moved toward us threateningly.

Fiona stepped away from me, not even looking at Vance, and she and Douglas disappeared outside the door, sliding the lock behind them.

"What was that all about?" I asked, looking at Vance to see the same perplexed look on his face that was on mine.

He shook his head while he stared at me.

This time we heard the metal plate on the door open. We turned to see Douglas standing behind the barred opening.

"Fiona informs me that Portia is not with child," he said with a disapproving look on his face.

"And?" Vance asked with a raised eyebrow.

"You haven't been sleeping with her," Douglas stated flatly.

"Oh, I've been sleeping with her," Vance replied sardonically. "It just so happens that's all I've been doing."

"I admit. I'm surprised," Douglas said. "I didn't think you'd be able to resist her this long."

Vance moved forward, stepping closer to toward the door, a menacing look flashing over his face. "When it comes to my wife, I'll do anything it takes to protect her." He glared at Douglas, his sultry voice sounding low and deadly.

"Well, you might want to consider this then," Douglas answered. "We've been very kind. There's nothing preventing us from taking you out of here and performing a demon conversion on you. That would guarantee that you would have relations with your wife."

"There's only one problem with that," Vance replied, not backing down an inch at the threat. "If you convert me, the chances are I'd kill her before I'd get around to being intimate with her."

Douglas paused for a moment as if considering this, before shrugging his shoulders nonchalantly.

"I guess we'll have to go with plan B then," he said turning to gesture toward something unseen.

"Which is what?" Vance asked suspiciously.

"That if you won't sleep with your wife, then we'll get someone else who will," he said with a grin.

Brian Fitzgerald's face appeared in the doorway with a smile.

"It would be my pleasure, uncle," he said, his grin widening, and he looked lustfully over at me.

Vance moved and was at the door faster than anything I had ever seen in my life, anger rolling through him.

"You stay away from her!" he growled, reaching through the bars to grab Brian around the neck. "So help me I'll kill you right here if you even so much as look at her again!"

I could see his hand begin to heat up to the violent red color it did when he had melted the doorknob at Damien's penthouse when he came to rescue me.

Brian began choking violently, and Douglas grabbed his shoulders to force him back out of Vance's reach.

"Do you hear me?" Vance was still yelling through the door. "If you even speak her name, you're dead!"

Douglas stepped back up toward the opening, being careful to stay at arm's length, out of Vance's grasp.

"If you don't do what we've asked, then this is what will happen, no matter what you threaten," he stated flatly.

Vance threw a fireball, causing them to dive to the side before some unseen person slammed the metal plate shut once again, forcing him to yank his arm back inside before they locked it firmly in place.

He was shaking with rage when he turned to face me, crossing to me instantly and grabbing me into his arms.

"I'll never let them take you!" he said, crushing me to him, and I could actually feel him trembling. "Never! I'd have to die first."

He kissed me roughly, then, hard and passionate, and I knew he was really afraid for me—us—him.

"What do we do now?" I asked, breaking the kiss after a long moment.

He pushed my hair back from my face and searched my gaze. "I don't know, Portia. Of course I want to be with you in the way they're demanding, but we just can't," he said. "We're going to have to try to plan an escape somehow. I won't let them give you to Brian."

His hands were shaky against my face. He was having a very hard time controlling his emotions.

"I love you," I said, wanting to ease his frustration somehow. "I'll do whatever you feel is best for us."

He dropped his hands from my face, moving to continue his pacing. Had the floor been carpeted, he would've worn a hole in it by now.

"That's the problem," he answered me. "I have no idea what's best for us."

The room was silent for a moment as we both contemplated our situation.

"Vance? Do you think my parents might be here by now?" I asked. "I mean we've obviously been missing for some length of time. Surely someone has noticed by now that we're gone."

"I've thought a lot about that," he replied. "I'm certain if they were aware we're missing then they're probably here."

"How could they not be aware?" I asked, puzzled.

"They could have demons impersonating us for all I know," he replied with a slight shrug of one shoulder.

I hadn't thought of that. It was true. Damien had once sent a demon to Vance who was impersonating his mother. While shape shifting demons were very rare, it was definitely possible. Douglas and Fiona would be being very careful now to cover any loose ends.

"You're probably right," I agreed. "They wouldn't want anyone to come looking for us."

My heart sank when I realized there was probably no one who knew we were even gone. We were all on our own.

"Don't fret about it, baby," he said, and he came back over to me, wrapping his arms around me again. "We'll figure out something."

It was several days later when the door to the cell opened again and a whole host of people entered. Vance immediately jumped up, moving to stand in front of me.

Douglas, Fiona, Colin, and Darcy along with a couple of other people we had never seen before came into the room.

"We're going to have a little celebration this evening," Fiona said, with her hands primly folded in front of her.

At precisely this moment Douglas grabbed Vance by the arm and Colin reached out, grabbing me. They quickly injected us both with some type of serum.

"What the heck is this?" Vance yelled, and he roughly jerked his arm away from Douglas.

"It won't harm you, I promise," Fiona said with a smile. "In fact, you might actually enjoy it."

Vance glared at her, growing even angrier. "What is it?" he asked, seething, his jaw clenched.

"Don't worry. It's just a little something that will make you more compliant for the evening. We want you both to have a marvelous time." She continued to smile unnervingly at us.

I felt the first wave of dizziness wash over me, and I reached out toward Vance to steady myself. I realized he was experiencing the same thing, because I could suddenly feel his emotions wash over me.

"We have to be extra careful tonight," his words penetrated into my head through the quickly thickening haze.

I only nodded at him, and I was suddenly unable to keep track of what I had been going to say in reply.

"It's starting to work," Colin said to Fiona while they both stood there staring at us.

"I don't know if the two of you are aware of the date, but tonight is the Festival of Beltane," Fiona continued.

"What is that?" I heard Vance mumble as he shook his head, struggling to stay alert.

"Well, the festival itself celebrates the renewal of the earth and its fertility, and invites all to share. We're going to be performing a fertility ritual on your lovely wife this evening," she explained.

"Leave her alone," Vance muttered softly.

Fiona laughed. "We wouldn't dream of harming her," she replied, waving the comment away with a flick of her hand, which all of a sudden made me feel dizzy. "In fact, you'll be the only one who touches her."

At this time, Colin and Darcy came forward with the other two individuals and began removing our clothing. I wanted to protest, but found that I couldn't— instead, I woodenly obeyed their commands.

The two women dressed me in some sort of long, woolen, red robe that wrapped around me and belted closed with a rough rope. There was a large hood that was lifted over my head. I wore nothing underneath.

My brain vaguely realized Vance was dressed in something similar, only he was in green.

We were both led out of the room and I found it hard to even focus on where we were going. Somehow I understood we had been led outside, where we were placed into a vehicle.

I couldn't keep track of where we were traveling to or even how long it took us to get there. In the fog of my mind I did become aware at some point, however, that Vance reached over to hold my hand.

Suddenly it seemed as if everything around me was on fire. I eventually realized I was no longer in the vehicle, but standing on a hillside next to a raging bonfire, though I had no memory or recollection of how I had gotten there.

There were a lot of other people standing in a circle around the fire, all in black hooded robes. I couldn't distinguish the faces of any of them since they were hidden in the shadow, but I felt a little nauseated because my vision would shift violently every time one of them moved.

Someone was standing next to me holding my elbow, and another person was standing next to Vance doing the same. These individuals started leading us around the bonfire inside the circle.

I could hear uniformed chanting, and I realized it was a spell of some sort that was increasing in volume, but my mind couldn't grasp what words were being said.

When we stopped circling the fire, I noticed the hooded individual next to Vance pulled out another needle and injected him once again. He didn't protest or try to stop them, so I figured he was just as hazy as I was.

The circle parted, and the two of us were led out of it. We walked a small distance on the exposed hill, guided by our handlers before we entered a thickly wooded area.

Our guides continued on this way with us until we reached a very small clearing in the trees that was lit by a few small torches. I could see a makeshift mattress, made of straw and covered in blankets, that was on a small wooden platform. Some thin poles held a twig canopy over the top of the bed, and red and green ribbons were hanging from it twisting together in the light warm breeze of the evening,.

The two of us were led over to the bed where our companions had us sit down.

I realized Fiona had been the person at my side when she leaned over to whisper into my ear.

"Seduce your lover," was all she said, her voice penetrating clearly through the fog of my mind, before she and the other figure backed away, and we were left there all alone.

I sat still for a moment as her words sank in. In the fuzzy state of my brain I knew something was wrong, but I couldn't remember what it was.

I turned to look at Vance for help, but I couldn't see his face under the hood, so I lifted my arms and pushed it back from him.

My breath caught in my throat.

Has he always been this handsome? The soft firelight lit his chiseled features to perfection as he looked back at me. I knew I had to kiss him.

I leaned forward, gently placing my lips against his mouth, tenderly sighing at the contact with him. Suddenly it was as if my touch awakened a raging inferno inside him.

His bright eyes instantly sprang to life, as if fire were racing through them, and he yanked me toward him in a crushing grip against his hard strong body, without breaking the kiss.

I responded equally to him, wrapping my arms around his neck, deepening the kiss as much as possible, and I was vaguely aware of the sound of my voice moaning in response to him.

His hands were tangled in my long hair, and he roughly grabbed it, jerking my head to the side, trailing love bites and kisses down the side of my face to my neck, and I lifted my chin higher to give him better access.

I could feel him move his hands, sliding them to my waist, working to release the knotted rope.

The thought flashed through my mind that we shouldn't be doing this, but I lost it as my hands found their way against the bare rippling muscles of his chest when his robe slid off his shoulders.

He tossed me back onto the straw mattress, continuing his trail of kisses over my feverish skin as the firelight danced over us.

All night long he made love to me, over and over again, unable to stop, until we finally collapsed—exhausted—into a deep sleep.

Sometime later, we were roughly awakened. Several people in dark hoods were throwing our robes back over our exposed bodies.

"Don't speak," someone next to me whispered into the night air. "You aren't safe here. We're here to rescue you."

I didn't recognize the voices speaking around us, and I kept shaking my head as I tried desperately to understand what they were talking about.

What was happening? Why were we awakened by strangers? Why did Vance and I need rescuing? My mind couldn't grasp it.

The hooded individuals wrapped their arms around us, helping us to our feet, only to begin hurrying us through the dark forest, pulling and dragging us along with them, running.

I could feel the skin ripping on the bottom of my tender feet as we were moved quickly through the untamed brush.

We reached a small clearing where there was a vehicle waiting in the darkness. The engine was running, and the headlights blinded me as we were propelled toward it. We were ushered inside, followed by the others who were with us.

"Gas it, Crispin," a male voice said roughly, and I thought the voice sounded vaguely familiar.

The engine revved, and the car was thrown into gear, spewing gravel into the air as we sped off down the road.

Chapter 13

Vance and I both came to at the same time in the unfamiliar room which surrounded us. I blinked my eyes a few times before my mind caught up with what I was seeing.

"Where are we?" I asked with a gasp, quickly sitting up.

He slowly rose up at my side, looking around at the soft quilts which covered us in the comfortable bed we were lying in.

"Are you okay?" he asked, turning to look at me before running a hand down my arm, and I knew he was checking me with his powers.

"I think so," I replied, stretching my neck and back, not feeling anything amiss about myself, other than my tender feet. "Are you?"

"Yes." His hand continued its slide down my arm until he found my palm and slipped his hand in mine, squeezing it slightly.

"I don't remember anything. Do you?" I searched his eyes for answers.

He shook his head with a barely perceptible movement. "Not much, although some images of the two of us involved in some pretty intimate situations are suddenly beginning to pop into my head," he replied, not looking too happy about it.

Some of the fog lifted at his words. "They forced us together, didn't they?" I said closing my eyes, feeling a wave of nausea wash over me, wondering who else might have been a party to our situation last night.

"I'm afraid so," he replied, leaning over to rest his head in my lap. "I'm sorry, Portia."

I reached out and stroked his wonderful hair while he lay there, looking at his perfect form in front of me. "Don't be sorry. I love being with you. I just hate being manipulated." I sighed, wishing I could comfort him somehow. "Where do you think we are?" I asked again, looking around the green and white bedroom.

At that moment the door to the room opened, and I stared into the handsome, concerned face of my debonair father.

"Dad?" I squeaked out, jumping off the bed, relief pouring through every cell of my being at the sight of him.

He was over to me in two steps, folding me into his arms, crushing me hard in his embrace. "Hi, Pumpkin," he said softly, and I began to cry into his shoulder, unable to stop myself.

He allowed me to let the flood gates open on him, and he stroked my hair, murmuring soft words to me.

"It's okay now, Pumpkin. You're safe. I won't let them harm you anymore," he said reassuringly.

I pulled away from him, and Vance joined me at his side, giving Dad a hug also, and they patted at each other hard on the back.

"How did you find us?" I asked, truly wondering how he had managed to locate us.

He didn't answer the question, though, instead pointing over to the dresser where some clothes were sitting on the top.

"Why don't the two of you change out of those robes and join me in the other room. You were drugged pretty badly and you've been asleep for a long while. There are a lot of people waiting to see you. We'll talk in there," he replied.

"All right," I said, and he headed for the door, giving me a soft smile as he moved away. I had to grab him one more time, just to make sure he was real. "I love you, Daddy," I said, and I hugged him and he laughed gently.

"I love you too, Portia, and I'm not leaving you." He chuckled while he squeezed me tightly one more time. "Now hurry and change."

I watched the door close behind him before turning to Vance.

He smiled at me, and I rushed into his arms. "We're safe!" I placed a kiss against his neck, nuzzling my face there in the warmth of his skin.

"Yes, for now. But this isn't even close to being over," he cautioned me, before he lightly kissed me back on the lips.

I nodded, understanding what he was trying to explain, but not really wanting to contemplate it at the moment.

"I know. But having someone on our side sure takes a huge weight off."

"I agree," he replied, before kissing me proper, and I could feel the relief flowing through him also. His hands drifted down, moving over my scantily clad form before he pulled away from me. "Let's get out of these awful robes," he said.

We opened the door and stepped out into a narrow hallway with a low ceiling. Following the sounds of murmuring voices, we moved on until we reached a living area. There were easily twenty people in the room waiting for us, most of them we didn't recognize.

"Mom!" I called out when I saw her. She stood and rushed toward me.

She grasped me tightly, and I let the tears fall freely down my face, as did she.

"I've missed you so much, precious!" she said, holding my face in her hands and kissing each cheek.

"I love you so much, Mom!" I replied, kissing her back, a small well of happy laughter bubbling up in my throat.

Grandma Milly was right behind her waiting for her turn, as well as Brad and Shelly. Once they were done hugging me, they moved right on to Vance. It was a very emotional moment for all of us.

A tall man with curly blond hair from the remaining group, stood and made his way over to us.

"My name is Crispin," he said extending a hand to both of us, and he offered a warm smile. "We met briefly, earlier this morning, though you may not remember it. I'm the leader of this coven here," he said turning to gesture to the others who were seated in the room.

"Crispin and his coven were instrumental in getting you back this morning," my dad explained to us.

"Thank you," Vance said, his eyes moving graciously around the room. "We're deeply indebted to you."

"It was our pleasure," Crispin replied. "I'm just sad we were unable to do it sooner. We've been watching the

Cummings residence for a long while, but no opportunity ever presented itself."

"How long have we been prisoners exactly?" I asked. "We were unable to keep track of time."

"It's the first of May today. You've been held for about three and half months now," he replied.

I looked at Vance. Three and half months, gone, lost.

"How did you know where we were?" Vance asked him.

"Well, apparently we have a double crosser in our coven. You may know him. His name is Brian Fitzgerald," Crispin explained looking a bit forlorn as he spoke.

I gasped at the mention of Brian and turned in time to see the angered look which flashed over Vance's face.

"Brian is in your coven?" he asked flatly.

Crispin shook his head. "Not any longer. We were unaware he was Douglas's nephew. Apparently Douglas sent him as a spy to infiltrate our coven and keep a watch over what we were up to. We've always been openly opposed to the Cummings family."

I saw Vance's face fall a little at this remark, before he masked his expression once again. "I'm sorry my family has caused everyone such hardship," he apologized, his eyes quickly darting over every person.

"Vance, none of this is your fault," my dad interjected with a shake of his head. "Stop taking responsibility for it. We're just happy the two of you are safe and we were able to get you before any real harm was done."

"Let's just take them home and get out of here!" my mom spoke up, with a pleading expression on her face.

"We can't leave," I said.

"Why not?" she asked. "The safest place for the two of you is as far away from here as possible."

"My mom is here," Vance replied.

"Your mom?" my dad asked, perking right up at this bit of information. "You found her?"

Vance nodded. "She's been a prisoner at Bell Tower Hall almost since the day she gave me up."

"So it was a demon shape shifter you killed," Grandma added.

"Yes. I won't leave her behind, either. She's helpless. She has no powers to protect herself with either. My father performed a demon kiss on her as punishment for defying him."

An audible gasp went through the room.

"Why have they kept her in her current state?" my dad asked, perplexed by this revelation.

"They've been trying to breed her," Vance spoke with a disgusted look. "Apparently she carries the blood of the white witch, something Portia also happens to have in abundance. They want Portia and I to have a baby so they can receive something called the Awakening."

"So that's why they performed a Celtic fertility ritual on you last night," Crispin muttered.

"Yes," Vance replied with a sigh. "And if my memory serves me correctly, they were very successful at it."

"Actually, they weren't," Crispin said with a knowing smile, looking directly at Vance.

"Oh, I assure you, Portia was well … loved last night," Vance said, shaking his head in disagreement.

There was an awkward pause for a moment before Crispin spoke again. "I am—how shall I say it—um … aware of that fact," Crispin said a bit uncomfortably at the blatant referrals to the intimate moments Vance and I had shared. "What I was referring to was the fact the ritual was never completed."

"There was more?" I asked, wondering what else could have possibly been done that hadn't been.

Crispin nodded in the affirmative. "In the ritual, the woman, that would be you, has to wash herself in the first morning dew after seducing her lover. That never happened. We took you well before the morning dew had fallen."

"So I won't get pregnant?" I asked, hopeful.

"Well, not because of the ritual," Crispin pointed out. "But as your husband pointed out, you did have plenty of ... exposure of the regular kind. Anything could happen."

I couldn't help blushing a little at his comments, before another woman in the group spoke up.

"We could give you some herbs or something that wouldn't allow the pregnancy to continue if you've conceived," she offered.

"Absolutely not!" I said in offense before I placed my hands protectively over my stomach. "If there's a baby in here, it's my baby. Mine and Vance's, born out of a strong love. I would never let anything happen to it."

"Sorry," the woman amended, casting her eyes about nervously. "I didn't mean to upset you. I was just trying to offer a suggestion."

Vance reached over and pulled me up close against his side, placing his arm tightly around my shoulders. "Portia's right," he said, matter-of-factly. "If we have conceived a child, getting rid of it is not an option."

I looked at him, and tears pooled in my eyes, threatening to spill over down my face.

"Thank you," I said into his head.

"I love you," he replied back in the same fashion, and he squeezed me gently, giving me a loving look.

My dad piped up, breaking the moment. "We need to make a plan, people," he said, snapping his fingers together in rapid succession. "I want to know everything there is to know about this Awakening thing and what it's all about. We also need to figure out a way to rescue Krista from these people in the process. It's time to put our heads together."

Everyone nodded, and talk began rippling throughout the group.

My dad motioned for Vance and me to come sit by him. "What do you know about this Awakening?" he asked, directing the question mainly to Vance.

"Not much," Vance replied. "I don't know where, when, how, or why it happens. I just know that the power of it goes to the witch or warlock with the most amount of white witch blood in them. My grandparents want this power. They believe if they combine the white witch blood I have with the blood from Portia, it'll create a child with an extraordinary amount of the heritage. They want to drink the blood of the child. It's the only way they can assimilate the white witch power. It has to be mixed in with their own bloodline in order for it to work."

"So, they're basically cannibalizing their own offspring," Dad said while he rubbed his hand over his face in a frustrated gesture.

"Pretty much," Vance said, a look of complete disgust passing over his features.

My dad looked at me. "I really hope you aren't pregnant, Portia," he said flatly, his eyes flickering briefly down toward my stomach.

"Me too, Dad, but it won't matter to them if I'm not," I replied with a slight shake of my head.

"What do you mean?" he asked, not following.

"If I fail to conceive, they'll just go back to their original plan," I said with a shrug.

"Which is what?"

"They'll try to use Vance. He already carries the bloodline mixed with their blood. They're just hoping to make that bloodline even purer through me," I explained.

Dad looked a Vance for several moments before he answered. "This isn't good, son," he said with concern.

"I know," Vance replied with a sigh.

"We really need to get you both away from here," he said, his voice sounding more insistent.

"I can't leave my mom behind," Vance said stubbornly. "I won't leave her behind," he amended a moment later.

"Well, you being here isn't going to help her either. If they catch you, things go from bad to worse, for everyone involved," Dad countered, trying to persuade him otherwise.

I could see Vance had that look in his eye when he was not going to be easy to reason with. I decided maybe I should give it a shot.

"Look, Vance," I said softly, hoping I wouldn't anger him by moving to stand with my father on this. "Krista has been with them all these years, and they've never hurt her. She herself said she's absolutely no threat to them without her powers. They probably hardly even notice her at this point."

He was giving me a hard stare, and I swallowed the lump forming in my throat.

"I'm not asking you to leave her behind. I'm asking you to consider what she'd tell you to do about this," I said, wishing I could somehow make him understand what I was trying to say.

He folded his arms over his chest, looking back and forth between me and my dad with a slightly angry expression, and I could see he was really struggling with this.

"Fine," he said, dropping his hands to his sides in defeat. "But I won't go far, maybe to Ireland or England, but no farther. We stay there, find out everything we can about this Awakening, and we come back for her as soon as we possibly can."

"Done!" my dad said, and he patted Vance on the back. "Trust me. I'll do everything in my power to get her back for you."

Chapter 14

We ended up renting a couple of apartments at the plush Milestone Hotel in London. Vance paid for the rooms, but we put them under Brad and Shelly's names to try and help avoid detection, just in case anyone came looking.

Once we were settled in, we spent most of the daylight hours each day searching through old documents in libraries, trying to find anything we could that would give us information on ancient rituals performed in Celtic ceremonies.

In the evenings, we all spent our time strolling through, and exploring, Hyde Park, sometimes venturing out before dusk to work our way through Kensington Gardens also before they closed.

Vance and I usually retired to our room early at night, just to enjoy being alone with one another. Our relationship resumed all of its normal aspects—however, we were very careful to use some form of birth control now, just in case I hadn't conceived during the Celtic ritual.

"If I have to dig through one more library, I think my head may explode," I complained one night while we were crawling into bed together.

"I know exactly how you feel," Vance said, and he reached over to pull me up next to him so he could cuddle with me.

"What should we do?" I asked, feeling exasperated. "It seems we're getting nowhere fast."

Vance stared off into space, thinking things over for a moment before he answered.

"I'm thinking we must not be looking in the right place," he said. His eyes flitted back over my face. "I mean, sure, we're finding things about the history of witchcraft, but nothing to do with actual spells or rituals. We need to find someplace with things like that."

"What about shops that deal specifically in Pagan or Wicca materials and supplies? Surely they'd have some things pertaining to historical rituals or prophecies," I suggested.

His face widened into the sexy grin I loved. "That pretty little head of your is as quick as ever," he said, placing a kiss on my forehead. "I think it's a good idea. We'll look up some places tomorrow and see what we can find here in London."

"I also think we need to start thinking more like Douglas and Fiona. Where would they have stumbled across this prophecy? What kind of places do they get their information from?" I added.

"Another great idea," Vance agreed.

"I mean it's obvious this Awakening is not a well-known thing. No one seems to have heard of it. It makes me think it's a practice that's fallen by the wayside. You know, sort of obsolete. Who knows if it really even happens?" I continued on, the thoughts rolling around in my head.

"Good point," he said. "I'm thinking we have at least a few months before it might begin. They had enough time for a full-term pregnancy to occur, as well as waiting a few months to see if you'd conceived."

I nodded. "So what happens if I'm pregnant?" I asked, glancing down at my stomach before looking up at him, changing the subject.

"We'll cross that bridge when we come to it," he replied without hesitation, looking directly into my eyes.

"Will you be upset about it?" I asked, a little worried since I didn't really know how he felt about the matter.

"Not because of the baby," he answered honestly. "I'd be upset about the danger it would place you and the child in. Plus, we're young, and I'd hoped to spend a significant amount of time as just the two of us before we started a family."

"So you'd be disappointed," I said, casting my eyes down as I drew a lazy circle with my finger on his bare chest.

"I'd never be disappointed with something you and I created together," he said, catching my trailing finger and lifting it to his lips to kiss it. "I'd just miss these kinds of moments we're getting to have together now," he replied.

"We'd still have them," I said, looking up at him.

"Yes. But not as often as I'd like. A baby has a way of changing those kinds of things, and I like all the alone time we have right now."

I couldn't argue with him on that subject, since I loved being alone with him, too. Even with all the crazy things we had going on around us, our moments together were always magical.

"Don't get me wrong," he continued. "I greatly look forward to the time we start expanding our little family. It'll be awesome to see you holding my baby on your hip, or nursing, or even changing diapers. You'll be a beautiful mother, I know it. I'd just planned on waiting until you were at least a legal adult before I knocked you up," he laughed, and he winked in jest at me. "Even then you'd still be a statistic ... you know, teenaged pregnancy."

"You're crazy," I said, and I lifted to kiss his lips with a quick peck. "I love you."

He grabbed me and flipped me over onto my back, effectively pinning me beneath him.

"You know what they say, practice makes perfect," he smiled, dipping his head in for another kiss.

"Is that what they say?" I asked, and I playfully turned my head so his kiss missed, landing somewhere in the vicinity of my ear.

"Ohhhh!" he laughed. "And she's going to play hard to get! All right, I'm up for this game!"

He proceeded to attack me with vigor, and in the end, I wasn't sure which one of us had lost and which one had won, but we both had a great time together anyway.

"Have I told you how much I love you, today?" he asked as he cuddled next to me a couple of hours later.

"Only about a thousand times," I replied with a tired voice. Smiling, I closed my sleep-laden eyes.

"Well, I'd better make it a thousand and one," he whispered, and he placed a light kiss against my hair, somewhere near my ear, "Because a thousand just isn't enough. I love you, Portia."

"I love you too, Vance," I responded, still smiling to myself, and I slowly drifted off to sleep.

I awoke in the morning stretching my arm out in search of Vance's warm body next to me, only to find him missing from the bed. My eyes popped open, and I stared at the empty spot in confusion, before looking up to glance around the room, pushing away my disheveled hair as it fell in a curtain around me.

He was sitting over at the small writing desk, still shirtless, dressed in a pair of sweatpants and drinking a glass of orange juice, while he was hunkered over a laptop reading something.

"What are you doing?" I asked groggily, and I rubbed absently at one of my tired eyes.

His head turned, and he glanced back at me.

"Hey, beautiful! You're awake!" he said, coming over to me. He slid his hands into my hair on either side of my head, lifting my face to him so he could give me a light kiss on the lips.

When he was finished he sat down on the bed next to me. "I've been searching for stores like you suggested last night," he responded, draping himself casually over my still-blanketed legs, then propping up on his elbow.

"Did you find some?" I asked, reaching my hand over to rub through his wonderfully messy hair.

"Yep. There are about five I think," he replied, smiling back at me.

"Sounds good. I'll get up and get ready so we can go check them out," I replied. I playfully pushed him backward so he had to roll off my legs, then stood up and made my way toward the bathroom.

"Hey!" he called after me, sounding way too chipper all of a sudden. "Care for some company?"

"I guess," I said, drawing out the words, and I sighed heavily, acting as if I were irritated.

He laughed and jumped up, hurrying to join me.

Breakfast was in full swing when we finally made our way into the small kitchen area.

"Look!" Brad called out in a teasing voice directed at Shelly. "The newlyweds decided to join us."

Vance shot him a look. "We'd be all too happy to leave right now and resume what we were doing if you'd prefer," Vance countered. He grabbed my hand and turned back toward the bedroom.

"No! No!" Brad protested. "I don't want to spend the rest of the morning waiting for the two of you to get your fill of each other. Been there, done that."

"Jealous much?" Vance said with a grin. He looked over at me and winked, his eyes dancing with amusement.

"Show off," Brad muttered under his breath, and Vance burst out laughing, thoroughly enjoying the ribbing he was dishing out.

"Don't worry, bro," he said patting Brad on the shoulder as he passed by. "Your day will come, and when it does you'll realize it was worth the wait."

I cleared my throat a little nervously. "So how's the food this morning?" I said trying to change the subject before Shelly turned to her fourth shade of pink in embarrassment at the conversation.

"It's delicious!" she replied with a grateful look before sliding a plate of muffins in my direction. "By the way, your family is having breakfast in their room next door this morning."

"All right," I said. I reached for a fat blueberry muffin. "Does my dad have any plans for today?"

She nodded, looking completely dejected. "More of the same, I'm afraid."

"Portia had a great idea last night," Vance said. "Maybe the two of you could help us out with that today."

"What's that?" Brad asked, looking up from his food in interest.

"She thought we should hit up some specialty shops in the city that deal with magic, rituals or occult-type things. Maybe we could find something more there."

"I'm game for a change of pace," Brad replied. "How about you, babe?" He looked at Shelly.

"Anything besides what we've been doing sounds great to me," she said after swallowing a mouthful of muffin.

"It's settled then," Vance replied. "We'll tell Sean our plan after breakfast."

My dad was a little less than enthusiastic about us going off just the four of us. He felt there was better safety in numbers, so we decided everyone would make the trip to the shops Vance had addresses for, since we had been having little luck with the library thing.

We followed the directions to a little out-of-the-way shop called Lankton's. The shopkeeper came in from the back of the store when we entered through the front door, sounding a little bell.

She was very friendly while Dad told her how we were interested in looking through any old texts she might have dealing with rituals, prophecies, or history of the white witch society.

The woman led us up a small curved spiral staircase to a tiny loft that overlooked the rest of the store. There was volume upon volume of ancient looking books up here. Some were neatly organized into shelves, and others were in various sized piles around the room.

She told us to help ourselves to anything we could fine and if we needed something to just call for her.

Each of us picked a pile to start on and began the slow tedious job of looking through the books.

We read through the first pages of the ones that had a table of contents, looking for any one thing that might seem related. Most of the books, however, didn't have contents listed in them, and we were forced to turn page by page through the giant tomes to see if we could find anything.

It was well after three in the afternoon when I finally had to stop and stretch my cramping legs. I walked down the stairs and out the front door into the fresh air outside. I noticed a juice bar down the block and decided to walk over there and get some type of refreshment, thinking that might help my impending headache.

I hadn't gone two steps before Vance's arms snaked around my waist, as his head appeared over my shoulder.

"Going somewhere, baby?" he asked, he breath moving warmly though my hair and up against my neck.

"Sorry. I should've said something," I apologized, and I turned to look at him. "My head hurts, and I thought maybe some fresh air and some juice would help." I gestured down the street toward the store I had been heading to.

"That does sound good," he agreed. "Do you care if I join you?"

I smiled at him. "You know I wouldn't love anything better," I said, and he reached around to thread his fingers through mine.

"I have to apologize for falling down on the job."

"What are you talking about?" I asked in confusion.

"I should've sensed you were getting tired and called for a break," he said, a concerned look in his eyes.

I laughed. "Vance, when will you get it through that thick skull of yours that I'm a big girl and I don't need you to cater to my every need? I'm okay, really." I nudged him playfully with my shoulder.

"But I like catering to your every need," he said with a serious look before he smiled at me again. "In fact, I honestly can't think of anything else I'd rather do more."

I stopped, turning to him on the sidewalk, releasing his hand and wrapping my arms around him tightly.

"You're too good to me," I said, and I nuzzled against his shoulder. "Thank you for all that you do."

"It really is my pleasure, Portia, believe me." He smiled before he leaned in to kiss my lips.

My stomach chose this moment to begin protesting loudly, rumbling in anger at its emptiness.

I felt the laughter rumble through Vance as his lips held mine for a few seconds longer before breaking away. "I think you're going to need a pastry with your juice, too," he commented. He patted my stomach with his hand.

"I think you're right."

He took my hand and began to walk a little more determinedly toward the juice shop.

We were inside placing our order when the rest of the group wandered in behind us.

Shelly plopped into a chair by a small table, telling Brad what she wanted to order.

Brad came up to stand by Vance in line, so I wandered back to sit and visit with Shelly.

"How are you holding up?" I asked.

"This research stuff is brutal." She grimaced and rubbed her hand over the small of her back.

"I'm sorry about all this. Would you and Brad like to go back to Sedona? I hate to have you sucked into all this and miss the rest of your school year." I felt badly about how they were always putting their lives on hold for our benefit.

"Brad and I are finished with school for the semester," she responded to me casually.

"How's that?" I asked, a little shocked at her comment.

"We've been here quite a while ... since we came to help look for you two. We had tutors the whole time, and we finished the required work for the semester. Your dad already sent everything back to the school so we'd get credit. Our parents have been telling everyone we're studying abroad, which I guess has been the case," she explained.

"Oh, well that's good for you guys. Vance and I are going to be miserably behind by the time we can get back," I replied feeling a little downhearted.

"Why don't you use our tutor through the summer?" Shelly suggested. "I'm sure you could finish up all of your credits in that amount of time."

"That does sound like a good idea. Thanks," I said as Vance and Brad joined us, carrying our food.

They sat down next to us and handed us what we had ordered.

I ate quickly because I felt like I was starving to death, and I felt like quite the pig when I finished before everyone else.

When they were all done, we stood to leave, and I picked up our trash so I could throw it away in the receptacle. A sudden wave of nausea washed over me and I covered my mouth with my hand.

"You okay, baby?" Vance asked, eyeing me closely.

I shook my head and ran into the bathroom where I began puking my guts up.

CHAPTER 15

One long nap, four over-the-counter pregnancy tests, and one magical medical exam later, I finally convinced Vance I wasn't pregnant.

He whisked me out of the juice bar, not even letting me walk on my own two feet before placing me in the car and rushing me back to the hotel.

I kept trying to tell him I had just gone too long without eating anything and then I had eaten too fast when I did.

He'd been almost certain I was expecting a baby, and I thought I felt a distinct moment of disappointment flash through him once he was sure otherwise. Staying by my side, he catered to my every need until I had finally fallen into an exhausted sleep.

When I woke up a couple of hours later it was to find him lying next to me, staring at me with concern. I burst out laughing at his expression of worry which caused him to make a face at me.

"I appreciate your concern, but I really am fine," I said, and I reached out to stroke the side of his face.

He grabbed my hand, holding it there. "I was really worried," he said. He searched my eyes intently, several things plainly written in his for me to see. "I couldn't live with myself if something were to happen to you."

"You're very sweet," I said with a soft smile.

"I mean it, Portia. I know I'm driving you crazy with my constant hovering over you, but you're everything to me," he replied apologetically. "I'm sorry if I'm bothering you, but I need you to know how I feel when it comes to you. Nothing is more important than your well-being."

"I understand," I said seriously, not wanting to hurt his feelings by making light of his mood. "But I'm not going anywhere."

I gave him a long lingering kiss so he would know I meant it. He wrapped his arms around me, pulling me up tighter against him, and I could feel his panic and unease at the situation.

"I love you," I said when we broke the kiss, and he continued to stare longingly at me.

"I love you, too," he replied. He reluctantly released me and moved to get off the bed. "Do you think you could eat something now?" he asked, and he walked over to the writing desk and picked up a tray with cheese and crackers on it.

"I can try," I said. I sat up to fluff the pillows behind my back, scooting up against them.

He placed the tray onto my lap, before sitting on the edge of the bed next to me. He would break off pieces of cheese and lay them on the crackers before handing them to me.

I tried to keep the smile from spreading across my face since I knew I could have done this tiny task by myself, but he seemed desperate to help me somehow, so I didn't say anything.

"Where is everyone else?" I asked, changing the subject away from myself, trying to direct his attention elsewhere.

"They went back to Lankton's," he said. He reached over to the nightstand, picked up a glass of juice, and handed it to me. "They said for you and me to take the evening off and just enjoy resting here together."

"That was sweet," I replied, swallowing a small sip of the drink before biting into another cracker. "I know Shelly was getting pretty worn out with all this, though. I feel bad creating more work for everyone else."

"I know. But we really need to figure out what's going on with this Awakening thing."

I agreed with a slight nod while he continued to feed me. I finally had to beg him to stop, telling him I was too full to eat another bite.

He, however, complained I hadn't yet eaten enough. He relented, though, when I told him I was going to get sick again if he kept force feeding me.

After that, he insisted upon drawing me a bath to relax in, which I completely enjoyed since he lit a couple candles and put on some soft music from a station on the television. I quickly fell asleep once more in the soothing environment.

When I finally managed to make my way out of the bathroom, it was to find the bedroom transformed, lit by the light of scented, glowing candles on almost every surface of the room. The aroma was intoxicating.

My eyes drifted past the new covered food tray on the end of the bed and over to my sleeping husband. He looked a bit like a Greek god who had decided to grace the earth with his very presence.

He had removed his shirt, which was casually tossed on the floor next to his shoes and socks, and his long jean-clad legs were stretched out, crossed loosely as the ankles.

His hands rested behind his head, causing his biceps to pop out, perfectly defined in the flickering light. My eyes traveled slowly down his sculpted bronzed skin, and I almost licked my lips in anticipation while I watched him. Had he not been sleeping so soundly, I would have accused him of setting up this scene with the express intent of seducing me.

The funny thing was I knew this wasn't the case since he had been desperately trying all day to make me rest. Had he not been in the picture, this would have been the very scene of extreme relaxation. Instead his presence had the exact opposite effect on me, causing my pulse to jump to an ever-increasing tempo.

I tightened the knot at the waist of my robe, before quietly tiptoeing around to the foot of the bed to pick up the food tray he had left there for me. I carefully moved it to another surface without even bothering to check what was making the delicious aromas coming from the steam hole on the top of the plate cover.

Determined not to wake him, I turned from the tray and made my way around to my side of the bed, sitting down as softly as possible, gently swinging my legs up onto the bed as I lay back on the pillow.

I held my breath for a few seconds when I felt him stir ever so slightly, but he didn't wake up. After several moments passed I rolled over onto my side so I could look at him.

I watched in awe while the candlelight danced and flickered over his skin, wanting to reach out and touch him so badly, but refraining from doing so because I knew he had really been pushing himself lately.

His face was relaxed in sleep, and I loved the way it looked, as if he didn't have a care in the world—all traces of the worry lines, scowls of deep concentration, and tension wiped away from his features. It had been months since I had truly seen him this relaxed. I often wondered if he ever really rested while we were being held captive. He had always been so concerned with everything and how he was going to protect me in a hostile environment. It was a joy to my heart to see him like this.

I lay perfectly still for a very long time, just watching him, letting my eyes travel up and down every inch of his perfect physique, wanting to capture every part of him in my memory forever.

My eyes started to get a little heavy themselves, and I slowly turned to go put out the candles before I fell asleep. I was just getting ready to use a little magic to extinguish the tiny flames when I felt his arm snake out and capture me around the waist, pulling me back up against his chest. I let out a little squeal of surprise.

"Where do you think you're going?" he said in a sleepy voice.

"I'm sorry. I didn't mean to wake you up," I said, and a broad smile slipped over my face. "I was getting sleepy and thought I'd better blow the candles out before we burned the place down around us. Thank you for setting the room up so nicely for me, though. It was very sweet."

"I'm sorry I fell asleep before I could enjoy it with you," he replied, and he nuzzled his nose against my ear before nibbling slightly there, causing a flash of goose bumps to run over my entire body.

"Don't feel bad. You've needed some good rest, probably more than I have. I was happy to see you so relaxed."

"Did you eat your dinner?" he asked me, brushing my damp hair back from my neck so he could reach it better, kissing his way from my ear to my throat.

"No," I replied honestly, and the shivers he was causing danced over my skin, to which I was rewarded with an exasperated sigh.

"Portia, you need to eat so you can keep your strength up," he said, and he paused in his tender assault of me.

"I was devouring something with my eyes instead," I replied jokingly.

His eyes registered a moment of confusion before the light of understanding flashed into them.

"You were, were you?" he said, and a seductive grin spread over his face. "Did you like what you saw?"

"It was the best visual buffet I could ever imagine," I replied, and I flashed him a grin over my shoulder. "I was practically salivating."

"Really?" he said with a quirk of his eyebrow, and he turned his head, his gaze traveling slowly down the length of my body and back up again. I could feel the heat of it as if he were touching me with an actual flame. "Because it couldn't have been better than the visual display I see laid out before me. Only I think looking isn't going to be enough. I'm going to need a taste."

"Only one taste?" I asked, flirting back brazenly, and I could feel my skin flush with excitement.

He rolled me onto my back, observing my blushing reaction, and I heard a low chuckle emanate from his throat.

"Girl, you have no idea what you're doing to me, but, yes, baby, I promise it'll be more than one taste," he replied, and his eyes burned a look that was unmistakable into my own.

"Mmm, it sounds ... delicious," I murmured, my breaths becoming more rapid as I fell under his seductive powers.

"Oh, it will be," he promised before his lips descended to claim mine, and I was not the least bit disappointed.

We ended up going to all the little bookstores Vance found over the next four days, spending many hours searching, yet finding nothing.

Vance insisted on everyone taking regularly scheduled breaks to stretch and keep our strength up with some sort of refreshment, not taking any chances with anyone's health or well-being, especially mine.

We had finally come to the fifth store on the list, and we were all sitting in a small, stuffy, windowless attic space covered in dust. It appeared these books hadn't been touched in a long while.

The shopkeeper at this location hadn't been too keen on letting us look at his collection, but had finally been persuaded to let us have a go at it after Vance promised we would definitely be purchasing from him.

We had been here for several hours, sifting through the musty smelling items, when Grandma finally spoke up.

"I think I may have found something," she said passing a very old, large book over to my dad.

Dad looked carefully at the brittle worn pages. "Yes. This is definitely something about the white witches," Dad agreed, his eyes intently searching over the yellowed page while he ran his index finger carefully over the writings.

Vance stood up, brushing himself off slightly, and came to look over his shoulder for a moment.

"I'll go down and see if we can't persuade the shop owner to let us borrow or purchase it," he said after a few seconds of perusing the book in interest.

He made his way out of the narrow doorway to head down to the lower floor of the store. He had only been gone for a few moments when he hurried back up the stairs in a hushed manner, holding his fingers to his lips.

"Quick! Everyone drop what you're doing. Go down the stairs and out the back as fast as you can," he said, waving his arm to hurry everyone along, not offering any other explanation.

To his credit, not one soul questioned him. Dad closed the book, tucking it under his arm, and we hurriedly made our way down the staircase toward the outside. When we were out the door, I turned to Vance who was dragging me down the narrow alleyway, breaking into a run.

"What is it?" I asked breathlessly, the others running alongside us, quickly trying to put distance between ourselves and the shop.

"Brian Fitzgerald was in the building," he huffed as we rounded a corner, out of the line of sight from the building.

"Brian?" I asked breathlessly. "What could he have possibly been doing there?"

"He was asking about that book," Vance said pointing to the one my dad was carrying under his arm still.

"But why would he want the book?" I asked while we made our way around to where we had parked the vehicles.

"I didn't stick around to find out," he replied. "He didn't see me, and I knew I needed to get everyone out of there before we were discovered. The others could've been with him for all I know."

He held the door to the car open for me, ushered me inside, and climbed in beside me. We were soon on our way down the road.

As our group was in two separate vehicles, we decided to split up and take alternate routes, weaving through town in random directions just in case someone was trying to follow us.

We didn't see anyone making any obvious attempts to mark our movements, so after about thirty minutes of driving we finally turned back toward the direction of the hotel.

We arrived without further incident, and we all met together in the safety of our apartment. Dad placed the book on the dining room table while everyone gathered around to read over his shoulders.

"The Society of the White Witch," Dad began reading aloud to the rest of us. "The first coven of this society was made up entirely of female witches, with no male warlock members admitted.

"These witches were concerned about the rising discord in the public eye where witchcraft was concerned. They set out on a quest to perfect their magic and use it only for the good of themselves and for the benefit of others they might meet. They were hoping to dispel the unrest that was beginning to stir through the masses, showing that witchcraft was not something to be feared but something to help all.

"These witches began purifying their magic and rituals to the point that they began to accomplish many great feats that had never been heard of before. Much of this magic revolved around the healing of others.

"The white witches claimed their powers had improved so much because of their belief in God as a higher power than themselves. They maintained all their gifts were from him and gave him all the credit for the work they had done.

"This caused much speculation in the magical community as most witches and warlocks believed only in the worship of Pagan deities, not one almighty God, though most of the Pagan covens were content to peacefully let them worship as they wished.

"However, it is said that several covens which dealt more in the dark art of things came up against these white witches in order to destroy them and prevent them from turning other witches toward their teachings.

"These covens attacked the white witch coven, which refused to fight back against those who assaulted them, feeling like it would be forsaking all the blessings they had received from their God, to injure another being. Each member of the white witch coven was slain until only the coven's high priestess remained.

"Legend has it that she called to her God in the skies, asking for mercy on her behalf. Her God heard her cries and sent an archangel who held the wicked covens at bay. The archangel presented her with a box which held a gift called the Awakening, which was likened unto the gift of immortality.

"He told her if she chose to open the box and accept the gift, she would live a very long time so she could continue the work that she had started. She would be protected from illness and even death for a time. When her time on earth was complete, she would be taken to heaven and the Awakening would be offered to one of her descendants, who could then continue her righteous mission here on Earth, passing the power for good down through the generations of time.

"When the high priestess finally died centuries later, she left detailed instructions on how her descendants could receive the Awakening by performing a certain ritual with the box.

"They were to place the box on the altar in the circle of stones and open it during a full moon when there is a lunar eclipse taking place. The box was not to be opened until the lunar eclipse was starting to pass and light began to shine on the moon's reflective surface once again, thus symbolizing the Awakening of light.

"The witch in the circle who carried the purest strain of white witch blood would then be the recipient of the enhanced powers and longevity of life.

"It was soon discovered that even though all the descendants of the white witch might be present at the ritual, that did not always mean they carried the purest strain of the blood. The magic of the white witch was selective and often skipped several generations at a time, only to reappear stronger in certain individuals of different generations. The Awakening would subsequently choose one of these individuals to transfer its power to.

"The last known white witch to receive the Awakening was actually a warlock descendant. He left the bonds of this earth over two centuries ago, and it is unknown if he was ever replaced in his calling.

"The box, upon which the ritual was founded on, has since disappeared."

Dad sat back from the book as we all silently absorbed what we had just heard.

"You know what this means, right?" Vance asked to no one in particular. "My grandparents have the box." He started pacing the room.

"We need to find out when the next lunar eclipse occurs during a full moon," I added.

"It's in July," Brad spoke up. "Shelly and I studied about it in science with our tutor."

"That can't be right," I said. "There's no way I could've delivered a baby by then. They were very specific in their desire for me to produce a child."

"That's it, though!" Vance said, turning suddenly to face me. "My mom said they couldn't drink your blood unless it was mixed with their own. If you had gotten pregnant that would have fulfilled that."

Everyone in the room just stared at him with blank looks, trying to comprehend what he was saying.

"Don't you get it? They had no intention of ever letting you go to term! It was your blood mixed with mine that they wanted. A baby just enhanced everything! They could drink straight from you or the fetus."

"I think I'm going to be sick," Shelly said suddenly. "They'd really just slice her open and take her unborn child right there?" she asked with a horrified look on her face.

"Yes, if they deemed it necessary," Vance replied without any hesitation, turning to look over at her.

"No offense, Vance, but your family sucks!" she said with a nauseated glance, and she placed a hand over her stomach.

"I happen to agree with you," he replied softly, and my heart ached at his comment.

"All right, everybody calm down, and let's think this thing through. We need to lay out our facts and look at them. What stone circle are we talking about here? Stonehenge?" my dad interjected offering a suggestion, and he looked around at all of us.

"Actually there are over one thousand stone circles in the British Isles and western Europe," Grandma Milly spoke up with a slightly dismayed look.

"You're kidding!" Dad replied in amazement. "How are we going to find out which one is the right one?"

"Maybe it doesn't matter which one," my mom suggested. "Maybe it can be any stone circle."

Dad walked back over to the open book on the table, silently reading down the manuscript again.

"I don't think so," he disagreed while he looked over the text, pointing out the one phrase that had caught his eye. "It specifically says 'the circle of stones' like it's speaking of one in particular."

"So now what do we do?" Shelly asked with a sigh, plopping down into one of the dining chairs dejectedly.

"More research," Brad said absently. He stuffed a day-old muffin into his mouth and licked his fingers.

"Ugh," Shelly grunted in reply, not looking at all happy about that statement, flashing Brad a disdainful glance.

"I know everyone is tired of all the digging we've had to do lately, but the good news is we should be able to research several of these places on the Internet. We'll get all the information we can on the stone circles from there. Those that we can't find out much about we'll drive to. It'll be an educational field trip of sorts," Dad said, trying to encourage everyone.

"We need to find out the geographical origin of the white witch coven. If we know what continent they started on, then my guess would be that the stone circle referred to would possibly be in the same place," I suggested, trying to think of anything that might help us out.

"Or we could try to find out where the first white witch left this world. Perhaps that would yield us a clue," Vance added. "Who knows if she moved around from place to place in her life? If she knew she was going to die, wouldn't she go to the place where she knew her powers would be transferred?"

"Those are both very good points," Dad agreed. "I also think we need to keep reading through this book and see if we can find anything more to help answer these questions. Any volunteers?" he asked, and he looked around at all of us.

"I'll do it," Grandma said, piping up instantly. "All this history is very interesting to me, and it's clear this is part of our ancestry. Maybe it'll yield some clue to our own heritage."

"It's all yours," Dad said, gesturing toward the book before he stepped out of her way. He continued on. "Vance and Portia, why don't you go hit the laptop in your room while Mom and I take Brad and Shelly to the Natural History Museum to see if we can find anything clues about these stone circles, what they were used for, and how they were created."

"Yay, a museum," Shelly said sarcastically, without any enthusiasm in her voice as she rolled her eyes. "Because that's so much better than a library."

Chapter 16

Vance and I climbed out of the car, the dim moonlight washing over us while we moved toward the giant stones in the circle ahead of us. Dad had divided us all into separate research parties to check out different locations, and Vance and I had been given the assignment of going to explore Stonehenge. We had been on a guided tour here earlier in the day, but Vance had wanted to come back when the place was deserted and explore it more at our leisure, so after having dinner in the nearest town we made our way back out to the isolated area.

The large towering stones loomed up out of the night as we entered the edifice. We walked around each of the massive pillars together, running our hands reverently over them as we passed, feeling their hewn textures move under our skin.

We were silent as we moved, listening to and feeling the energies that flowed around us until we had made our way into the inner circle of stones.

"Do you feel it?" Vance asked while he held his hands out from his body, closing his eyes and taking a deep breath.

"Yes," I replied, knowing instinctively he was talking about the humming pulse that was filling the air around us.

It was as if magic was alive and beating in the very air here.

"Something very powerful is at work here," Vance said, and he lifted his palms into the air in front of him.

I watched him in amazement when sparks began generating from the tips of his fingers. There was a loud snapping sound, and suddenly the air burst into electrical currents around him.

He chuckled, and the currents spread through the air, twisting, zipping, and arcing in all directions until there was a current attached to every stone in the circle. I felt like we were standing in the middle of an electric storm ball, and I could feel the static electricity in the air begin to even lift the hairs on my head.

"Come here," he said with a grin while he continued to manipulate the magic.

I walked toward him, and the streams of electricity danced harmlessly away from my body as I approached, until I was standing right in front of him.

"Lift your hands up," he commanded me, and I did as he asked.

He moved his hands until our palms were almost touching, but not quite, and I felt him link with me mentally.

Sparks began shooting from my fingertips the second his mind attached to mine, and I jerked a bit as a wave of the most intense power I had ever felt coursed completely through my body from head to toe.

My breath caught when I suddenly realized this was his magic flowing through me. Never could I have imagined the strength or the level at which he operated. I had always known he was strong and gifted magically, but I would have never dreamed it possible at this magnitude.

A stronger surge moved through me. I felt my hair lift and swirl away from my body as it did, and I realized with awe that he was playing. What I was feeling was not even the full extent of his power! I wondered how he could possibly contain it all. My body was trembling at the invasion of it, and it continued to pulsate through me, causing magical reactions from my own power. I noticed the tips of my fingers had now turned to solid ice.

The air churned and throbbed with the electric streams that lifted from our bodies, twisting together. I watched the display around us in amazement. It was a phenomenal sight to behold, to be a part of.

He stepped forward, locking his fingers with mine, and I felt more than saw the explosion of electricity when his lips touched mine. My knees buckled under the power of his magic. He released one of my hands and caught me easily around the waist before pushing me backward with his body until my back was pressed against one of the ancient stones.

He lifted the one hand he still held up over my head, pressing it up against the rock too. He ran his free hand down my arm, sending actual sparks over my skin, raising huge goose bumps there, before he took my free hand and threaded it around his waist.

Lifting his hand, he touched my face, running his thumb over my lips while he looked at me. He looked like some sort of mythical god standing in front of me with the very air crackling and swirling around him.

Suddenly his fingers felt very cold on my lips, and I looked down to see that the tips of them had ice on them also, and I realized my powers were transferring to him as well.

"Look at the two of us." He grinned seductively while continuing to run his thumb over my lower lip. "Fire and Ice ... literally."

"How are you doing this?" I asked him.

"I'm not. It's this place. It's intensifying everything," he replied dipping in to replace his thumb with his ever so hot lips.

Another shock of power rolled through me, and my knees buckled so badly I would have fallen had he not had me so firmly pinned there with his body. He kissed me feverishly, twisting his free hand into my hair, and I could feel the heat of his magic roll through me with the contact.

He burned so hot it was almost unbearable for me. I never realized how cold my magic felt before this point, but getting to experience him in this way was shedding a whole new light on him for me.

He kissed me for a long, long time until I started to notice that both of our lips were becoming icy as well.

He broke the kiss with a laugh.

"We're going to have to stop this, or you're going to turn me to a block of ice." He grinned.

"I don't think that's possible since my insides are currently on fire with your magic," I breathed heavily.

"This has certainly been an interesting exchange of power between the two of us, hasn't it?" he said, his gaze flitting over my face.

"Yes, it has been very enlightening," I agreed.

He let out a sigh, leaning his forehead against mine, and I stared deeply into his blue eyes.

"I think I want to kiss you here all night long," he said.

"That sounds divine," I replied, watching him.

"Does it?" he asked, quirking an eyebrow at me slightly. "I've never been so hot and cold all at the same time before in my life! I'm afraid if I continued, you might freeze off some of my body parts!" He winked, and I laughed out loud at him.

It was then I noticed he actually had frost on his eyebrows, and I smiled, reaching up to brush it off.

"I guess we could always take the kissing someplace less magical," I suggested to him.

"Kissing you is always magical, Portia, no matter where we are. And what tends to follow it is even more so."

"You know what I mean," I said, shoving at his shoulder slightly with my free hand.

He just laughed, swinging me up into his arms. He proceeded to carry me, electrical storm and all, to the edge of the circle.

As it turned out, while we easily concluded Stonehenge definitely had a magical influence, none of us had any luck with our assignments. We found nothing that indicated whether any of the stone circles we looked at was the one the white witch had been speaking about.

We had gone on numerous amounts of the so-called "field trips" to visit some of the stone circle sites we had not been able to research from London. For weeks we toured properties and listened to lectures from informed sources on the histories of said places.

After a while the information we were hearing began to run together. No one knew why these circles were constructed, when they were constructed, or what they were used for.

Several had theories about their being used as astrological calendars, ritual places, or even something that marked the passing of someone into death. No one was really sure what they were all about.

The only thing we could consider as marked progress on the subject was a reference that Grandma had found in the book she had continued to study. It had said the high priestess of the white witch coven had never left Scotland during her immortality. We had concluded from that little tidbit of information that the stone circle spoken of must be one that was in Scotland.

We all decided we should probably relocate back to the area. Dad had done a lot of research on places in Scotland, and with the help of Crispin, we finally located an old Scottish keep currently under renovations to be made into a hotel.

They had one wing that was finished, but not yet opened to the public. We were able to get permission to stay there in the keep, thus removing ourselves from a place Douglas and Fiona might continually be searching for us.

Dad had been in touch with the rest of our coven who were still in Sedona, and they informed him there had been some foreign people who had been asking after our whereabouts. We were certain they came from Douglas and Fiona.

“I’ll give them credit for being persistent,” Vance grumbled when he heard the news. “Is everyone in Sedona all right?”

“They said everything has been going along as it normally would,” Dad replied nonchalantly, though I could see a small flicker of worry cross over his face which he hurriedly disguised.

I sighed, knowing he was feeling concern over several issues and wanting to keep everyone safe.

Later that evening, when Vance and I were lying in bed together, I asked him a question.

"Why do you think Douglas and Fiona want this power so badly? History says the power has always been used for good."

He shrugged, considering before answering. "I just assumed it was because of how much it would enhance their powers. Plus the longevity will help them to rule with those powers over their followers."

"There's one problem with this, though," I said while I trailed my fingers up and down his arm.

"What's that?" he asked, watching me through half-lidded eyes.

"They can't both receive the power. It would only go to one of them, whoever had the most of the blood source in them."

"You're right," he said, and the emotions danced over his face while he pondered my comment. "Either they've designated one or the other to be the recipient, or they'd have to betray each other when the time comes."

"That's what I was thinking," I replied with a smile. "That would make them divided against one another. Which one would the rest of their coven follow, or would they be divided also?"

"You're thinking that they could be easier to fight if they were fighting against each other, aren't you?" His eyes flashed over me in appreciation.

I nodded. "If they have to fight each other and us, how could they possibly win?"

"That's a really good point. Now we just have to hope this is the course they're on. If they've chosen one to receive it, then it'll have the opposite effect, uniting them even stronger."

"You're right," I replied as I climbed off the bed, walking over to look out the window. "Is there some way we could try to figure out which way things are leaning?"

"You mean start spying on them?" he asked with a slight frown. "I don't know how safe that would be."

"What about Crispin's coven? They've been spying on them for years. Douglas and Fiona are completely aware of it, too. It wouldn't be anything out of the ordinary," I said, turning to look at him.

He got off the bed and came to join me at the window, wrapping his arms around my waist.

"I think that's a good idea. I'll talk to your dad about it in the morning," he said, bending to kiss my lightly scarred neck.

I enjoyed his touch while I watched the moonlight wash over the landscape outside. It really was beautiful here. Too bad everything was so shrouded in mystery right now; we might've actually been able to enjoy our stay.

As it was, Dad hardly let Vance and me out of the keep for fear that someone we met at the reception would see us and tell Douglas and Fiona about it. He made it very clear we were not to stray from the grounds.

We spent several days entertaining ourselves by exploring around the ancient place and some of the outbuildings. On many occasions I found Vance sitting alone in the crumbling old Kirk, silently contemplating things.

I could tell he was slipping back into some of his old habits where I was concerned. Often his mind would be fettered in front of me as if he were trying to protect me from something.

Though it was frustrating, I also knew he was a lot more worried than he was really letting on. I didn't bring it up again since I didn't want to add to his burdens, but I was disappointed. I knew it was hard for him to let me in anyway, since he had been so practiced at shutting himself down completely before we had met. It was his way of protecting himself, too.

I had seen the richly intricate person he really was, though. His emotions sometimes threatened to completely overwhelm him. He considered that the ultimate sign of weakness. He had to be in control.

I looked forward to the day when he would realize it was those emotions I loved so much about him. It was all of his little imperfections that made him real to me in a way I wished I could make him understand.

For some reason, though, he was determined to be the savior and champion in this relationship. It was a role I knew he could execute because I had seen him do it on several occasions. But I wanted to be his partner, his lover, his friend, not his damsel in distress.

I sighed heavily. Maybe it was just a man thing. He had said to me once before that it was his job to take care of me. That comment had resulted in our largest argument to-date and was one of the major reasons I hesitated to bring up the fact that he was shutting me out again.

"You're upset with me," he said, and he pulled away from me, turning me from the window to face him.

"No, not really," I replied, feeling a bit angry with myself for letting him read me so easily.

"Tell me what's on your mind," he encouraged, and he led me over to sit on the loveseat near the fireplace in our suite.

"It's nothing." I smiled trying to dismiss the subject with a wave of my hand, wishing he would just let it drop.

"Portia, talk to me. If something's bothering you, then I want to know what it is," he said softly as he squeezed my hands in a quiet gesture.

I waited a moment before I spoke, trying to compose my emotions so I wouldn't upset him.

"I noticed you're worried about something and the walls are starting to go up again, that's all," I said, looking down to where our hands were intertwined together and resting in my lap.

When he didn't respond to me I risked a glance up into his eyes, to gauge his reaction, feeling a bit nervous. I was surprised by the love, and the hurt, I saw there.

"I'm not doing it intentionally," he responded, his eyes staring straight into mine.

"I know you aren't. That's why I hadn't said anything about it."

"I don't like to hurt you in any way," he said remorsefully. "That makes this a tricky road for me. If I tell you about things that worry me, I risk hurting you, and if I don't, then I hurt you, too. How can I change that?" he asked me, seemingly anxious for my opinion on the subject.

"You're going to have to start realizing you can trust me with whatever you have to say. We've been through a lot together. I haven't run off yet," I smiled so he would know I was teasing.

"You've been a trouper," he agreed, and he squeezed my hand tighter in response.

"Don't take this the wrong way, but I feel you have this need to be the super macho, protector guy in this relationship. While I love everything about you that is so totally 'guy' about you, I tend to view this relationship more in the terms of a partnership." I looked at him seriously.

"Well, I hope you'll understand this," he began. "I want to be your protector. You're my wife, and I love everything about you. I completely consider you an equal partner in this relationship, but I won't lie. If it came down to you or me, I'd put my life on the line to save you."

"That's what scares me," I replied honestly. "I know you'd do exactly that. I don't want a life without you. I'd rather die with you."

"And I don't wish to deprive the world of the most beautiful creature it has ever known," he said, and he released my hand so he could place both of his on the sides of my face.

"Whatever," I said, and I rolled my eyes, thinking he was completely delirious. "Are you going to tell me what's bothering you or not?"

He let his hands drop away from my face and just sat there looking at me for a moment before giving a large sigh.

"It's about the Awakening," he replied, and he stared off into the distance as if he were searching for something there.

"What about it?" I asked curiously, not knowing where he was going with this.

He stood and started his pacing, the way he always did when something big was weighing on his mind.

"I'm assuming that we'll have to actually go to the ritual to stop whichever of my grandparents from receiving it," he said.

"That seems logical," I replied.

"Well, in order for them to not receive it, then someone else has to, right?" he asked me.

"If the ritual has already been started, then yes, I'd suppose so," I said trying to follow his train of thought.

"So the person with the purest blood in the circle would be you, correct?" he asked, turning to stare at me.

I instantly understood what had him so upset. If I accepted the Awakening, then I'd become nearly immortal, subject to live for a very long time. He would not be, thus forcing our eventual separation by death.

My eyes widened in fear. "I don't want it. I won't live without you," I said, wrapping my arms around him.

"That's the problem. If you refuse it, then it'll pass to me," he replied, and I realized he would be the one living a hundred lifetimes without me.

"No!" I whispered in angst. "There has to be another way! Surely fate wouldn't let us go through all these things just to be together for a few short years before ripping us apart again?"

My head was spinning while he held me, and I felt the tears threatening to come. His grip tightened protectively around me.

"There's only one other way I can think of to change all this," he said, and he lifted a hand to stroke my long hair.

"Which is what?"

"We need to end this before the Awakening can happen," he stated flatly.

"How can we do that?"

"I'm thinking we're going to need to find a way into Bell Tower Hall. I need to take a look around."

"No! It's too dangerous! That's their domain, the place where they'll be the strongest," I argued.

"I know that!" he said in frustration. "But unless we can find some way to draw them and their entire coven out of there, I see no other way."

"What about the box?" I asked him.

"I don't follow," he replied with a slightly confused look crossing his features while he watched me.

"They have it hidden away somewhere. What if someone else is aware of the location? We'll still have the exact same problem. If that box falls into any other demon hands, they can try to enforce the ritual upon themselves ... same results, different people."

He stood, digging his hand through his hair like he always did when he was frustrated about something.

"You're right, as usual," he said, and he turned from me with another sigh to start pacing. "We have to figure out where they're keeping it."

"I'm assuming they've had it in a very safe place for a very long time. This ritual was put into motion before you were born. They must feel very secure about its whereabouts."

He didn't reply this time, only nodding.

I watched him as he continued on his track, back and forth.

"We just don't have enough information still," he said throwing his hands up into the air before letting them fall helplessly to his side in defeat. "I feel completely overwhelmed at times. I don't know what to do!"

"Let's talk to Crispin tomorrow," I suggested to him, standing. "He's been following your grandparents' actions for a long while. Maybe he can tell us where they store important things or where they go and the company they've been keeping lately. Let's use the resources we do have."

He stopped pacing and came back over to hug me, wrapping his finely toned arms around me.

"Have I told you how smart I think you are?" he asked, and a whisper of a kiss was placed against my forehead.

"Not today," I smiled, and I reached my arms around his waist, laying my head against his sculpted chest. "But this is why you shouldn't shut me out. We need to talk to each other so we know what we're dealing with."

I could feel his chin on the top of my head as he nodded slightly.

"Message received, Portia," he replied softly. "Can you ever forgive me for treating you so wrong?"

"You haven't been doing it on purpose, and I understand that. It's hard for you to break several years' worth of habit for my benefit. I'm doing my best to try and look at where you're coming from, which was why I didn't want to say anything to you about it in the first place. I didn't want to upset you."

"So instead, you'll walk on eggshells around me trying to keep the peace?" he asked. "I won't have things that way either, baby. Never fear saying what you have to say to me. I want it. I need it."

I looked up at him. "I love you," I said.

"I know," he replied. "And I'm the luckiest person on this earth because of it."

He tipped his head down, kissing me softly on the lips while he hugged me even tighter. He pulled back after a moment, resting his forehead against mine, and he slowly rubbed the tip of his nose back and forth against mine.

"Gosh, I love you, Portia," he said with a sigh. "I don't know if you'll ever really understand how I feel about you, and I don't know if I'll ever be able to properly show you, but you make me feel things in a way I never dreamed possible."

I didn't say anything in reply, not wanting to break the tender moment of his declaration while he kissed my cheek with slow deliberate movements before he moved down my neck to rest his face gently there. I could feel his hot breath feathering against my throat while he nuzzled up against me.

"I love you," he whispered softly again, and he placed a kiss against my skin.

Chapter 17

Dad called Crispin the next day, and he agreed to come meet us at the keep early in the afternoon. When we were all settled into the sitting room, he started to speak.

"So, Sean asked me for some more information on the Cummingses' activities. Our coven has kept tabs on them for a long time, searching for some way to trip them up and expose them.

"I can assure you that Douglas and Fiona are very careful individuals. Members of their coven extend from their household staff to corporate contacts from the community. They're very high-powered individuals even without their magical influences.

"They have complete control over their followers. Some demon covens let their members run wild on bloodthirsty rampages, not Douglas and Fiona. They run a very refined operation that probably resembles something like being a member of a wine-tasting society.

"They prefer their coven members remain in human form as much as possible and that they do everything possible to maintain an appearance of normalcy. They are upper crust to the core.

"That in itself speaks to their control over their powers as most demon covens operate on a more crazed and bloodthirsty level.

"Most of their ritual dealings take place in their home, so it's made observing their practices difficult, if not near impossible. We've never ventured onto the property uninvited."

"You've been invited before?" Dad asked with a quizzical look.

Crispin nodded. "Once or twice, when business dealings couldn't afford my being slighted at one of their functions, they allowed me a visit. They were dinner parties where I was surrounded by many, many people, thus insuring my safety."

"Did you notice anything unusual at that time?" I asked curiously.

"No. Like I said before, they were the picture of propriety. Now you say you're looking for a certain artifact, some type of box?" he replied.

"Yes," Dad explained. "It would be something that is, at the very least, several hundreds of years old."

Crispin reached up to scratch lightly behind his ear while he pondered this for a moment. "I assume you're aware the son, Damien, was a very successful antiques dealer?" he asked looking back and forth between my dad and Vance.

Dad nodded. "We're aware."

"Well, I wouldn't even know where to begin searching for an antique box in that house." He gestured toward

Vance and me. "As I'm sure the two of you know there's hardly an item in that house that isn't an antique."

"You bring up an interesting point, though," Vance said. "Perhaps my father is the one who originally came across the artifact in his business dealings."

"I think that could be very probable," Crispin acknowledged. "I'm less familiar with his dealings, however, since he was around the world quite a bit, until more recent years after they brought his wife to Bell Tower Hall. He visited her quite frequently, which I found interesting since we were sure they were an estranged couple. I understand the reasons now that we've met you."

I saw a brief look of anger flash over Vance's face before he successfully shuttered his emotions again.

Crispin was a complete gentleman and pretended not to notice, though.

"So have you ever noticed anyone in my family keeping a separate or special storage space somewhere else?" Vance asked.

"I've never seen anything that would suggest that," Crispin answered. "I think Bell Tower is a vast enough estate that they could store or hide anything they could possibly want and no one would find it for centuries, if ever."

"That's what I was afraid of," Dad said. "There isn't even really any point to trying to sneak onto the property to look for something unless we have some sort of starting point. We'd just be putting ourselves in danger."

"I'd suggest you stay completely away from the property," Crispin agreed. "There's just no need to risk yourselves. Let my coven continue to keep tabs on everything, and if we notice any activity picking up or anything out of the ordinary, we'll contact you right away."

We all stood when Crispin rose from his seat, shaking his hand and thanking him for his information. Dad walked him out to his vehicle.

"Well, that was completely useless," Vance muttered to me. He reached for my hand. "He's been watching them for years. I doubt my grandparents would be stupid enough to start revealing things now."

"I agree with you," I replied sadly. "I don't know where else we could look for information either."

"Maybe we should try following some of the demon contacts they have. You know, the ones Crispin told us about," he suggested.

"It's worth a shot, I guess," I said with a shrug. "I'm sure Dad has plenty of his surveillance stuff here with him and could do something like that."

We discussed things with Dad when he came back in, and he agreed to get a list of the Cummingses' associates to see if we could find anything out from watching them.

Vance and I spent the rest of the day looking things up on the Internet trying to find out any information we could on his family and their past dealings. Most of the things we found revolved around his dad and the projects he had been involved in on the archeological scene. Vance was surprised to learn his Dad actually started out his career on quite a few digs and trips of exploration.

"Sounds like he was a regular Indiana Jones," he commented a bit sarcastically.

"Maybe that was how he came across the box," I suggested. "Is there anything out there in particular which says he spent any time here in Scotland looking for stuff?"

"Nothing that I've seen so far," he replied. He kept on searching, moving through site after site.

I got up from my chair and stretched. "Wow! It's after dark already!" I said, looking out the window. "I'm going to go down to the kitchen to see if I can scrounge us up some food. I'm totally famished! Would you like something?"

"Sounds good," he mumbled, his eyes continuing to skim over the page in front of him. "Hurry back."

"I will," I replied, going to give him a peck on the cheek before I wandered out the door, closing it behind me.

I walked down the large original stone staircase and made my way through the hall into the kitchen area.

Since the hotel wasn't staffed yet, the owners agreed to let us use the main kitchen as our own. We enjoyed having many dinners in there together since our return to Scotland.

There were large preparation areas, just like the kitchens of five star chefs. Every kind of convenience was available. Pots and pans, of every size and in coordinating colors, hung from designated hooks on wire racks over the metal countertops. There were knives of every length and width arranged neatly into holders on every surface throughout the entire space.

The large ovens and stove tops were my favorite part because we could cook all the dishes we were preparing at once which allowed dinner to get ready in a much faster time.

Tonight, however, everyone had gone with Mom and Dad to do some grocery shopping since we were running out of things to cook. I was tired of waiting for them to get back.

Walking through the large space, I flipped on one small light so I could see to make my way to the refrigerator. I opened the door and started rummaging through the shelves, looking for something that seemed appealing.

I was bent over peering into the bottom shelf when I felt his arms slide around my waist. He caught me off guard, and I giggled.

"I didn't hear you come in," I said and straightened up, shutting the door while I turned to face him.

I stumbled backward into the fridge when I stared up into the face of, not Vance, but Brian Fitzgerald.

Hysteria bubbled up inside me, and I opened my mouth to scream, but he quickly placed his hand in a hard grip over it.

"No screaming now," he said quietly, and he slid his sharp double edged athame in a feigned slicing motion across my throat.

He may have stopped the scream from leaving my mouth, but it was still ringing loudly in my head.

Slowly, he removed his hand from my mouth, keeping the knife carefully placed against my jugular.

"I was so very disappointed when you escaped," he whispered seductively into my hair, and he placed a whisper of a kiss against it, while running his free hand down my arm until he reached my hand, locking his fingers with mine. "I was looking forward to getting to know you better." He chuckled softly.

He lifted my hand high over my head and pinned me with his body against the icebox.

Think, Portia, think! I commanded myself, trying to remember the training sessions I'd had with Vance.

I flicked the fingers of my free hand toward the rows of knives and several popped out of their holders to fly straight at Brian's back.

He anticipated it, though, throwing a shield up around himself, and the knives all bounced harmlessly off the unseen barrier, clattering with a great noise to the floor all around him.

"That wasn't very nice, Portia," he said with a slight shake of his head as if he were berating a naughty child. "But I do like your fire. You know, I've been looking for you ever since you left." He inhaled the scent of my hair. "I was serious when I said I'd happily take Vance's place."

"I'll never leave him," I said, and I stared up into his demon red eyes, swallowing slowly as he pushed the knife a little harder against me.

"Don't worry about that. I'll do my best to help you change your mind," he smiled harshly, and his gaze flitted down my face and to my throat.

"I think Douglas and Fiona have other plans for me," I said, trying to change the subject and direct his attention to a safer subject.

He laughed. "They don't even know where you are. I'm the one who had the bright idea to start following Crispin to see if he'd lead me to you, and guess what? He did," he replied, his eyes flashing

"Where are they keeping the box?" I asked him point blank, trying to glean any information from him I could while I was stalling.

"What box?" he replied, not really listening to me, and he leaned in closer to my neck.

"The one for the ritual," I said, angling my head as far away from him as I possibly could.

"I don't know what you're talking about," he responded. He moved over me, placing his lips against my mouth. I yanked my head hard to the left, trying to get away from him.

"That's all right, Portia," he whispered in a low voice. "Your neck will work just fine, too."

I could feel his teeth sharpening against my skin, and he licked over the scar that was there.

"I think you'll make a lovely demon bride," he said, lifting his head back for a second before he moved in to bite me.

Shoving hard at him with my free hand, I closed my eyes, waiting for the pain, but it never came.

I heard Brian grunt, and I opened my eyes just in time to see him ripped away from me and flung clear across the room, hitting the far wall.

"Portia, get out of here!" Vance yelled at me before he turned his attention back toward Brian, and I felt the murderous rage that threatened to consume every fiber of his being.

I couldn't move, though, because my legs turned to jelly. I sank to the floor in semi relief at his appearance.

Brian hopped up in an instant, easily jumping onto one of the large metal preparation counters in the room, before flinging himself across the open space toward Vance.

He hit Vance in his midsection, and the two of them skidded across the floor, slamming into the opposite wall.

Brian rolled away quickly, before Vance could get a good hold on him, standing to throw his athame with deadly accuracy.

Vance immediately shielded himself, causing the knife to hit and bounce away from him. Brian reached out with his hand toward the knife as it slid, and it immediately jumped back into his outstretched hand, but he wasn't finished. All the knives in the entire kitchen suddenly lifted and shot straight at Vance.

Vance stood quickly raising his arm and waved it in a circle over his head, pointing directly at Brian.

The knives turned and headed back toward Brian who stood shocked for a moment before throwing a barrier up around himself.

Suddenly one of the metal countertops loosened, flipping off its surface, plowing through the air toward Vance.

Vance threw his hands out in front of him and released a giant arc of flame into the metal, stopping it in mid-flight while Brian kept pushing at it with his magic from the other side.

The metal surface was frozen in place between the two forces that struggled over it. Soon it began to overheat and started to melt in the middle, until it snapped into two pieces.

Brian used the momentum to hurtle the severed sheets at Vance from both sides. They just missed slicing him by mere millimeters, continuing on past him, where they slammed into the wall, sticking into the ancient stones.

"Impressive," Vance said, and the two circled, facing each other in a standoff, each looking for an opening against the other. They were both breathing heavily from their exertions.

"You haven't seen anything yet," Brian smirked, taunting, attempting to bait him.

"Yeah? Like what?" Vance replied, though never letting his guard down for a moment.

"Like how I'm going to steal your Portia over there and make her forget she ever knew you existed." He grinned while he goaded him, looking over at me with a seductive wink.

"Wrong answer!" Vance replied, seeing his opening. He ran toward Brian and levitated, launching himself into the air before somersaulting past Brian, to land behind him in a crouch.

Before Brian could register what had happened and turn around, Vance stood quickly, reaching out to grab him around the neck with one hand, yanking him hard against his body. He held him prisoner with only one arm, his muscles flexed and bulging.

Vance's eyes were hard pinpoints in the dim light.

"I told you if you ever spoke her name I'd kill you," he stated flatly, his voice sounding deadly, and his hand began to glow the molten color I had seen it do before.

Brian lifted his arm, trying to swing it backward so he could stab Vance with his athame, but Vance yanked the arm hard behind him and I heard the bone snap in two.

Brian screamed, and Vance released the arm, which flopped down to dangle limply at his side. Brian reached up to his neck with his good arm, clawing desperately at Vance's now flaming red hand.

I could smell the sickening scent of burning flesh when the skin on Brian's neck and face began to smoke under Vance's grasp.

Brian continued to claw and grab, unable to loosen the strong grip that held him, and suddenly I heard him gurgle, and blood gushed out from between Vance's fingers.

Vance didn't let go. I could see the light fading from Brian's eyes as death overtook him. Still, Vance continued to hold onto him until I actually heard bone crunching beneath his fingers. Brian's head suddenly sagged and fell off his body to the floor with a loud thud.

Vance finally released Brian then, letting his body tumble carelessly to land near the severed head.

I sat, frozen in place, with my hands clasped over my mouth, my eyes wide in horror as Vance turned to look at me.

I could feel the deadly fury that moved through every part of him with each beat of his heart. His eyes locked with mine, and I felt sorrow shoot through him when he took in my expression.

He took a faltering step toward me before stopping. “I’m sorry, Portia,” he said, swallowing hard when I continued to look at him, completely aghast.

I was unable to answer him after what I had just witnessed.

He stared hard at me for a few moments before he walked briskly out the door.

Chapter 18

I was still sitting on the kitchen floor, staring at Brian's gruesome corpse, when my family arrived back with the groceries.

Dad flipped on all the lights as he entered the room, stopping cold when he saw the scene in front of him. His eyes trailed over the body and across the floor to where I sat shaking against the refrigerator. Shelly screamed when she came into the room behind him and dropped the bag of groceries she had been carrying. She buried her face in Brad's shoulder.

"Portia!" my dad called to me, quickly setting his bags on the counter. He rushed over to my side. "Are you okay? What happened here? Did you do this?" he asked in rapid succession.

My teeth were chattering as I tried to talk. "Brian snuck up on me. He threatened me and tried to bite me. Vance found us. They fought, and Vance ...Vance ... he ...," I trailed off, looking at the body in front of me.

Grandma dug through a drawer, finding and grabbing a linen tablecloth. She pulled it out and began to cover the body along with the severed head.

My dad shook me hard trying to get me to focus.

“Portia, did Vance kill Brian?” he asked me staring straight into my eyes with a look of concern.

I nodded.

“Where is he now?”

“I don’t know. He left,” I said, and my voice quivered uncontrollably with the shock of what I had witnessed.

“He left you here? Alone? With this?” he asked incredulously, gesturing to the scene behind him.

“Yes,” I said, and a sudden wave of guilt washed over me. “But it was my fault.”

“How’s this your fault?” my dad replied, moving to stand over me, crossing his arms over his chest.

“I’ve never seen anything like that before, let alone coming from Vance. I mean I’ve always known he was powerful, but ... he scared me,” I explained. “He saw the look on my face afterward, apologized and then left.”

My dad turned to the others who also had stricken looks on their faces as they stared back at me.

“Brad, Shelly, go find Vance,” he ordered. “And tell him I said to get back here right now!”

“No!” I said, and I slowly rose up to my feet, trying to summon up my courage. “Let me go.”

“Are you sure that’s the best thing to do?” my mom spoke up. “What if there are more people from Douglas and Fiona’s coven out there?”

“Brian was said he was looking for me on his own. No one else knows where we are. He was gloating over how he found me without their help. It’ll be fine, Mom,” I said, and I hesitated over the sheeted body.

"Portia, we've got this taken care of," my grandma said. She placed a hand of restraint on my shoulder. "Go find your husband."

I looked at the sheet one more time, wrapped my arms around myself and headed out the door.

I knew exactly where to look for him. I exited the keep and headed out into the night air.

Slowly, I moved across the grounds of the massive structure until I reached the remains of the old crumbling Kirk.

I could see his outline in the darkness. He was kneeling over the ruins of the ancient altar, his head held in his hands.

Moving quietly, I walked up the stone-strewn aisle, until I reached his side and knelt beside him.

He didn't move or acknowledge my presence, and the wall in his head was firmly up between us.

I stayed there for a long while waiting for him to say something, anything. But the words I waited for never came.

I finally decided to speak. "Lord," I prayed out loud, and I looked up to the starry heavens that showed through the giant holes in the beamed structure. "I'd like to thank you for all the many blessings I have. I'd especially like to express my appreciation to you for my loving husband, who would do anything in his power to protect me from harm. Please, *please* let him know how much I love him, even when things scare me unexpectedly. I love him with all my heart. Amen."

I knelt with him for a while longer as he continued to wrestle with his demons. Sometime later when he still hadn't spoken to me, I stood up and walked out of the church. I went back to the keep, thankful that I didn't pass anyone as I made my way up to the bedroom.

Closing the door behind me, I changed into my night clothes and crawled into the massive bed, pulling the down comforter over my head.

I snuggled into the cozy space and waited for him.

It was a long time before he finally crept quietly back into the suite. I heard him move toward the bathroom, and soon the sound of the shower was running behind the closed door.

A short while later, I felt him lift the covers and slide into bed with me, and the air filled with the sweet smell of his aftershave, soap and shampoo.

"You didn't have to wait up for me," he said with a sigh, not touching me with any part of his body.

"But I wanted to," I said a little sleepily, and I rolled over to lie across his chest, letting my hair spread over him in the way I knew he liked.

I heard his breath catch in his throat when I touched him, and I knew my gesture meant a lot.

"I'm sorry, Portia," he apologized again, and he lightly reached out to stroke the strands of my hair.

"Sorry for what? Saving me?"

"No, for being so brutal about it ... for scaring you. I let myself get carried away with anger. I couldn't stand that he touched you."

I lifted my head to look at him in the dark, laying one of my hands against the side of his face.

"Vance, had the tables been reversed and someone who was purely evil was making moves on you, I would've felt the same way," I said, lightly stroking his face. "The fear came from the fact that I've never really seen the full extent of your powers before. Everyone is always telling me how you're this super powerful warlock, but other than a few isolated incidences, I've never seen you at maximum capacity. For a single moment it made me question whether or not I really knew who you were. I didn't recognize you."

He was quiet for a moment before he spoke. "I never meant to scare you. I'm sorry I did. And just for the record, you know all the important things there are to know about me. Who cares about whether or not I have strong powers. The strongest things inside me are my feelings for you. Brian threatened those tonight, and I reacted accordingly, completely violent and with unnecessary roughness."

"You don't need to try and explain to me. I get it. I just want you to be happy with yourself. Yes, you were brutal, but the fact is Brian was evil and needed to be destroyed. It was something we knew we were going to have to do eventually. It just happened sooner rather than later."

"When I heard you scream in my mind, it was as if my heart stopped beating and my blood ran cold," he said, and I felt a tremor move through him. "I was so frightened while I was running to you, feeling like everything was moving in slow motion, and I couldn't get to you fast enough. I was so afraid he'd kill you before I could get to you."

"It's over now," I replied, and I kissed his lips softly. "Put it from your mind. There's no sense in reliving it."

We were both quiet for a minute before he spoke again. "Thank you for your prayer," he whispered. "It meant a lot to me. I thought I was losing you."

"Never, ever," I replied, kissing him again.

He hugged me tightly to him, and when the kiss was over, we spent the rest of the night together in a soft, tender embrace, just holding one another, until we drifted off to sleep.

The morning light found us much too soon since we didn't want to get up yet to face another day.

I was happy to see Vance was much more like his usual self than he had been last night. Every now and then I would catch a look of question in his eyes, though, when he would stare at me. I could see he still had doubts about whether or not I was really okay with everything. I was going to have to do my best to prove it to him.

"You know I love you with every fiber of my being, right?" I asked him once when I caught him in the middle of one of those reflective stares.

He didn't answer me for a minute, and he brushed his hand lightly over my head, moving down the surface of my hair.

I started to worry then. "You do know it?" I asked again, feeling my heart flutter a little.

He stared straight into my eyes when he answered. "Yes, I know you love me with every fiber of your being. I just wonder if you feel safe around me now with the same kind of intensity. Or do I scare you completely?"

"I know you'll always protect me and never try to hurt me," I answered in a matter of fact tone.

He gave a small smirk, before slightly shaking his head from side to side in disagreement. "You're dancing around the question," he stated, staring at me. "Give me a straight answer."

He wasn't going to make this easy on me.

I sighed. "Yes, I feel safe around you, and yes, you scare the crap out of me," I said honestly.

I could see the sadness creep into his eyes.

"But," I added, "there have always been some dangerous things about you that have scared me a little. I mean let's face it, all the demon stuff you've been through.

You killed the woman you thought was your mother. You killed your father. Then there's the whole demon kiss thing, and now this. You're dangerous." I paused for a moment before continuing, placing my hand over his chest. "Here in your heart, though, is the desire to be a really good person, and I love that about you. That and the fact I've never met a girl yet who didn't enjoy having a guy who could be a bit of a bad boy on occasion, myself included."

I smiled at him, trying to make him understand.

"That's the problem, though," he replied seriously. "Under the right circumstances, I could be a very bad boy, so bad I could even kill you."

I shook my head. "I don't believe that for a moment," I said firmly. "You've had the opportunity to kill me on a couple of occasions in the past, and both times you chose to try and save me instead."

He grunted in disgust. "Yeah, after I'd helped myself to drinking your blood and then basically begged you to make the demon conversion with me. I'm not some super hero, Portia," he replied with a frown.

"That was the bloodlust talking, after the fact. It doesn't mean anything. It wasn't real," I said dismissing his comment.

"It wasn't real?" he argued back, his eyes suddenly flaring with a heated emotion. "It felt pretty real to me. I can tell you honestly that there were times you'd lay in my arms and I burned with the need to bite you, drink you, even to the point of killing you. I wanted to so badly it hurt, and then it would all tangle in with that horrible sex drive. You have no idea how much I ached to do these things to you, all while you lay so trustingly in my arms."

I was shocked by his bluntness. I hadn't realized how hard I had been pushing him. I didn't know what to say.

"Even now things are still difficult for me. While I may not have the desire to kill you like I did before, the physical needs are still driving me crazy. I don't think it has diminished at all!"

I smiled then, pursing my lips to keep from laughing.

"What?" he asked, looking annoyed at me.

"Have you ever considered that maybe we just have really strong chemistry?" I asked.

He shrugged his shoulders, and he glanced away from me.

"Well, consider this then," I whispered, and I moved as close as I could to his face, turning his head back toward me. "I burn with the same desires you do, and I've never tasted a drop of demon blood. Explain that."

I looked at him triumphantly when he struggled with a comeback, but couldn't find one. "See? This connection has nothing to do with your dark past. We're linked together because we're soulmates, plain and simple."

He sighed, giving in completely. "I don't know how. You and I are complete opposites."

"It's our opposition that works for us," I replied, tapping the end of his nose lightly with my fingertip. "I'm a woman, you're a man. I'm a witch, you're a warlock. You're an Aries, I'm a Virgo, and though we aren't completely opposite there, it's close. Your magical powers rule from fire, and mine from ice. You know what they say...opposites attract." I smiled impishly at him. "Even wise philosophers say there must be opposition in all things."

He laughed. "I don't think they were referring to our relationship," he said, and he smiled broadly.

"I don't care," I replied while I stared at his beautiful blue eyes and flashing smile. "I just want you know, without reservation, that I love and trust you completely."

His smile slowly faded, and he reached a finger under my chin, pulling me toward him, kissing me gently.

"Thank you," he said. "That means more to me than you'll ever know."

Chapter 19

We sat around the large dining table with everyone else while the food was being passed around for dinner from one hand to the next.

We had discussed the fact Brian had not known about the box for the ritual when I questioned him about it. This led to the general consensus that there was a good possibility the rest of the Cummingses' demon coven was unaware of the box also. This made sense since it would have eliminated the possibility of someone else wanting to take the box for themselves.

"I think we should look for Darcy," I said popping into the conversation after listening to several suggestions from the others.

"Why's that?" Dad asked with a curious glance.

"Well, we know she worked closely with Damien in Las Vegas. He wanted the Awakening for himself. That's why he hid Vance from Douglas and Fiona. It's also why he was performing the demon kiss. He knew the Awakening would greatly enhance any powers he was carrying. He was stealing as many as he could so he could be even that much more powerful. I assume Douglas and Fiona have probably done the same thing."

"What does that have to do with Darcy?" Shelly asked with a slightly confused look crossing her features.

"Damien was actively preparing for this event. I think it might suggest he was the one in possession of the box. Think about it. Darcy has now been accepted into the welcoming arms of Douglas and Fiona after she served their wayward son. What could she have possibly offered them that would've made them interested in her?" I asked, looking around the table at each of them.

"That could make sense," my dad said. "It could also mean she's the only one besides Douglas and Fiona who knows where the box is. However, I'm inclined to think perhaps Damien was still working with his parents. Otherwise, why would they have helped him out with Krista?"

"That's true. Either way we need to get hold of Darcy. I'm sure she could help us with answers," Vance interjected in a no-nonsense tone of voice, as if kidnapping a demon was an everyday discussion. "She's a housemaid now at Bell Tower. Surely she must have time off or run errands. I doubt Crispin and his coven would watch her much, probably thinking she's insignificant."

"You're right," my dad agreed as he looked back at him. "They've tended to focus on the more influential members of the coven. Perhaps it's the ones they're overlooking that are actually carrying out the dirty work, so to speak."

"It's a crafty idea," Vance said, agreeing with my dad's assumption. "If there's one thing I learned about my grandmother while I was there, it's that she's definitely cunning."

"I agree," I added softly, thinking of the prim and proper Fiona who in reality was probably one of the most devious people I'd ever known in my life, which was really saying something since I had met her son.

Vance looked at me with an apologetic glance, reaching over to pat my leg under the table.

"It's settled then," Dad said, while he buttered his roll with a knife. "We go after Darcy. We need to set up a containment area somewhere too in the event that we find her. It would have to be someplace that wouldn't alert the construction workers that are in and out of this place."

"Well, this is a Scottish keep," Vance said, a mischievous smile spreading across his face. "Portia and I had an excellent time exploring the dungeons underneath here. They haven't been touched at all, and it's my understanding they're to remain that way since the owner wishes to use them as a point of interest for the guests who stay here."

"Hmmm, holding a prisoner in the dungeon? What a novel idea," Dad smiled before he bit into his roll.

"You boys are having way too much fun with this idea," my mom said, shaking her head.

Vance and Dad looked at each other and chuckled, while I blushed at remembering the ever-so-hot kisses Vance had shared with me during our exploration of the dungeon.

Vance noticed my blush immediately and sent a seductive little wink in my direction, which caused me to flush even harder.

"I'll get started on our guest preparations right after dinner," Grandma said, giving a disapproving look to Vance and my dad before glancing at me also. "I'm going to need the magical help of you two and Portia, though, when it comes time to reinforce the cell. Hopefully that'll be enough power to contain her."

"I don't see why it wouldn't be," Vance replied with a slight shrug. "I got the impression she was a less than desirable subordinate."

"Now you sound like a snob," I whispered over his shoulder into his ear, and I elbowed him lightly in the ribs.

"What?" he replied, turning to look at me, his eyes flashing over me. "I'm just telling it like it is." He grinned widely at me.

"You are being a snob!" I said in shock, and I looked at him in amazement, never having seen him in this light before.

He turned back to take a bite of his food. "Maybe," he replied with a smile, and he quirked a handsome eyebrow at me while he chewed his food.

"You're a *bad* boy," I said, my eyes widening at his teasing behavior.

He swallowed and then leaned over close to my ear. "You like that, if I recall correctly." His grin took on a completely seductive light, and I suddenly realized he was grandstanding for my benefit.

"You're a chauvinistic pig." I smirked back at him.

He laughed and placed a quick kiss on my cheek. "Thank you," he said with all the machismo in the world.

This was definitely a new surprising side of him I'd never seen before. He had never been self-boasting—always modest. While it made me nervous, it kind of turned me on, too, mostly because I couldn't argue with it. He really was as good as he thought he was.

"Don't over analyze it, Portia," he said into my head. "I'm just messing with you."

"Why?" I asked back, curiously.

"Because it's fun." He chuckled.

I reached out and slugged him hard in the arm, making everyone at the table look over at me in disbelief since they hadn't heard our mental conversation.

"You all are my witnesses," Vance said, pointing around at them, waving his arm in a sweeping motion.

"Witness to what?" I asked him incredulously.

"Spousal abuse," he said and grinned even broader, and I slugged him again.

"You're just building my case." He laughed. He raised his arms, crossing them in front of him as if he were warding off an impending attack.

I stood up and wrapped my arms around his upheld ones reaching behind his shoulders, wrestling him to my chest.

"You're going to get a beating for real now." I laughed, and he squirmed in my grasp.

"Quick!" Brad said, suddenly grabbing Shelly's plate from in front of her. "Let's get out of here before they start making out on the table."

Everyone started laughing at us then.

The light was dancing in Vance's eyes, and he looked up at me with a mischievous smirk, arching an eyebrow at the suggestion as if it were a wonderful idea.

"Are we really that obvious?" I sighed, releasing him and plopping back into my chair.

"If the two of you were any more obvious, we'd have to give you an x rating," Brad replied dryly.

Vance laughed right out loud, and I blushed to my roots. "I'll take that as a compliment," he said with a boyish grin, winking at me before turning to look at Brad.

"You would," Brad replied, with a shake of his head.

Brad suddenly reached out and grabbed Shelly, plastering a giant kiss on her lips, right in front of everybody, before releasing her so quickly she almost fell out of her chair.

"See. I can act like that, too. How does that make you feel when you have to watch it?" he said, directing his comment at Vance.

"I'd say it's about dang time," Vance replied, a huge grin spreading widely across his face, and he winked in Shelly's direction.

This time Shelly blushed, and everyone laughed again.

"Enough of this conversation," Mom scolded us with a small smile. She stood and began clearing dishes. "Milly, why don't you and Sean head downstairs to the dungeon and start working on things there while the kids help me clean up things here? I'll send them down when they're finished."

"That sounds good," Grandma agreed, turning to my dad. "Sean, you want to help me get my things?"

"Sure thing, Mom," he replied, wrapping an arm around her shoulders.

She reciprocated, wrapping her arm around his waist, and the two strolled out of the room together.

Clean up was easy since we all chipped in with a little magic to get the work done in the kitchen.

Thankfully, Dad and Grandma had been able to combine their magic to restore the damaged kitchen back to its original condition after Vance had attacked Brian. No one would ever realize that a magical battle had taken place here.

When we were done, we all made our way to the small wooden door that opened to reveal the stone steps into the dungeon.

There was no electricity in this part of the building. A bright torch was lit on the wall to light our way, and it was as if we had stepped back in time about two hundred years.

We carefully made our way down the narrow stairs, Vance holding my hand as he led me, Brad leading Shelly behind me.

We reached the bottom of the steps and stepped off onto the hard-packed earth. More torches were lit in the passageway. We followed them through the labyrinth of tunnels until we arrived at the furthest cell.

Dad and Grandma had the door to the cell open and had cast a circle inside. They were performing a ritual to purify the space. They walked around the circle waving special herbs and chanting quietly together.

We watched in silence while they moved in perfect unity, their magic twisting together to do the work that was asked of it.

When they were finished, they released the circle and invited us to join them inside.

Grandma explained how they were going to reinforce the structure with a magical glass, much the same as when Vance had been contained during his near conversion.

We would all be placing our hands together, one pair next to the other, and we actually would cause the surfaces we were touching to become solidified.

Once that was complete, the cell would only be able to be breached from the outside and not the inside.

We did as we were instructed on each of the walls. When we were done, Grandma added an electrical current that would shock from the inside also, thus discouraging the prisoner from touching the surface.

Once we were done, the cell was closed up, to await its possible captive. Dad and Grandma placed a cloaking spell in the hallway.

This spell made the hallway appear to be completely normal and untouched in the off chance that someone wandered by. It would work also, even if Darcy were in the cell.

"Looks good," Dad said to no one in particular, stepping back to survey their work. "I think it'll pass."

"I agree. Good job," Grandma replied, and she draped her arm around him. "Now we just need our guest."

Dad nodded. "We'll start working on that first thing tomorrow. We'll set a plan together at breakfast."

"Sounds good," Grandma said before turning to the four of us. "Can I get you all to help carry these supplies back upstairs?"

"Absolutely," Vance said, stepping forward.

When we had gathered everything together, we headed up the stairs. We placed everything in Grandma's room and headed off into the different directions of our own rooms.

Vance smiled and nudged me when we saw Brad stop at Shelly's door, waiting for us to pass so he could kiss her goodnight in private.

We walked slowly past them, and Vance sidled up against me, pulling my face over to his so he could kiss my check with a loud smack.

I giggled softly. "You're so bad," I said, nudging him in the ribs with my elbow.

He couldn't resist turning back to look at Shelly and Brad.

Brad was glaring at him, while Shelly was nervously toeing the carpet beneath her feet.

"Just kiss her already," Vance said with a grin before he turned back around and we continued on down the hall.

When we reached the door to our room, he opened it and ushered me inside, closing it behind us.

I only walked about two steps away from him when he grabbed me roughly by the arm and pulled me back, shoving me up against the door.

He placed both hands on either side of my head and leaned over me, staring at me with a smile. "I was just thinking about how much I enjoy being married. No more holding back, having to say goodnight at the door like that schmuck out in the hall is doing right now. But then I got to thinking about how I really enjoy the passion of a goodnight kiss, and I thought maybe I should kiss you goodnight anyway. You know—see if the fire is still there."

I started laughing as he eyed me, his sexy grin plastered on his face, his hot gaze trailing over me.

"That might've been the lamest stunt to get a kiss I've ever seen," I said, and my eyes started watering a bit with my mirth.

He hung his head and shook it slowly from side to side. "I knew it," he said in feigned sadness, and he took a deep sigh. "I'm losing my touch."

"You sure are," I replied, and I ducked under his arm, walking past him, biting my lip in anticipation of what I knew would follow.

I didn't make it far before he grabbed me again, pinning me up against the door with his body this time.

"Where do you think you're going?" he asked totally serious now, running his hands over my shoulders and down my arms.

"To bed?" I answered with a question.

He nodded slowly. "Yes, you certainly are, eventually," he replied, his voice thick with desire.

He dipped his head in for the kiss, I wrapped my arms around his neck, and his mouth moved over mine. He bit my bottom lip gently. I closed my eyes, opening my mouth to enjoyed the taste of him. There was no question; the fire was definitely still there.

The kiss went on for ages, and I never wanted it to stop. He kept me pressed hard against the door with his body while his hands held the sides of my head, tangled in my hair, his mouth never leaving mine for an instant as he ravaged it with heated enthusiasm for several long minutes.

He broke away from me, looking intensely at me. "Well?" he asked a bit breathlessly.

I was completely honest. "That was the best goodnight kiss I've ever had in my life," I said, looking up at him, my quick breath matching his own.

He smiled, continuing to look down at me. "Would you think I was bragging if I said I thought so too?" he asked with his sexy grin.

"Not at all," I said, my arms still wrapped around him, and I toyed with some of his hair at the nape of his neck.

"Shall we try to top it?" he said.

"Please," I responded.

He dipped his head in again, and I kissed him with everything I had in me, until it felt as if the very air was sizzling around us. I wasn't at all surprised when, without breaking the kiss, he swept me off my feet and carried me to the bed.

That one turned out to be the best kiss I ever had.

Chapter 20

Dad began laying out the plans for the day.

Brad and Shelly were going to be joggers running on the street in front of Bell Tower Hall. They were going to place a surveillance camera near the entrance so we could watch the comings and goings at the property.

Dad would set up equipment that would relay the signal to our location, while Mom and Grandma would alternate driving up and down the road until Shelly and Brad were in the clear and they could come home.

Of course, Vance and I were stuck with the usual, manning the fort. While I could see he was going crazy with having to stay behind, this was one time I agreed with Dad. I didn't want Vance anywhere near those people.

We went into the sitting area after everyone had left. Dad had the monitor for the surveillance set up in there. We were supposed to watch it and let them know if the signal relayed okay.

"You want to watch some television?" Vance asked absently, picking up the remote and clicking it toward the large set. "I imagine it'll be a while before they need us."

"That's fine," I said, and we both sat on the sofa together.

Vance put his arm on the back of the couch and his feet up on the coffee table. I decided to lie down and put my head in his lap.

He continued clicking the remote, but moved his other hand down where he gently rested it over my shoulder. He slowly began to run his fingers through my hair over and over. I wondered if he even knew what he was doing, or if it was just a natural reflex with him, but it felt good nonetheless. It was extremely relaxing.

He was very restless, I could tell, since he didn't linger long on any one channel, surfing his way through the entire selection.

I closed my eyes when he started the process over, just enjoying being next to him even if he was a little agitated.

I didn't realize I had fallen asleep until I felt him move gently from underneath me, laying me softly back onto the sofa.

Slowly, I opened my eyes to see him walk over to the monitor, which was right next to the television, and adjust a few knobs. Suddenly a picture of Douglas and Fiona's driveway snapped clearly onto the screen.

"Got it, Sean," he spoke into a small handheld walkie talkie Dad left for us.

"Is the picture clear?" my dad's voice came back.

"Looks perfect," Vance said after he watched the screen intently for a few moments.

"Great," Dad's voice crackled over the radio. "We'll be back shortly. You want to take the first shift?"

"No problem. I've got it under control," he said.

He placed the radio next to the monitor and headed back to the sofa.

"Sorry. I didn't mean to wake you," he said, and he looked at me with a soft expression of regret on his face.

He sat down next to me, gently lifting my head into his lap, and I snuggled comfortably up against him once again.

"How long was I asleep?" I asked with a yawn.

"About forty-five minutes," he replied. "Everything is done now. The others should be back shortly."

"I heard," I said.

I continued to lie in his lap, and he absently stroked my face and hair while he alternated between watching the water sports on the television and watching the monitor. They were close enough together we could easily keep tabs on both.

We sat in comfortable silence until the rest of the family came into the room.

"See anything yet?" Dad asked excitedly.

I could totally tell he was in his government agent mode.

"Not a thing," Vance replied. "But I did have a question."

"What's that?" Dad inquired.

"If we see Darcy leave, how are we going to follow her? We're here, and by the time we could get into a car to follow, she'd be completely out of the area," he said with a concerned look.

Dad just grinned. "Oh ye of little faith," he replied. "Have I ever let you down yet? I set up sensors for several miles in both directions. They'll alert us to the direction of travel. When we do find the car, we'll tag it, too, even though we'll take Darcy. That way if

Douglas and Fiona use the vehicle again we'll be able to follow them with pretty efficient accuracy, without them discovering we're tailing them."

"You're right, Sean. You don't disappoint," Vance said with a grin.

"Something should be happening soon," Grandma spoke up. "We're only a week away from the eclipse now."

"You need to be careful," I said, looking up at Vance. "They'll be doing everything in their power to find you now."

"I'm counting on it," he said.

"Please don't go off and do something crazy," I replied. "If they got hold of you now, I'd be terrified."

"I don't have any plans to do anything like that." He chuckled as he patted my head. "You don't trust me very much do you?"

"I'm speaking from past experience," I said, frowning at him. "You tend to suffer from white knight syndrome, running off to help someone in need without thinking things through first."

"Portia, you have my word that I'll be careful and try not to do anything rash," he promised.

"Good," I said, and I settled back into his lap. "It'd better stay that way," I added for extra emphasis.

"We'll watch things for the next few hours," Vance said to my dad. "I'll call you if I see anything."

"Great," Dad said. "I'll go put this other equipment up then."

Grandma and Mom followed him out of the room, while Brad and Shelly came to have a seat in the two chairs next to the sofa.

"So how was your run?" I asked Shelly with a smile.

"Actually it was a nice jog." She laughed. "The air was great, and the scenery was beautiful. If it hadn't been for the fact I knew we were running along the fence line of a demon coven, it might've been enjoyable."

"That was the part I liked best," Brad said looking at her. "All that adrenaline pumping through me, knowing we were there to thwart them right under their very noses."

"You're so crazy! Such a guy!" Shelly laughed at him and reached out to hold his hand.

Brad took her hand and squeezed it, rubbing his thumb over the back of her hand, a sweet gesture that didn't pass by neither me nor Vance.

"Well, we're glad both of you are back here safely," I said with a smile.

"Yes," Vance replied. "And I want to thank you for everything you two have done on our behalf. You've placed yourselves in danger to protect us. It's something I haven't agreed with, but I do appreciate."

"Anything for a friend, right?" Brad replied, and Vance nodded.

We turned back to watch the water sports on the television.

"The lochs around here sure are beautiful," Shelly commented while we watched the gorgeous water on the screen in front of us. "We should go on a picnic by one sometime."

"That sounds like fun," I agreed, thinking it was a great plan. "Maybe we can when my dad finally lets Vance and me off house arrest."

"I guess we could do something here on the grounds for lunch," Shelly suggested. "What do you think?" she asked, turning to Brad.

"It sounds fine to me," he said with a shrug.

"Call it a double date then." I smiled speaking up for Vance and myself.

When it was lunchtime, my parents came in to watch the monitor.

"I made some sandwiches and laid out some other things for your picnic in the kitchen," my mom said.

"Thanks, Mom. That was really sweet of you."

"Didn't see anything, I'm assuming?" Dad asked looking directly at Vance.

"Nope, sorry," he replied.

"Well, take this radio out with you just in case we need to get hold of you quickly," Dad said, giving a handheld to Vance.

"See you in a little while," I said. We exited the room and made our way to the kitchen.

Mom had gone above and beyond herself this time. She had dug up a large wicker basket from somewhere, and had it laden with sandwiches, sweet meats, fruits and other snack items, as well as a few bottles of water. Next to the basket was a large blanket folded neatly on the counter.

"Mmm. Life is always good when Stacey's around," Brad said when he peered into the overstuffed basket.

The rest of us nodded, looking at the mouthwatering items inside.

Vance picked up the basket, Brad grabbed the blanket, and the four of us headed toward the front door of the keep.

"So where do you want to go?" Vance asked when we entered the courtyard.

"I was thinking about that little door in the back wall that leads out onto the hillside," I said. "There's a beautiful view from there of the mountains and the loch in the distance."

"I don't know about that," Brad said. "Technically that's outside the keep. Your dad wouldn't like it."

"That settles it," Vance said with resolution in his voice. "That's definitely where we're going."

I laughed at him and his attempted rebellion against his restraints. He was going to push the limits as far as he could possibly get away with.

"Well, I think the fact that we could see anyone who wanted to sneak up on us for miles before they could actually reach us will make it okay," I said with a smile, looking over at the others.

"I know," Brad replied with a grin. "I was just kidding anyway. I like messing with Mr. Macho over here occasionally."

"I know," I said, smiling back at him and adding a wink.

"Hey!" Vance said, yanking me up against his side. "Quit flirting with Shelly's boyfriend."

"Whatever!" I replied' and I sucker-punched him in the abs.

He doubled over as if I had really injured him, letting out a loud groan, before he popped back up laughing at me.

"I didn't believe you for a second," I said, making a silly face at him and sticking out my tongue like a child.

"Guess I'll have to work on my acting skills," he said still laughing.

"I guess so!" I replied, always enjoying ribbing him a little.

We reached the small door, and Shelly pushed it open. We walked out into the glorious sunshine that was splaying over the rolling hillside, stretching out to the beautiful valley beneath us. We went out onto the grassy decline a little ways, where Brad shook open the large blanket. Shelly and I helped him to spread it across the ground before we all climbed onto it, and

Vance sat the basket of food in the middle so we could all reach it.

We enjoyed the delicious items my mom had packed, stuffing ourselves to the brim.

"This is really nice out here," Vance said moving to lie on his back, resting his arms behind his head.

I joined him, laying my head on his stomach, looking up at the blue sky overhead with its puffy white clouds that trailed across it like clumps of cotton balls.

"Thanks for suggesting this, Shelly," he continued. "It's very nice to get out of the keep for a while."

"You're welcome," she replied, and Brad moved to sit behind her so she could recline against his chest.

We were quiet, just letting the breeze move over the four of us, watching the clouds roll by, while they cast shadows out over the landscape.

After a while I sat up and started to place items back into the basket. That was when I noticed it.

"Look!" I said, pulling a Frisbee up out of the basket. "Mom must have put this in." I laughed. "I wonder where she found it."

"Let's do it. I need some exercise!" Vance said, jumping quickly to his feet, followed by Brad and Shelly.

We decided to play as teams, which gave Vance and me a bit of an unfair advantage since we often used magic to make things interesting. Brad and Shelly did a pretty good job at using their magic to keep up with us, though. I was actually surprised at how good they had gotten.

Of course, the guys had to step it up a notch from that, showing off their physical prowess since they had a captive audience.

I didn't mind, though. I watched Vance somersault through the air to grab an extremely high throw from Brad.

I could watch him move like this all day. The guy was positively breathtaking!

He pitched the Frisbee back to Brad from his peak in the air before tumbling back to the earth, landing easily on his feet.

I cheered for Vance when Brad missed the Frisbee, but was amazed when Shelly popped up behind him, catching the disc easily and returned it artfully to us.

"I'm impressed!" I called out to her, really meaning it. "You're totally a natural!"

Shelly grinned widely back at me. "Who knew I could be so athletic?" she replied with a wide smile.

We played for a long while, each of us trying to outdo the other until we collapsed into a tired heap on the blanket.

"That was fun!" I said breathing heavily, trying to catch my breath.

"It really was," Vance agreed. "You two were awesome! If I didn't know any better, I'd think you were a full-fledged witch and warlock."

"Really?" Shelly asked with a genuine smile, before sobering slightly. "Or are you just being nice?"

"Would I do that?" Vance asked, huffing.

"Probably," Brad interjected with a grin.

"I'm wounded to the core," Vance said, slamming his hand into his chest as if he had just been stabbed or something, falling backward onto the blanket. "Quick! I think I might need mouth to mouth," he said, reaching out to grab me, pulling me onto his chest.

"I happen to know rescue breathing," I said hovering seductively over him. I blew hard into his mouth instead of kissing him, catching him by surprise, and he gagged and started coughing.

The rest of us burst out laughing, and I jumped up to run away, knowing I would be in trouble now.

I made it about a yard away before he tackled me, and we went rolling several more yards down the steep hill together.

When we stopped, we were laughing hard at each other.

"That was fun," I said a little breathlessly.

"It was fun. I sure love you," he said with a big grin.

"I love you, too," I replied smiling back at him.

He leaned in to kiss me, and my breath caught when his lips touched mine. I wound my arms around his neck and pulled him closer to me, opening my mouth in invitation to him. He let out a soft groan, kissing me back hotly.

"You're going to start something I'm not going to want to stop," he whispered against my lips, his eyes flashing open to look into mine.

"Fine by me," I countered, and I pulled him back, kissing him harder.

He happily obliged me, kissing me with the same fervor I was dishing out. "What brought all this on?" he asked quietly, but with a mischievous glint in his gaze.

"Watching you in action, of course, and you know it. You were doing it on purpose, hoping it would have exactly this type of effect on me!"

"I'm thinking it's nap time all of a sudden," he chuckled, not bothering to deny it. "What do you think?"

"I think it sounds like a delightful idea," I replied and he nudged my nose with his. "If we can get away without hurting their feelings," I added, nodding up the hill toward Brad and Shelly.

"Well, then, let's get up and see what we can do about that," he countered, but he stopped to kiss me breathless once more before he stood up and offered me a hand.

I slipped my hand into his, and he pulled me to my feet.

"This picnic was a wonderful idea," he commented casually, locking his fingers with mine. "I haven't had this much fun in a while."

I looked at him with saucer-round eyes, trying to portray hurt feelings.

"Why I'm totally wounded by that comment!" I said mockingly, placing a hand over my heart.

He started laughing, pulling me into his arms once again and kissing me roughly, threading his fingers into my hair with one hand and holding me tight to him with the other.

"You were not included in that previous remark," he stated hotly. "Nothing is ever better than my time with you."

I felt my skin flush in response to his words, and he let out a low sound when he moved to kiss me again.

It was at this moment that Brad hollered out at us.

Reluctantly we both turned to look up the hill toward him.

"It's Sean!" he shouted, pointing to the radio. "They've spotted Darcy!"

Chapter 21

The four of us raced back to the keep as fast as we could. We burst in through the massive wooden doors and nearly collided with my dad.

"We're on our way out," Dad said to Vance. "You and Portia stay here. Shelly and Brad come with us."

I heard Vance sigh in frustration, and Brad and Shelly turned to follow Dad and Grandma out the door.

Standing at the doorway, I watched them while they pulled out of the bailey, speeding off down the road.

I turned to look at Mom. "What happened?" I asked.

"A car with a driver pulled out of the estate turning toward town. We could plainly see Darcy sitting in the back," she replied.

"Why would a driver be taking Darcy somewhere? She's the maid. Doesn't that seem a bit odd to anyone?" I asked.

Vance shrugged his shoulders. "I have no idea," he replied with a briefly thoughtful expression. "So what's the plan?" he asked Mom.

"They're going to follow them and see if they can get her alone somewhere. When Milly and Sean grab her, they want Brad and Shelly to place the tracking device on the vehicle. They plan on using a serum on Darcy to knock her out so she won't be combative," my mom explained.

"I'm familiar with the stuff," Vance said with a grimace, and he looked at me. "We'd better go light the torches in the dungeon and get things ready before they get back. Stacey, are the construction workers still here?"

"No," she said. "I think they left to go work on another job for the rest of the day."

"Perfect," Vance said, grabbing me by the hand. "Come on, let's go."

He led me to the stairs that entered the dungeon, touching each oil-soaked torch when we passed, making them burst into flame. Soon the place was ablaze, and we were standing in front of the cleverly disguised cell.

We passed through the illusion, stepping up to the real cell.

"Let's open it," he said, placing his hands against the glass barrier.

I placed my hands next to his, and together we melted a hole big enough for Darcy to be carried in.

"What now?" I asked him.

"Now we wait," he said. He grabbed my hand and led me back through the tunnels, up the stairs and out into the hall. "We need to make sure that this door is always secured from here on out, too, so no one accidentally wanders down into the dungeon."

He waved his hand over the lock, magically securing it.

"Let's go find your mom," he said, continuing on down the hall.

We made our way through the keep to the sitting room finding Mom sitting next to the monitor.

"Did you see something else?" Vance asked her when we came up beside her. He glanced quickly at the screen.

She shook her head, holding up the portable radio.

"I just heard from Sean. They have her pinned down. They're just waiting for an opportunity to drug her where no one will notice," she said, looking up at us. "I'm nervous for them."

"It'll be okay, Stacey," Vance replied reaching out to place a hand on her shoulder. "Sean is an expert in this cloak-and-dagger kind of stuff. He knows what he's doing."

Mom just nodded, not answering.

I went and sat on the couch. Vance began his traditional pacing across the floor. Things were weighing heavily on his mind.

In the end we didn't have to wait long at all.

"We have her," Shelly's voice crackled over the radio. "We're on our way back now."

"Everything is ready for you," my mom answered her.

"This is it," Vance said, rubbing his hands together in anticipation. "Finally we can get some answers."

"I wouldn't get too excited," I admonished him. "When you were given this injection you were out cold for hours."

I saw a brief look of disappointment cross his face, before he nodded.

He was waiting at the front door when the car pulled back into the bailey, rushing down the steps to meet them to help as they pulled Darcy from the vehicle.

Vance lifted her from Sean and carried her petite form easily into the keep. I stepped aside so he could enter.

"Portia, come get the door for me," he said as he passed.

I moved in front of him and hurried to the sealed door, waving my hand over the lock to release it. I pulled it open, and Vance brushed past me heading down the steep stone stairs.

I let the others pass through the door before I closed it behind me, sealing the lock once again.

We moved quickly down the passageway, trying to catch up with Vance. He was already placing Darcy on the cot inside the cell by the time I rounded the corner and stepped through the illusion barrier.

He came back out immediately. Grandma, Dad and I joined him, and we resealed the glass shield around the cell.

"That should hold her good," my dad said, stepping back to survey everything. "I want someone with her around the clock until she wakes up," he added. "Who wants to go first?"

"Me," Vance said without hesitation.

"All right," Dad said, placing a radio into his hand. "Let us know when you need someone to trade places with you."

"Will do," he said, turning to look at me. "Do you want to stay with me?"

"Yes, but I think I'll run upstairs and get us some chairs to sit on first so we can be a little more comfortable," I replied.

"Oh!" Grandma spoke up, turning to the neighboring cell. "I forgot we have an extra cot in here that you can use."

She went inside and pulled it out, setting it against the wall for us.

"Thanks, Grandma," I said.

Vance and I both sat down on it leaning back against the stones behind us.

"No problem," she said, and she patted my shoulder. "Just let me know if you need anything else."

"Okay," I said, watching the group disappear from sight.

Vance put his feet up on the edge of the thin mattress, resting his arms over his bent knees and leaning his head back against the wall, closing his eyes.

"Are you tired?" I asked him.

He opened his eyes to look over at me through hooded lids. "Not really," he answered. "Why, are you?"

"No," I replied to him. "You just seemed tired."

"I'm tired of waiting on everything," he acknowledged. "I'm just ready for all this to be over. I want to get my mom and be done with place. I just want to move on and live our lives."

"Hopefully that will happen soon," I replied with a small smile.

He reached over and patted me on my knee. "There she is. My ever-the-optimistic lover," he smiled softly at me, before he closed his eyes again.

When he didn't remove his hand from my leg, I slid my hand over the top of his, threading my fingers through his before I leaned my head onto his shoulder to rest against him.

I didn't close my eyes, though, instead looking at the blood pulsating through his veins, signifying that he was real, alive, and he wanted to be with me. I kept wondering when I would wake up and find he had only been a figment of my imagination.

"You don't need to worry," he chuckled softly. "I'm real, with all of my flaws, and yes, you're the only one I want." He squeezed my fingers with his.

"I just love you. You make me so happy. I feel like I don't deserve to be this blessed. I keep waiting for something to come and rip it all away from me," I explained.

"I'm not planning on ever leaving you for any reason," he assured me. "But can I point out one thing?"

"Go ahead."

"Even if the worst were to happen and we were somehow parted, let's say by death even, you and I have experienced a love most people wait their whole lives just to have a small taste of," he said.

I thought about that for a few seconds. "Yes, but that's what makes me so scared. It's such a wonderful thing I don't ever want to lose it."

"So would you rather not have ever had the taste than to risk knowing what you'd be missing?" he asked me.

I didn't have to think long about that one. "No. I'd take every second with you I could get before you had to leave," I replied and I wrapped my free arm tightly around his.

"Well, then my suggestion is we live each moment we have together as if it were our last, and then whenever the end does come, we won't have any regrets. Besides, death will only be a short separation for us. I fully plan on being with you in the next life," he said seriously.

"Do you really believe all that stuff?" I asked him.

"What? God, religion, and the afterlife?"

"Yeah."

"Absolutely, don't you?" he asked me.

"I always have," I said. "It's just scary to me now when I don't have any proof. What if something happened to you, and that was it? Poof, the end?"

"Have faith, Portia," he said, squeezing my hand. "What kind of cruel God would send us here to earth if he didn't have some sort of plan for us? I don't believe he'd do that. Plus I plan on you and me living together until we're very old anyway." He smiled.

"Great!" I said facetiously. "Then I'll have to worry about all of my wrinkles and whether or not I'm able to keep you interested in boring old me."

He laughed. "Have you ever looked at your family?" he asked me. "They hardly share a wrinkle between them. I think you'll age just fine, and you could never, ever be boring to me, even if you tried. The real question is whether you'll still love me when I lose my six-pack and have a beer belly instead."

"Yeah right. You're Mr. Perfect Physique. That'll never happen," I replied with a smile. "Your family looks pretty fit too."

He sobered up at that comment.

"I just wish they had the personalities to offset their looks," he replied with a faraway look in his eyes.

"Your mom does," I said, trying to cheer him up.

"Yes, she does, doesn't she?" he responded.

"She does, and I really like her," I replied.

He gave a small laugh then. "Isn't it ironic? You always hear about the horrible mother-in-law stories, and she's the only person in my family you even like."

"I probably would've liked the others, too, in the beginning," I said. "They just made some bad choices and ended up losing themselves as a consequence."

"Yeah, all choices have consequences, whether they're good or bad. They just happened to make all the wrong ones."

"That's what is different about you. You try to make good decisions. Your mom tries too."

"It hasn't helped either of us much though, has it?" he answered. "We're still wrapped up in everyone's bad choices around us."

"But still you fight for what you know is right. You're a warrior for what's good." I smiled, and he laughed out loud.

"I wouldn't exactly call myself a warrior," he stated humbly.

"What would you call yourself then?" I asked, truly wondering how he would describe himself.

He thought about it before he answered me. "A dreamer," he replied, and I was surprised because I never would've thought he'd choose that word for himself. "I dream of a wonderful life in a wonderful future with the people I love surrounding me."

I could feel the rawness in his soul as he spoke, and I knew he revealed his most tender emotions to me.

"Well, then I'll make that my dream, and we'll dream it together," I said to him.

He let go of my hand and wrapped his arm around my shoulders, pulling me toward him so he could kiss the top of my head.

"I love you," he said as he hugged me.

"I love you, too, more than you'll ever know." I smiled.

"Are you sure I didn't just lose all of my appeal to you, though," he said with a chuckle. "I know how you enjoy being married to a bad boy. Now I'm just a dreamer," he teased.

"Regardless of whatever you think you are, I want every part of you there is to have, Vance. Bad boy, dreamer, lover, tease, I'll take them all," I said seriously. "I want you to know I love all of it."

"Good, I'm glad," he said with a smile. "Because I want to give it all to you—I enjoy giving it all to you."

I laughed at him, choosing to turn his words back on him playfully.

"And I've certainly been enjoying the 'getting' of it," I flirted, and I turned to face him better, pulling his face to mine so I could kiss him.

He chuckled and wrapped his arms around me, pulling me up onto his lap, thoroughly kissing me back while he wound his fingers through my hair and held my face gently up next to his.

I let my arms twist around his neck when he deepened the kiss, sighing, and I leaned in closer.

"Ugh!" An unexpected voice broke into our moment. "I see the lovers are still going at it. Give me a break and get a room."

We both stopped immediately and turned toward the cell.

Darcy was awake.

Chapter 22

Vance slowly slid me off his lap, stood, and walked over to the cell. He looked Darcy up and down.

"Well, you're awake much earlier than expected," he said, sliding his hands into the pockets of his jeans.

"I assume you're referring to the little drug I was given? You should know demons are much more powerful than regular witches and warlocks. We recover from things much quicker," she goaded him.

"Is that so?" he said, and he removed his hands from his pockets to fold one arm across his chest. He rested his other arm on it and raised a finger to tap on his lips. "Nope. I just don't recall those demons I killed being more powerful than I was." He turned to look at me. "What do you think, Portia? Should we dig up Brian and ask him?" He turned back to Darcy. "Oh, that's right! We can't because he lost his head. Unless he's still recovering, that is."

I could see that, despite his proclamation otherwise, Vance's inner bad boy was still running strong and flaming to the surface.

Darcy's face twisted into her demon form. She let out a large hiss and jumped, slamming her body against the glass.

Instantly, the current running behind the magical pane shocked her, and she fell backward to the floor.

Vance looked at her, a long, low, wicked-sounding laugh coming from deep inside him while he watched her climb to her feet.

"Is that the best you've got, Darcy?" he baited her, his eyes flashing in enjoyment. "I've got to say, I'm still not impressed."

"You killed Brian?" she asked, her disbelief evident in the tone of her voice.

"Yes, I did. Would you like to see?" Vance said in an accommodating voice, and he waved his hand slightly, gesturing toward the hallway behind him. "I could run out and get him for you real fast."

"I believe you," she said, hanging her head in a way that almost made me feel sorry for her.

"Are you sad, Darcy? Surely a demon isn't capable of any real emotion," he continued to push her.

She lifted her head to glare at him. "He was my lover!" she spat at him. "The two of us shared something special together!"

"Did you now?" Vance asked, stepping up to the glass, and I could feel the anger course through him. "Then perhaps you could explain to me why I caught him here, trying to feel up my wife!"

"You're lying!" she screamed, her voice making an earsplitting sound. "Brian would never leave me!"

"Well, Darcy, apparently you weren't meeting his needs well enough because he was definitely off looking for greener pastures than you have to offer," Vance replied with irritation. He had to turn away from the glass for a moment to cool down. The very thought of Brian in the kitchen with me was threatening to overwhelm him again.

"He was the one who came to comfort me," she said, raising her chin a notch, "after you killed your father."

Vance turned quickly back to the glass at that remark.

"What are you saying, Darcy?" he said seriously, a glowering look crossing his face. "Were you intimate with him, too?"

She paused for a moment as if she were weighing her answer. "Yes, not that it's any of your business," she answered, returning his stare. "He was good to me. I think he even loved me," she added almost as an afterthought.

Vance let out a quick choked laugh. "Boy, Darcy, you're really off your mark when it comes to judgment, aren't you?" he asked incredulously.

"What do you mean?" she asked, her eyes narrowing.

"You are aware my father was still married and he was flying here to Scotland to have regular relations with *his wife?*" he asked her, not sugar-coating it at all.

"Yes, but he didn't like it. He said it was just a means to an end," she replied haughtily. "He said I was the only one for him, his soulmate."

Vance laughed out at this comment.

"What's so funny?" she asked.

"I was wondering if you knew why he was also putting the moves on Portia then while she was his prisoner. He made it very clear he intended to take her as his lover." He scratched behind one ear as if completely puzzled.

Darcy turned her glare to me. "You're lying! She was just a pawn to him. I don't know why anyone would ever want her." She sent me a sizzling look of pure hatred.

"Well, I could personally give you a thousand reasons off the top of my head," Vance returned. "But that isn't why we brought you here."

"Why did you bring me here?"

"We need some information."

"And why would I tell you anything?" She smiled, baring her rows of uneven teeth.

"Well, because if you don't I might be inclined to melt your head off your body just like I did to your sweet lover boy, Brian," he replied in a voice that sounded way too chipper about the idea.

She looked at him hard for a moment, as if gauging how serious he really was, before a look of fear flashed through her face.

"What do you want to know?" she asked, swallowing hard.

"Where's the box?" Vance asked bluntly, jumping straight to the point.

Another moment of fear shot through her face before she shuttered it again behind her demon red eyes.

"What box?" she answered. She nervously flashed a look over in my direction before flitting back to him.

"Now, now, Darcy," Vance said, stepping up within an inch of the glass. "Let's not start playing games. We were getting along so well."

"I really don't know what you're referring to," she replied, trying to give him a nonchalant look.

"Is that so?" Vance said, looking at her with a hard stare. "That's funny, considering my father's the one who had the box while he was importing witches and warlocks from all over the world to perform a demon kiss on so he could steal their powers. He was doing that specifically to give him more powers to be enhanced by the Awakening."

When he said that word, her eyes widened in surprise.

"That's right, Darcy. I know all about it. I know he had the box and you brought it here to give to Douglas and Fiona, using it to get into their good graces. I know they intend to use it in the circle of stones next week during the eclipse. I also know they're desperately looking for me at this very moment so they'll have the vessel they need to complete the ritual. So what I need from you is the location of the box so I can keep this abomination from happening." He looked straight into her glowing eyes.

"Why do you think I'd tell you anything?" she asked. "You've made it perfectly clear that you intend to ruin my life. If you get that box away from Douglas and Fiona, I'd have nowhere to go. They'd kill me for telling."

"And I'll kill you if you don't," he threatened her in a soft voice that belied his meaning.

"You'll kill me if I do," she stated flatly.

"Well, I can't just let you live to stir up more trouble now, can I?" he asked. "I let you go once before, and now look at all of us. Here we are stuck in this dungeon trying to fix all the problems you've put into motion. What would you have me do?"

"Let me leave," she pleaded. "I'll go get the box and bring it to you. You can do whatever you need to with it. I promise I'll leave and you'll never see me again."

"There's only one problem with that scenario," Vance complained with a shake of his head.

"What?" she asked.

"I don't trust you. I know as soon as I let you go you'll run straight to my grandparents and let them know where we are," he stated.

She shook her head violently. "I wouldn't! I promise!"

Vance laughed at her again. "It's never going to happen, Darcy, so don't bother trying. Just tell me where the box is," he said. "Your fate is going to be the same either way you go, so what do you care? They'll kill you or I will. Even if I let you go, they would never believe you didn't tell us anything. Face it, you're dead." He shrugged his shoulders in defeat and stepped away from the glass, turning to leave.

"Wait!" she called out in desperation. "Don't leave yet."

Vance halted but didn't turn around. "I'll make a bargain with you," she spat out after waiting for him to acknowledge her.

He turned and walked back to the glass, and I could feel a self-assurance roll through him when he realized his interrogation tactics might be working with her.

"Lay out your deal then," he said matter-of-factly, acting as though he were truly interested in any proposition she might offer.

"I'll tell you where the box is if you let me stay here, with you," she answered, looking straight into his eyes.

Vance gave her an incredulous stare. "What the heck would I do with you?" he asked completely amazed by her suggestion.

"I could be ... your mistress," she offered, and she slid a quick glance over toward me.

"Excuse me?" Vance answered in shock, his eyes widening dramatically, and I could see she had thrown him completely off his game with the suggestion. "You're joking, right?"

"No. I'm very good at what I do. You're a young virile man who could easily handle two women," she said with a shrug as though this were no big deal.

I was off the cot and at the glass in one stride. "You stay away from him!" I said, lifting my finger up to the barrier, anger flushing through me at her ludicrous proposition.

Vance reached out and pulled my hand back down. "I've got this, Portia," he said, and he turned back to the glass with a completely calm demeanor. "Darcy, there's nothing you could possibly do, or say, that would ever induce me to even consider such an arrangement, with you or anyone else. Why would I trade in absolute perfection for a whore like you?" His eyebrow quirked up in question, and his face went completely dead of any emotion.

Darcy was instantly out of her crouch, screaming, and she hurtled herself at the glass once more, only to be shocked and sent flying once again.

"Come on, Portia. We're done here," Vance said, and he grabbed me by the elbow, turning me around so we could leave.

"Wait!" Darcy called to him again, but we kept walking. "Wait! Please! I don't know where it is!"

He stopped this time, letting go of my arm and turned to stride back to the glass.

"What?" he asked harshly.

The tears rolled down her face in earnest now. "I don't know where the box is. That was part of the deal when I brought it to them. They got to keep it and I could stay as long as I didn't ask about it, tell anyone about it, or try to find where they'd put it. They said they'd kill me if I did," she sobbed.

Vance considered these things for a moment, and I could see how hard he was clenching his hands. He ground his teeth together before he spoke to her again.

"Well, you've just sealed your fate with them then, haven't you?" he said accusingly.

"What do you mean?" she asked, wiping a tear away with the back of her hand.

"You just told us about it. That's a breach of contract with Douglas and Fiona. You've signed your own death warrant, I believe. I guess I can send you back to them now."

He grabbed my hand and led me out of the magical illusion. She screamed at the top of her lungs behind us, begging us to not send her back.

Her cries echoed through the tunnels while we made our way through the twisting labyrinth to the stone steps that lifted us up out of the bowels of the earth to the magically secured door.

Vance unlocked it and strode down the hall to the sitting room where we found the rest of the family.

"What's going on?" Dad asked hopping to his feet when we entered the room, noticing our concerned expressions immediately.

"Darcy is awake," Vance informed him.

"Already? I expected her to be out for hours," he said looking very surprised. "Let's go talk to her."

"I already have," Vance replied, reaching out to grab my dad by the arm when he started to walk past him. "It's no use, Sean. She doesn't know where the box is. This is a dead end."

Dad looked down to where Vance was still holding him by the arm. Vance released him, letting his arm fall back to his side.

"How can you be sure?" Grandma asked. "It would be in her demon nature to lie."

"They had a very long conversation," I spoke up. "Darcy tried all of her tricks before she confessed the truth. She knows Douglas and Fiona will kill her if she goes back. Vance said he was going to send her to them. She's down there freaking out now."

"This is not good," my dad said. "If she can't tell us where the box is, we can't stop the ritual."

"Actually we can," I replied. "If they don't have Vance, the Awakening will do them no good. They have to have his blood in order for it to work. No one else has any white witch blood that they can assimilate."

"You may be on to something, Portia," my dad said as he nodded his head, shaking his finger toward me in agreement. "We need to get Vance as far away from here as possible."

Vance shook his head. "No. We still need to get the box and destroy it. Otherwise, they can just wait for the next time they can perform the ritual and we go through all this all over again. Portia and I would always be running, looking over our shoulders. I won't live like that," he said.

My dad looked exasperated. "But it gives us more time to find the box," he replied.

"They know that we know! We have the book. Do you think that box will ever come out of hiding into the open? No. It'll only be out at the ritual. It's the only possible chance we have of getting it," Vance said in frustration.

"That may be," my dad replied. "But you will not be the one doing the getting of it! You're to stay as far away from that ritual as you can possibly be, do you understand me? I hate to pull rank on you, Vance, but I'm still the leader of this coven, and you'll do as I say."

I could feel the anger boiling inside Vance at these remarks. "Fine," he said in a deadly calm voice, and everyone else in the room silently watched the strained interaction.

He didn't let go of my hand, and he led me out of the room behind him, heading toward our bedroom upstairs.

I didn't say anything while he towed me along, trying to give him some time to let his anger cool.

He pulled me into the room and closed the door softly behind me.

"I'm sorry," I said softly to him.

He looked at me, his gaze traveling up and down the length of me, then he pulled me hard up against his body.

"Don't talk," he said while he threaded his fingers into my hair and proceeded to give me a smoldering kiss that matched his smoldering demeanor.

I just stood there, letting him release his pent-up energy into the kiss. It was rough and bruising against my tender lips, hard and demanding. He pushed up against me until I was taking steps backward under the pressure, not stopping until he finally had me up against a wall.

He ravaged my lips with an almost uncontrolled desperation. His fingers tightened in my hair, brusquely tilting my head backward to give him better access while he continued to punish me with his mouth. My necked arched under the pressure, and his mouth moved down my skin where he placed several nips in a none-too-delicate fashion.

I gasped at the assault, feeling both desire and worry over his handling of me. He had never been this way with me before. I began to tremble underneath him, both from excitement and nerves, and I lifted my hands to run over his muscled arms as they held me.

I wasn't afraid of him. I knew he would never hurt me intentionally. I was just worried over how upset he had become with everything.

He released me, stepping several paces away from me.

"Sorry," he apologized with a hurt look on his face. "I don't want to use you in this way. You mean everything to me, and I'm letting my emotions excuse my rough handling of you. Please forgive me, Portia."

I walked up and wrapped my arms around him.

"It's okay, really," I said, reaching up to kiss him on the lips, and he let his arms slide back around me. "I want to do this, Vance. Will you let me do this for you?"

He stared at me for a moment with several emotions warring on his face before he swallowed thickly and nodded.

This time I grabbed his face in my hands and delivered a scorching kiss back to him.

I heard a low sound emanate from his throat, and suddenly I found myself pressed back up against the wall once more.

CHAPTER 23

Vance had spent the next several days pacing the floor in the sitting room while he watched the monitor of the Cummingses' driveway, waiting for any sign of life from the inside.

The tracker we placed on their vehicle showed it had returned to the house without Darcy. It appeared that it hadn't moved since.

Dad and Grandma spent a lot of time down in the dungeons trying to see if they could get any information out of Darcy.

She refused to speak to anyone except for Vance, and he refused to give her the time of day. Grandma even begged him to please go try to talking to her again, but to no avail. He wouldn't have anything more to do with her.

Relations between Vance and my dad were particularly strained ever since Dad ordered him to stand down. They both seemed to avoid each other on purpose now.

Vance and I had been eating meals in our room, rather than joining the rest of the family.

I understood why he was isolating himself. He was trying not to blow up at anybody. I was afraid it was only going to be a matter of time, though. His emotions were boiling just under the surface.

It hadn't helped matters when Dad entered the dungeon this morning to find Darcy had committed suicide sometime during the night.

He blamed Vance completely for it, saying if he had just gone down there and reassured her, this would have never happened.

Vance had turned and very calmly told him that the world was now a better place without Darcy in it, as far as he was concerned, before he left the room.

This made my dad very angry, and he shouted down the hall after him—something about Vance being an ungrateful hothead.

Grandma had finally pulled Dad over into a corner to try and talk him down. I'd gone after Vance, and everyone else had been walking on eggshells around the two of them ever since.

We were currently in our bedroom. I was sitting cross-legged on the bed watching him as he paced on the floor. I was beginning to think he was going to wear a hole in the carpet.

"Things just aren't making sense, Portia," he said. "The eclipse is tonight. We should've seen some type of preparations going on by now. No one has been in or out of that place since we took Darcy. Where's the rest of the coven? Which circle is the right one? Where do we go from here?"

There was a knock at the door, and Shelly entered the room, her face alight with excitement.

"Vance, your grandparents just left the estate in their vehicle. They had a driver and another woman with them. It was your mom. I'm sure of it. She looked just like the demon you destroyed before that you thought was her."

Vance was out the door and down the hall before I could even get off the bed. I ran down the hallway after him, clattering down the stairs and around the corner into the sitting room.

Dad was rewinding the monitor, showing Vance the image.

"That's my mom," he said. "We need to go after her."

"We will. The tracker on the car is working well. Let's get everyone into the cars so we can follow them," Dad said calmly.

"What if they're going somewhere far away?" Shelly asked. "Should we take our clothes?"

I could hear Vance literally growl in frustration under his breath. "We'll just buy new clothes wherever we end up," he said through gritted teeth, and he dragged me toward the doorway.

"Hang on," Dad said to him, and I could feel that it took every ounce of Vance's self-control to stop without screaming at everyone at the top of his lungs. "Shelly, you and Brad stay here and help Stacey gather up everyone's things just in case we need them. Mom and I will go on ahead with Vance and Portia to track the vehicle. We'll call you and let you know where we're going."

Shelly nodded, and Dad leaned over to give Mom a peck on the cheek.

"Be careful," Mom said softly to him.

"We will," he said, with a lingering touch against her face before he went out the door.

"Finally," Vance muttered in irritation into my head. "They could be halfway to the United States by now."

"Try to stay calm, babe," I said back to him, knowing he was very frustrated. "We'll find her."

The four of us hurried to the car, quickly climbing inside, Dad and Grandma up front and Vance and I in the back.

Grandma was the driver, while Dad watched his device and navigated which way to go. We soon found ourselves heading out onto open highway.

My dad called my mom and told her it did look like we would be heading out for a longer trip and to bring everything. He gave her our directions thus far and told her he would call her again when he knew more.

Vance was holding my hand, but he was clenching it so hard I felt like my fingers were going to fall off. I finally asked him to let go.

"Sorry," he said, and I placed his hand in my lap, trying to massage some of the tension out of it.

He was completely tied up in knots, both inside and out.

I gave up, laying my head on his shoulder, linking my arm through his.

His eyes never left the road as he stared straight ahead, watching for any sign of the vehicle ahead of us.

I knew Dad was keeping us out of line of sight on purpose. He didn't want Douglas and Fiona to know we were following them.

We traveled for quite a while before we came into an area known as Aberdeenshire. We tailed the vehicle into the town of Inverurie. We were just inside the city limits when Dad suddenly lost the signal to the car.

"No!" he said, and he hit the monitor on the side with his hand. "No! No! No! Not now! Come back!"

Vance sat white-knuckled for a moment, then threw his hands up in disgust and flopped back against the seat in defeat.

Dad had Grandma drive to the last location we received a signal from, but there was no sign of the vehicle anywhere.

"Now what do we do?" I asked my dad, feeling my own frustration at the situation mingling with Vance's.

"I guess we'll check into a hotel and see if they ever pop back up on the monitor. I'm sorry, Vance," he said with true regret written all over his face. "I don't know what happened."

"It isn't your fault. Hopefully this was their final destination," he said, completely dejected, and I could tell by his voice that he didn't think that was very likely.

We checked into four of the rooms at the Kintore Arms Hotel which was the closest place to where we had lost the signal.

Dad got a hold of the others who were well on their way here and gave them the final information.

The hotel was old and small, but under the current circumstances it worked for our needs.

Vance and I went straight to our room and plopped onto the bed, flicking on the television for a diversion from our anxious thoughts.

It was late afternoon now. We hadn't eaten since breakfast, and I felt myself losing energy quickly.

"You want to try to find someplace to eat?" I asked, and right on cue my stomach growled a little too loudly.

"Do you think your Dad will let us out by ourselves?" he asked sarcastically when he looked over at me.

"We won't stop to ask," I said, pulling him to his feet after me, and he flashed the first grin I had seen him give all day.

We quickly exited the building, walking down the street, entering the first pub we saw.

"You know this is a bar, right?" Vance said when I pulled him inside.

"They serve food, too," I replied, pointing to the writing in the window before I guided him over to a small table in a dark corner.

We ordered from a very friendly waitress, and before long we were served our food.

I began eating with relish.

"Don't eat too fast," Vance cautioned me, watching me. "Remember what happened last time?"

"Yes," I said with a sigh, taking care to eat slower and trying to actually enjoy the food.

The sun was dipping low in the sky before we finally finished, paid and headed back to the hotel.

The rest of the family had arrived, and Dad was frantic with worry because no one had been able to find us.

"You shouldn't be out of the hotel!" he said to Vance. "Someone could've seen you."

"Portia was hungry," Vance replied, not stepping down. "I didn't want her to get sick again, and I certainly wasn't sending her off to find food in a strange town by herself."

Grandma stepped in between the two of them. "Sean, did you tell him what we found out while they were gone?" she asked, trying to redirect their attention.

Dad let out a big sigh. "We got online and looked up stone circles in the area," he said with a hard expression.

"And?" Vance and I both asked at the same time.

"There are ninety such circles in Aberdeenshire."

"That's just great," Vance said lifting his hands before dropping them to his side in defeat. "Is anything going to work in our favor?"

He spun around and walked down the hall into our room, closing the door behind him with a slam.

Dad just looked at me, shaking his head, his face reddening. "He's really getting out of control, Portia."

"He's just nervous, Dad. We all are. That's why everyone is fighting. I'll go talk to him." I left Dad standing there in the hall staring after me.

I went into the room, opening the door softly and closing it the same way behind me.

Vance was lying on the bed watching the news.

I walked into the bathroom to splash a little cold water on my face, trying to calm myself down.

Things were coming to a head. I could feel it.

"What the heck?" I heard Vance say from the other room. "Portia! Come here quick!"

I walked to the doorway to see what he was talking about.

He was standing at the foot of the bed looking at the television. A news reporter was talking about a breaking news story on the screen. She was standing next to Douglas and Fiona.

"What happened then?" the reporter was asking Fiona who looked very distraught, but leaned in to speak into the microphone.

"It's just been so horrible," Fiona said, clasping her hands together and wringing them in a frustrated fashion. "We've been touring this part of the country with our daughter-in-law for the last two days. She went out to see the Easter Aquhorthies Stone Circle outside Inverurie yesterday."

Vance was instantly on his laptop, looking up directions.

"She never came home last night," Fiona continued. "She's a diabetic, and we're afraid she's sick somewhere."

A picture of Krista popped up on the screen.

The reporter spoke up again. "This woman was last reportedly seen on High Street in Inverurie. If you have seen her, please call our hotline number at the bottom of the screen. We need your help to return this woman to her family."

"What is this?" I asked, confused, and I stared at the screen. "This doesn't make any sense!"

"It's a message for us," Vance said while he began to write something down on a piece of paper. "Portia, go get your dad."

"All right," I said, hurrying out the door and down the narrow hallway to my parents' room.

I knocked briskly on the door, and my mom answered. "Did you see it?" I asked and pointed at the T.V.

"See what?" she replied.

"Douglas and Fiona were just on the news saying Krista got lost here yesterday after visiting Easter Aquhorthies Stone Circle. Vance said it's a message and to come get Dad," I replied.

Everyone jumped up in a flurry all at once and hurried down to our room.

"Dad's here, Vance!" I called out when I entered the room, but I didn't see him. "Vance?" I called out, and I went into the bathroom. "He isn't here!" I ran to the window. "The car is gone!" I yelled, and tears began to fill my eyes.

I turned to see Dad looking at Vance's open laptop.

"Get in the car! I have the directions!" Dad hollered, and we all ran downstairs to pile into the other vehicle.

CHAPTER 24

I was shaking violently, and Brad wrapped his arm around me.

"We'll find him, don't worry!" he said, trying to comfort me while Dad peeled out of the parking lot onto the dark road.

"Vance!" I screamed at him in my head. "Don't you dare do this!" I knew he could hear me.

"I have to, Portia!" he answered me immediately. "They'll kill her if I don't go!"

"Vance, they want to drink your blood! You could die, too! This is just a lure to get you there!" I argued with him.

My dad caught my expression in the rearview mirror. "Are you talking to him?" he shouted at me while we sped along.

I nodded.

"You tell him to pull that car over right now and wait for us! That's an order!"

I relayed the message, sure that Vance heard every word himself, but desperate to try anything to get him to stop.

"Portia," he said back to me, calmer than I'd heard him in a while. "I love you, baby, but I have to do this."

The dreaded wall was instantly back in place between us, and I could hear nothing but dead silence.

"He cut me off!" I cried out, my voice catching.

I looked out the window and could easily see the moon was almost in full eclipse on the horizon.

We were speeding out of town, driving recklessly. The road became increasingly narrower as we worked our way up into some small hills, finally pulling into a parking area.

I saw the car Vance had driven parked up in front of us with the driver's door hanging wide open.

My eyes followed the trail that led up the hill, and I could see Vance running up it at full speed toward the raised stone circle on the top.

"Get out!" I yelled at Brad, and I shoved him out of the car, climbing over the top of him and taking off after Vance.

I heard the others running behind me, but I didn't turn to look at their progress, only caring about my husband in front of me.

I could see the black-cloaked figures that stood in a circle around the fire burning in the middle. There was also a white-clad figure lying across a recumbent stone on one side of the circle. I knew instinctively it was Krista even though I was too far away to see for sure. She wasn't moving, making me wonder instantly if she had been drugged.

Vance was approaching the steps that led up into the ring in front of me. I saw him breach the circle, throwing both hands out to his sides, launching a stream of fire, incinerating at least four of the demons present, two on each side of him.

He ran straight to the recumbent stone, jumping up on a small rock next to it, shoving Krista off the other side of the altar, out of the circle and out of harm's way.

I was a few yards away from the steps when he turned to face the others. I saw the flash of a knife and felt the involuntary scream that was ripped from my lips when I saw Fiona slam it into his chest, right into his heart.

I stumbled to my knees, grabbed my own chest in pain, and saw the blood spray from him. Some of it gurgled up out of his mouth, and he registered a look of surprise, falling over onto the altar.

I could hear the others stop short behind me with a gasp.

I saw Douglas flip his hood back, and he leaned over to drink the pumping blood straight from Vance's chest.

Fiona quickly produced the box we had been trying so hard to find, flipping it open and setting it next to Vance on the altar.

To my surprise, Vance slowly lifted his head up, and I could see his eyes were flaming red now. I watched in amazement as his teeth lengthened into uneven fangs, something I hadn't seen since his near conversion. It was also something we assumed he had been cured of. Apparently the demon blood in him was still running full and strong. Vance reached out with one hand, grabbing Douglas around his neck. He whipped Douglas up against his mouth, sinking the sharpened teeth into his exposed throat. Douglas screamed as Vance began to drink heavily from him.

I could see the molten color seep into Vance's fingers, and Douglas's flesh began searing beneath them. He struggled desperately to rip them away from him, but Vance held him firm.

Fiona surprised me when she turned to stab Douglas in the back with the knife. She pulled it out quickly, and he arched backward, out of Vance's grasp. She swung the knife again in a wide arc, this time completely decapitating him, shoving his lifeless body to the side. Quickly, she turned toward Vance, just as the moon began to move out of full eclipse.

A white light swirled up out of the box toward the sky before drifting down toward Fiona, but began to go into Vance instead since she had not yet consumed any of his blood.

Vance weakly tried to push her away, while attempting to roll onto his side to remove his blood-pouring wounds from her reach.

She struggled to control him for a moment before she raised her knife and stabbed him again, causing a fresh onslaught of blood to burst forth, desperate to devour it.

"I love you, Portia," I heard his voice seep softly into my head. "I'm sorry."

His features relaxed, and I saw his arms drop loosely to his side and his head roll to the left, his body going limp.

"*No!*" I screamed, waking to the horror happening in front of me. I snapped out of my stupor, quickly regaining my footing and tore into the circle.

Several hooded demons moved to stop me from entering.

Without even thinking, I shot ice shards out at them, one after another, as if my hands were automatic weapons. The demons quickly fell to the ground. I didn't bother to check and see if they were all dead, knowing the others behind me would take care of them.

As soon as I crossed through the stones into the circle, the Awakening immediately moved away from Vance and shot across into my body. I paused for only a moment when the initial shock hit me. It was strong, but not painful. I could feel the energy as it moved through me changing things inside, but I couldn't allow myself to slow down. I continued running to the altar.

I was moving in machine mode now, and I came up behind Fiona, yanking her away from Vance. I felt no mercy as I slammed a large ice shard right through her back with my hand.

She arched back against me in a scream, flailing with her arms into the air. I reached to grab her own weapon, the athame she still gripped in one of her hands. I sank the knife into her soft flesh, slitting her throat from side to side, until I felt the athame hit bone. Then I threw her blood-spraying body to the side, on top of Douglas. I hurriedly climbed up onto the recumbent stone.

"Vance!" the scream tore from my very soul as I looked into his dead eyes. "No! No! *No*!" I said and I knelt over his body, covering my mouth over his, trying to breathe life back into his blood-slicked face.

I could hear the sounds of battle taking place around me, fighting, grunting, calls for help. The Awakening was still transferring into me from the box, but I didn't care about any of those things, only pounding on his chest, trying to restart his heart.

I placed both of my hands over the gaping wounds and tried to focus my magic to heal him. Nothing happened. The wounds would not heal.

"It's too late." I heard my dad's voice beside me, and he dragged me off the altar.

"*No*!" I screamed, sobbing when I felt Grandma grab my other arm, and they pulled me kicking and screaming out of the circle.

"Wait, Portia!" my dad yelled at me after we passed through the stones.

I realized what they were doing then when the Awakening instantly left me and reverted back to Vance.

I sank to my knees and watched as the remainder of the power moved into his body. As soon as it had stopped the transfer, I ran back into the circle, climbing over the dead bodies and onto the altar.

"Vance!" I cried, and I shook him, not looking up when I heard the others approaching us. "Vance!" I screamed at him again. "Wake up!"

I heard Dad and Grandma on the other side of the altar checking on Krista, but I didn't care about anything except him.

"Vance Mangum, you wake up this instant, do you hear me?" I whispered through gritted teeth into his ear.

Nothing.

I started pumping on his chest again not knowing what else to do. One, two, three, four, five, I counted, not sure if I was even doing it right. I leaned over and blew into his mouth twice. I repeated the action, tears rolling down my face.

"Wake up. Wake up. Wake up," I said through clenched teeth, continuing to pump against him.

I could hear Shelly whimpering beside me, and Brad climbed up next to me to help. He took over the compressions while I continued the rescue breathing.

The minutes wore on, but I couldn't stop.

After several minutes passed, Brad finally sat back, looking at me with a haunted expression.

"I'm sorry, Portia. I think it's too late."

"Don't you dare stop!" I screamed at him, and I continued pumping on Vance's chest.

Over and over again I worked on him while the tears rolled down my face, falling onto his open chest wounds. I felt the sweat dripping from my forehead and the exhaustion beginning to seep into my limbs.

After several more minutes, I felt my dad's hands cover mine, stopping them with a firm grip.

"Pumpkin, you need to stop now. He isn't with us anymore, honey. He's gone," he said softly, his voice barely loud enough for me to hear.

I looked over at him in confusion, seeing the tears that ran down his face and his trembling lips.

"No!" I said shaking my head in disbelief while I watched him. "It isn't possible. Not Vance!"

He struggled to hold his composure before he could speak again.

"Honey, look at him. He's bled out. There's nothing left to save," he tried to explain so I could understand. "Come down, and let's get him off the altar now."

"No!" I screamed, sobs wracking my body. I reached down and gathered Vance's limp form up against me, crying into his hair. "You promised!" I yelled at him. "You promised you wouldn't leave me!"

I rocked his body back and forth in my arms.

"You promised. You promised. You promised," I whispered against him over and over again.

Shelly was crying into Brad's chest, as my mom and Grandma held each other, letting the tears flow freely down their faces, Krista lying unconscious and unknowing at their feet.

"We were supposed to protect him!" I screamed at the top of my lungs while I looked at all of them staring at me. *"Does this look like protection to you?"*

I clenched my teeth together and threw my head back, screaming into the night air, and the sobs threatened to overtake me.

"Please take me with you," I said, and I kissed his dark wavy hair, my voice shuddering. "I can't live without you."

"Come on, Portia," my dad called again, and he held his arms out to me. "Let's take him home."

I held him to my chest, and I looked up to the heavens and shouted, "Can anyone hear me up there? *Please God*, I beg you, don't take him. Not yet! Please don't take my life from me!"

There was no answer from the star-filled sky as I sat rocking Vance against my body.

I held him for a few more minutes before I gently laid him back onto the stone altar, laying my head against his bloody chest. As I wiped at my swollen eyes, I spied the box that had caused all this misery still lying open on the altar.

I snatched it up, jumped off the stone and threw it in the fire. I watched it burn until there was nothing left of it.

"There!" I said turning to face the rest of the group. "Now this will never happen to anyone else."

I felt the rage flowing through me, and I stalked around the circle in my blood-soaked clothes, glaring at the dead bodies that were lying there. I began picking up each demon body by myself, dragging it over to the fire, and throwing them one by one into the flames.

My family just watched me, not helping me, knowing somehow I needed to do this.

I put all of my frustration into the task until I finally came to the last demon body. It was Fiona's. When I reached out to pick up her body, another set of hands came to join mine.

"I can do this myself!" I shouted, looking up into the face of the offending individual.

My dad looked at me with sad eyes before he released the body and stepped backward.

I dragged Fiona over to the fire, not using any magic, choosing to exert myself physically as much as possible. I tossed her unceremoniously into the flames, watching without emotion while they licked up and devoured her corpse. The air filled with the acrid smell of burning flesh.

I stood like a statue, in complete silence, and waited until every figure in the inferno disappeared, leaving no visible trace behind.

My dad and Grandma came forward and began using some of their magic to extinguish the flames. When the fire was out, they cast a spell out over the ground, making it appear completely untouched in the moonlight. One would never know there had been a fire here.

I felt someone's hands on my shoulders and turned to see Shelly's sympathetic eyes staring back at me. I looked away from her and up into the sky at the bright full moon that shone down upon us, before I turned back toward the recumbent stone altar.

"I'm going to take Krista down to the car now, and then I'll come back for Vance," I heard my dad's voice say.

I nodded slightly in acknowledgment. "Why don't you all go help him?" I added woodenly to the rest of the group. "I'd like a minute here alone before we move Vance."

No one answered me, but I saw that they slowly trickled out of the circle after Dad.

When they were all gone, I climbed back up onto the stone and knelt next to Vance's body.

Even in death, he still looked beautiful to me. I wiped at some of the blood that was smeared across his face, but it had dried too much already for me to remove it. I gently slid my hands beneath him and lifted his head to cradle it in my lap.

I slowly ran my fingers over his eyelids, closing them over the now-empty blue eyes that stared back at me. There were no traces of the demon face I had seen earlier when he was fighting for his life.

As I ran my fingers through his hair repeatedly, I wondered if this would be the last time I would ever be able to do this.

"I love you," I whispered softly to him. "Wherever you are, I hope you can still hear me. I'll never stop loving you. If I live to be a thousand years old, your name will still be on the first breath I take in the morning, and it will be the last thing I say at night." I paused for a moment, tracing my fingers over his masculine features. "Please forgive me for not being able to save you." I reached down to intertwine my fingers with his, lifting his hand to my mouth to lightly kiss each one of his fingertips.

When I was done, I gently laid my cheek against the back of his hand, trying to memorize the feel of it there. I stayed that way in silence for several long moments before my dad's voice finally interrupted me.

"Are you ready, Portia?" he asked from beside me.

"Yes," I replied, slowly.

I gently moved out from under Vance's head and slid down to the ground. I stood back while Dad reached up and pulled Vance's limp form into his arms. I couldn't help the little gasp that escaped my lips when his unsupported head fell backwards.

Grandma appeared next to me, stepping up to the stone and reciting something over it. Instantly Vance's blood that stained the rock began to disappear. She turned and placed an arm around my shoulders.

Without a word we followed Dad together, making our way out of the circle and down the path to where the vehicles were waiting.

Dad carried Vance over to where he parked his car just a short time earlier, the door still standing wide open the way he left it.

"Put him in the backseat with me," I instructed, and Dad nodded.

I climbed into the seat from the driver's side and scooted over so Dad could lay the body inside. Once again I cradled Vance's head in my lap.

Dad got in behind the wheel, and Grandma got in the front passenger seat.

"We decided to go back to the keep tonight. We'll have more privacy there than at the hotel," Dad explained.

"Okay," I replied, feeling numb.

"Do you feel comfortable enough for such a long trip?" Grandma asked me with a concerned look.

"I'm fine," I said, staring at the body lying next to me. "Let's go."

I was actually glad I was going to have the extra time to be with him. I wasn't ready to let go just yet. I reached out to place his hand in mine, and I could feel the coolness beginning to creep into his limbs now.

He was really gone.

I let the silent tears fall.

Chapter 25

My dad used his government contacts to procure us a private jet to fly home in the next morning.

A body bag arrived with the car that would take us to the airport. I thought my heart was going to fall out of my chest when I watched my dad pull the zipper up over the face of my sweet husband.

I was completely numb from head to toe now, running in robotic mode, while I sat next to the wooden casket that had been waiting for us on the plane. Thankfully, my family had the coffin placed at the far end of the plane and not in the cargo area. I was able to sit there next to it—by myself, alone with my thoughts.

I had run over the events of the previous night in my mind many times. The one thing that continued to stand out to me was the fact Vance's demon attributes had come to the surface after he had been stabbed. We were so sure he'd been cured from that.

I brought the subject up with my Grandma later that evening, wondering why it had happened. She didn't really have any answers for me, but she reminded me that we never really knew what had happened with him. We all just assumed that he had been completely healed somehow.

We were stupid to have thought that would be the case. After all, he had been fed demon blood again while we were staying with Douglas and Fiona. And surely having the strength to perform a demon kiss on his father must've meant something. Not only was he able to perform the kiss, but he also assimilated all of Damien's powers, as well as those Damien had stolen from other people. Maybe the reason he stopped having withdrawals after performing the kiss was just because the demon side of him was being fed something it needed from the transfer. He complained to me on several separate occasions about the difficulty he was having controlling his emotions.

I sighed heavily, glancing up the aisle a few rows to where Krista was still sleeping heavily. Whatever drug Douglas and Fiona used on her was certainly taking a long time to wear off. She hadn't even moved a muscle—didn't even know her son had died trying to save her.

I wasn't looking forward to having to tell her about it, yet at the same time I was hoping she might hold some of the answers to my questions. Not that any of it mattered. Answers were not going to bring him back to me.

Suddenly, I felt a little queasy, and I realized I hadn't eaten anything today. My mind instantly went to the day when I had gotten sick and Vance was sure I was pregnant. I'd give anything to be pregnant right now, just so I could have a little piece of him with me still. I knew that wasn't the case, though, since he had been very careful to make sure it didn't happen.

I stood up and walked down the aisle to where a tray of fruits had been set on the side board.

"Getting an appetite back?" my mom asked me casually when I reached out for an apple.

"No," I said. "I'm just starting to feel a little sick right now."

"Is there anything I can do for you?" she asked me with a concerned look.

"No, Mom," I said, and I took a bite. "I'll be fine," I added, over my mouthful of the crisp fruit, and I walked toward the rear of the plane, thinking I'd never be fine again and the painful ache I was feeling would always be with me.

I stopped to check on the sleeping Krista, before I made my way back to Vance's casket. I sat down and placed my free hand on the surface that covered his mortal remains.

I must have finally fallen asleep after I finished my apple because when I awoke, it was to find we were on final descent into New York for refueling. The tears popped instantly into my eyes when I remembered the last time I had been here was on the first day of our honeymoon.

"Are you okay?" Shelly's voice asked, and she slid quickly into the seat beside me, buckling her belt.

"Is it ever going to get any easier?" I asked, looking her in the eyes, the tears streaming quietly down my face.

"I honestly don't know," she replied reaching over to hold my hand. "I've never had to experience anything like this before."

"I just keep thinking about how he told me he wanted us to be together forever, beyond this life and into the next. He told me he couldn't believe a just God, who could create the universe, would send us here without some type of plan for us. I can't seem to find the justice in this, though. Look at all we've been through so we could have a life together, and this is how it's supposed to end? I can't accept this," I said searching her eyes for answers I knew she couldn't possibly have.

"I don't know why things happened this way, Portia," she responded honestly. "But I do know one thing, and that is Vance loved you with every fiber of his being. Most people on this earth will never get to experience the kind of love he had for you or you for him. You should treasure it as a great gift, even though it was a short one."

"I will treasure it always. It's the only thing I have left of him," I replied solemnly. "He told me once, if he were to die before me, he'd be waiting for me to join him on the other side." I laughed in disgust at the thought. "Do you realize that could be centuries from now? I'm going to outlive all of you! I couldn't die if I tried! I'm stuck here in mortality. Not only do I have to live without the love of my life, I'll eventually lose all of you, too. You'll have the chance to see Vance long before I ever will."

I could tell she didn't know what to say to me, so she just laid her head on my shoulder.

"I really am sorry, Portia," she said, the tears welling in her eyes. "I loved him, too."

"I know you did," I replied, reaching out and squeezing her hand tightly, and she turned her palm up so she could lace her fingers with mine. "We all did."

We sat in silence as the plane touched down and taxied off the runway. When we were at a complete stop, Dad unbuckled his belt and came back to check on us.

"You doing okay back here?" he asked. "Do you want to get off the plane while we refuel and stretch your legs a bit? Some of the others are going to."

"I'll be fine," I replied, not wanting to leave Vance or Krista on the plane by themselves. "You go ahead," I said to

Shelly when I looked down the aisle. "It looks like Brad's waiting for you."

"I can stay with you," she replied.

"No, go ahead. I'm fine," I said, trying to reassure her.

She squeezed my hand one more time before letting go and moving past me to go meet Brad.

"Portia, why don't you go, too?" Dad asked with concern. "I'll stay here with Vance and Krista."

"Dad," I began, and my chin quivered slightly, "there are only going to be a few more moments in my life that I'm going to be able to physically be next to him. I don't want to squander one minute of it. Please ... I need to stay."

"I understand, Pumpkin," he said, pursing his lips together for a second before he reached out to pat my leg. "I'll be right outside if you need me, all right?"

"Thanks, Dad," I said, attempting to smile, though I really didn't feel like doing such a thing at all.

Thirty minutes later, everyone was re-boarded and we were ready to take off again. After we were airborne, Brad unbuckled his belt and came back toward me, carrying something bulky under his arm.

"Here. I thought you might like this," he said, and he glanced quickly toward the casket next to me, swallowing as though he had a large lump in his throat.

He was holding out a fluffy pillow wrapped in a blanket.

"Thank you, Brad. This looks really comfy," I replied reaching out for them, and he placed them in my hands.

He kept standing there for a few awkward moments, his Adam's apple bobbing hard in his throat.

I waited patiently since I could see he had something he was trying to say. "He was ...." He clenched his jaw hard, trying to control his emotion. "He was my best friend."

"I know." I smiled slightly, and my lips trembled at his comment. "He felt the same about you, too."

"I'm sorry I couldn't do more," he said, pursing his lips together.

I looked into his glassy eyes and nodded. "It was his choice, Brad. There was nothing any of us could do about it," I reminded him.

"But I don't know what I can do to help you," he said, and a single tear finally made its way over the edge of his eye.

"You're already doing it," I said, reaching out to take his hand.

He leaned in then to give me a full bear hug. "Love you, Portia," he said quickly before straightening and walking briskly away.

"Love you too, Brad," I whispered quietly under my breath.

I watched him walk away, back to join Shelly before I undid my seatbelt and lay across the adjoining seats. I placed the pillow under my head while cuddling up with the blanket, and I closed my eyes, letting sleep claim me almost instantly.

I dreamed this time. I was standing alone in my purple field of flowers, and I twirled around looking for Vance, but he wasn't there. I sank to my knees, held my head in my hands and sobbed.

The last words I ever heard him say echoed over and over again in my mind.

"I love you, Portia. I'm sorry. I love you, Portia. I'm sorry. I love you, Portia. I'm sorry."

"I can't take this anymore!" I screamed at the top of my lungs in my dream. "Stop it! Stop it!"

Still the words kept coming. "I love you, Portia. I'm sorry. I'm sorry. I'm...Portia, help me."

I bolted awake, straight up in my seat, staring at the casket in front of me. I hopped out of my chair and quickly knelt beside it, throwing the lid open to grab the zippered bag inside.

"What's going on?" my dad yelled, and he raced back toward me as I yanked the zipper downward.

"He was calling me!" I shouted, and I moved the bag away from his face with trembling hands.

I sat back when his plainly deceased face came into my view.

"He was calling me!" I said in a choked whisper, and I placed my arms around my waist in an attempt to stop the shaking.

My dad dropped to his knees and pulled me into his embrace.

"It was just a dream, Pumpkin. I'm sorry. It was just a dream."

I buried my head into his chest and sobbed loudly, not caring who could hear me.

"I can't do this, Daddy," I cried, and my mom came to join us at my side. "I can't live without him."

Chapter 26

The hearse was there waiting for us at the airport when we landed. Dad, Brad, the pilot, and the man from the mortuary who had come onboard, carried Vance's casket off the plane. I followed numbly behind them, and we stepped onto the tarmac, into the hot July air of Sedona, Arizona.

There was a gurney at the bottom of the steps, and Vance's temporary casket was placed on that and rolled over to the back of the funeral vehicle. The gurney was collapsed, and the entire unit was slid into the back of the car.

"Thank you for your help," my dad said, reaching out to shake the attendant's hand.

"No problem, Mr. Mullins. We'll take care of everything from here," he replied.

"I do have one request," Dad spoke up again. "We already know what the cause of death was, so we'd like to ask that you do not perform an autopsy."

"Not a problem, sir. We already received an official fax from the coroner saying an autopsy was not necessary," the man replied.

"Wonderful," my dad said. "Also because of our religious beliefs, we ask that the body not be embalmed either."

"I'll be sure that's added into the notes, although it seems as if I remember that request already being on there," he replied.

"That's good," Dad said. "We'll be in touch with you over the final funeral arrangements soon."

I stood rooted to my spot while I watched the car carry Vance away from me and out of my sight.

My dad didn't rush me, instead waiting patiently beside me until I turned to go toward the waiting vehicle.

"A coroner never examined the body," I stated while we walked toward the car together.

"I know," he replied with a sigh. "I pulled a few strings. We don't know if Vance's demon DNA might have brought up unusual results in an autopsy. We figured it was best to bypass it."

He opened the door to the waiting SUV, allowing me to climb in the front next to him. Everyone else was already inside.

"We need to have the funeral as soon as possible, Portia," he added as he started the vehicle.

"Why?" I asked, not even wanting to think about it.

"Because we aren't embalming the body. He will ...," he glanced apologetically at me, "decay much faster."

I felt physically ill at the thought.

"Of course, we'll help you with anything you need," he offered.

"I don't think we should plan anything until Krista wakes up," I replied, running a hand through my hair. "He's her only child, and he died trying to save her. She needs to be involved in this, too."

"You're right," he said. "Hopefully she'll be awake before too long."

"Don't rush her into this hell," I responded softly. "Let her be blissfully unaware for as long as she possibly can be."

We drove unspeaking through town, and my eyes couldn't help but notice all the places that held memories of Vance for me. It became too overwhelming for me, and I finally had to close my eyes against the sight until we pulled up at our house.

When I opened my eyes again, though, it was to find the yard was covered in members of our coven and their families, who waited to greet us. I wasn't in the mood to meet anyone right now, but I knew they were all meaning well.

My dad got out of the car and came around to open my door. I stepped out of the vehicle and into the waiting arms of Babs who hugged me so tightly I thought I might never breathe again.

"I'm so sorry, Portia!" she cried into my hair, and my lips trembled unspeaking, as tears hit my face. "We love you so much."

I thanked her with a nod, and the scene was repeated with each of the remaining coven members and their relatives.

When we finally made it into the house, it was to the smells of delicious food dishes that had been delivered to the kitchen. My stomach revolted at the thought of eating right now, and I continued up the stairs, going straight into my bedroom, closing the door behind me.

My cat, Jinx, was instantly upon me. I grabbed her up into my arms and carried her over to my bed as she wrapped her white paws around my neck, and I nuzzled my face into her fluffy white fur.

I let loose then. "He died, Jinx! He died!" I cried into her fur, and I curled into a ball on the bed, holding her tightly against me.

She stayed there with me until I finally cried myself to sleep.

I was awakened some time later by a soft knock at the door.

"Come in," I said groggily and sat up.

The door opened, and Krista slipped quietly into the room, her red-rimmed eyes showing in the dim light.

"I'm sorry!" I said bursting into tears once again. She rushed to my side and swept me up into her arms. "I tried to save him! I did everything I could think of, but nothing worked!"

"Hush, sweetheart," she whispered in a choked voice, her tears falling upon my shoulder. "None of this is your fault."

"He loved you so much!" I said, and she continued to hold me close. "All he ever hoped for was to find you again and have some kind of life with you. He missed you so badly in all the years you were gone."

"I know. I felt the same way," she replied, her voice heavy with sorrow.

"When he found out where they had you, he wouldn't listen to reason. No offense, but I tried to stop him. I knew they were using you as a lure to get him there," I explained.

"That's my boy," she agreed. "He was always headstrong. Portia, you have to let this go. None of it was your fault."

"Yes, it was," I said, my voice shaking from the crying. "If I would've reacted faster when they first stabbed him, I might've been able to do something different, something that could've helped him somehow."

Krista pulled back then so she could look at me. "Portia, listen to me! Trying to have hindsight isn't going to change anything. What's done is done. Now we have to try to find a way to move on with our lives. Vance would want us both to do that. He loved us both, and he'd be miserable knowing we're miserable, too," she said looking into my eyes.

"I know that," I replied, and I hiccupped. "My head knows all the important things it needs to do. I just need someone or something to tell it to my heart," I choked out.

"Give it time to catch up, sweetie," she said, stroking her hand over my hair, similar to the way Vance used to. "Now I know this is a hard thing to do right away, but we need to plan this funeral. All of your family is downstairs. Do you think you're up to it?"

I slowly nodded, and we headed downstairs together, arm in arm.

The black casket with silver handles sat on one side of the small viewing room in the mortuary. I requested this first moment to myself. I walked timidly up to the opened portion at the top.

He looked like he was sleeping, and I reached out to touch him, just to make sure. He was so cold.

His hair had been textured perfectly into place, just the way he liked it, purposely messy. His face still looked just like him. I was going to have to compliment whoever had done his makeup. They worked well from the photograph I had given them.

He was dressed in the tuxedo he had worn at our wedding, just a few short months ago. His wedding ring was still on his finger, as was mine.

There was a beautiful spray of red roses that draped the lower end of the casket, with ribbon running through it that said “Beloved Husband & Son” on it.

I had heard someone once say the spirit never strays far from its body before it is buried, so I decided to speak to him one last time.

“I want to thank you for all the great memories you’ve given me,” I said, and I reached out to touch his hand. “You’re the most wonderful person I’ve ever known. I’ll always keep you right here.” I pointed to where my heart rested in my chest. “I want to hold you to your word. You said you’d wait for me. Please do. It may take a long time for me to get where you are, but I will come. I promise.” I stood there for a few minutes just drinking in the sight of him, knowing it would be my last private moment with him. “I love you,” I added finally, bending over to kiss him softly one last time.

I walked over to the door to let the rest of the family, who were waiting outside, in.

When they were done paying their respects, we stepped out so Krista could have a minute to herself with her son.

She soon reappeared, and two attendants from the funeral home went in to close the casket before they rolled it past us to the waiting hearse.

Once Vance was placed inside, we were ushered to a company limousine, which we rode in while we followed the hearse to the church.

The funeral service turned out to be fairly large. It was filled with a great number of teenagers from Sedona High School and several of their families. The program was short and consisted of a congregational hymn followed by a slightly fabricated version of Vance's life story. There was a solo performed by a friend of mine who was in the school choir, and she was followed by the minister who gave some remarks on dealing with life and death. Then it was over.

The male members of the coven were the pallbearers. They carried the casket out to the waiting hearse, which then led the processional to the cemetery.

The casket was removed upon arrival and placed into a liner before being set upon the motorized straps that would lower it into the plot. Some chairs and a canopy had been placed over near it. My dad led Krista and me over to them, while Mom, Grandma, Brad, and Shelly followed behind.

Once the crowd was assembled, my friend from the choir sang another hymn, and then the minister said a prayer to dedicate the grave. Afterwards, everyone was dismissed and invited to go back to the church for a luncheon that had been provided by one of the church's ladies organizations.

I spoke with a few well-wishers before I pulled my dad to the side and told him to go back to the church without me. I wanted to stay here until Vance was lowered into the ground.

He gave me a questioning look and told me to call him on his cell phone when I was ready for him to come get me.

I ducked into an out of the way spot where I could observe things from a distance, but not be observed myself. As soon as the cemetery was cleared, a few workers appeared with shovels, as well as a man driving a small tractor.

I saw the belts begin to move, and Vance's casket was lowered into the ground. My heart began to beat faster when it quickly lowered out of my sight, and I had to resist the urge to run after it.

The men soon had the belts up out of the pit, but nothing could have prepared me for the sound of that first shovel full of dirt hitting the casket liner beneath. I had to cover my mouth to keep from crying out.

I watched as the small tractor moved in and pushed most of the dirt back into the hole. When he had done as much as he could, the other men came in with their shovels to finish up the work. Afterward they placed a small metal marker at the head of the grave.

When they had all left, I made my way out from my hiding place, slowly walking over to where the soft mound rose up from the ground. I sank down to my heels and reached my hand out, placing it in the fresh dirt.

When I removed my hand, there was a perfect print of it left behind, showing I had been there.

"I love you," I said one more time, and I closed my eyes in sorrow for a moment, then stood and walked out of the cemetery.

I called my dad when I reached the gates, and he was there to pick me up shortly. I asked him not to take me to the church, but home instead as I couldn't handle any more people right now.

He dropped me off and went back to the church, since there were still many people in attendance and he offered to play host to them for me.

I walked into the empty house and went upstairs to my room. I changed out of my black dress and went over to my dresser to find something comfortable to wear. That was where I stumbled onto one of Vance's t-shirts and a pair of sweats he had left there. I gently, almost reverently, pulled them out of the drawer.

I held them up to my face, trying to find a hint of his smell on them. There was something faintly there. That was when I decided to wear them.

They were much too large for me, but I didn't care. The shirt sagged to my mid-thigh, and I had to tie the drawstring hard on the sweats to get them tight enough.

I slipped on a pair of my tennis shoes and wandered out into our garage where his massive black motorcycle was parked in one of the bays, next to my little green scooter. His helmet sat in the middle of the seat, on top of one of his leather jackets.

Both of these items did smell like him, and I slipped them on before I opened the garage door.

I climbed onto the bike, lifted the kickstand, and pushed it backward out into the driveway, then out onto the street. I kick-started the engine like I had seen him do so many times. I popped it into gear and took off, roaring down the street.

My body knew exactly where I was going without my mind really having to register what I was doing. I made a right at the highway and headed up into Oak Creek Canyon.

I drove easily, until I came to the small road I was looking for. I turned off, crossed the bridge and parked the motorcycle at the dead end on the other side. I took off the jacket and helmet since it was hot and left them with the bike, then proceeded to hike my way up to the large flat stone that marked our secret place.

The memories flooded over me as soon as I entered into the space. It was like I was watching a movie. I could see the first moonlit night when he had brought me here, when he had told me he believed we were soulmates. I saw the ritual in which he had performed his spell, binding our souls together for eternity. I saw the crisp, fall day when we had taken pictures in the changing leaves, when we had laughed and chased each other through the forest.

It was like he was alive here. I could see his smiling face as if he were standing before me. I could hear him telling me he loved me. I could feel his hugs and kisses. His magic surrounded me, and it was strong.

Flinging my arms out from my body, I twirled around in a circle, letting a smile spread out across my face.

"I love you!" I shouted while I spun around.

"I love you! I love you! I love you!" echoed back at me off the canyon walls.

After I had twirled until I was too dizzy to stand up, I sank down to the ground. I just sat there and let all the images I had of him wash over me.

I stayed that way, unmoving, until the sun sunk low behind the hills and the night sky began to take its place.

I decided I better go home before everyone became too worried about me. But I knew I would return tomorrow to visit the ghosts of my past again.

When I walked back into the kitchen from the garage, it was to a whole host of worried faces.

"Sorry," I said a little sheepishly. "I needed to get out for a while."

"Are you sure you're okay?" my mom asked, taking in my oddly dressed appearance.

"Vance left these in my drawer," I explained, and I ran my hand down the relaxed material.

"Where did you go?" Krista asked me casually.

I smiled at the memory. "Vance had a special place he liked to go to in Oak Creek Canyon. He used to take me there with him after we got together. When I went there today it was like he was alive again. His magic is strong there. I could see all the things we had done there together, as if I were watching a movie. I didn't want to leave."

"You seem happier," she commented, watching me.

"I was happy while I was there. Would you like to go see it?" I asked. "I don't know if it will affect you the same way, but it was a place that he loved."

"I would like that very much, thank you." Krista smiled at me.

"Come with me upstairs," I replied, and I gestured toward my room. "I have something else to show you."

She followed me up the stairs and into my bedroom where I pulled out the packet of pictures Vance and I had taken together.

"We took these in the canyon one day last fall. It was one of the best days in my life," I explained, and I handed them to her.

Krista took the pictures from me, slowly going over each one until she came to the one which was my favorite, where Vance was staring straight at me with that loving look in his eyes.

"He loved you a lot, didn't he?" she asked softly.

"Yes, he did," I replied, and the tears welled up in my eyes. "Those are the only pictures I have of him." Suddenly a thought popped into my head. "I'll be right back," I added, and I hurried out my bedroom door.

I ran down the stairs looking for my mom until I found her in the family room.

"Mom, did you ever get my wedding pictures from the photographer in Las Vegas?" I asked.

She gave me a sad look, and she nodded.

"I did, but I didn't think you'd be up to looking at them so soon," she said with a slight frown.

"Can I have them now, please? I really want to show Krista the wedding," I explained.

My mom stood up, walked over to one of the bookshelves, and pulled a large manila envelope off, handing it to me.

"Here you go," she said.

"Thanks, Mom." I smiled and ran back up into my bedroom.

Krista was still looking at the pictures on my bed.

"These are our wedding pictures!" I said, holding up the large envelope. "I haven't ever seen them before. Would you like to look at them with me?"

I opened the envelope with nervous fingers and dumped the contents out into the middle of my bed. My breath caught in my throat when I saw the many captured images tumbling onto the surface in front of me.

There he was ... my Vance. The photographer had captured the look on his face when he had first seen me coming toward him down the aisle. The very moment I had laid my eyes on him and he had stolen my breath away.

"There are so many!" I exclaimed with joy. "It's as if she captured every second of our wedding!"

The tears slid down my face, and I picked up each copy, carefully examining it like it was a priceless diamond.

"You look so beautiful in your dress." Krista smiled while she looked over them with me.

"Thank you," I replied, unable to look at myself since there were so many images of Vance.

"This is wonderful of you to share these with me. It's almost as if I was there with you," she said, holding up one image in particular. "Have you ever seen a boy more in love than this?" she asked laughing.

"No, not ever!" I smiled back. "I think that one is going to be my favorite of him! I can't wait to show him these!"

The words slipped from my mouth before I realized what I had said, and I saw Krista visibly flinch.

"Oh! I ... I ...," I stammered unable to think of the words I needed to say to cover my horrible blunder.

I ran out the room, down the stairs and into the garage. Tears were streaming down my face. I pushed the door opener on my way past, hopped on the motorcycle and pushed it out onto the carport.

I jump-started the engine and took off down the road into the dark night. I didn't really know where I was going this time until I turned off on the cemetery road. Once I arrived inside the gates I turned the bike off and strode out across the grounds toward Vance's grave. I needed to just be near him.

The way was lit dimly by the moon, and I noticed as I approached Vance's grave that he already had another visitor, which surprised me.

"Hello?" I called out to the person in the shadows, not wishing to alarm them with my late-night arrival.

The figure didn't move, and I began to wonder if my eyes were playing tricks on me.

"Hello?" I called out again. "Who's there?"

The figure did turn this time, stepping from the shadows, into the moonlight.

My blood froze. "Vance?" I said hoarsely, recognizing him instantly along with the tuxedo he had been buried in.

My eyes darted quickly over to the grave next to him, and I could see that the earth had been moved and there was now a slight depression into the ground.

"Vance!" I called out, running full speed to throw my arms around him, crushing him to me in a desperate grip.

He was covered in dirt, but I didn't care, and I kissed him full on the mouth, tangling my hands into his hair.

"You're alive! You're alive!" I said hugging him, and tears of joy began streaming down my face.

He reached up to grab hold of both of my arms, pulling them away from him so he could step back and look at me.

"Who are you?" he said roughly.

About the Author

Lacey Weatherford has always had a love of books. She wanted to become a writer after reading her first novel at the age of eight.

Lacey resides in Arizona, where she lives with her husband and six children, one son-in-law and their energetic schnauzer, Sophie. When she's not supporting her kids at their music/sporting events she spends her time writing, reading, and blogging.

Visit the official websites at:
http://www.ofwitchesandwarlocks.com
http://www.laceyweatherfordbooks.com
Follow Lacey on Twitter at:
http://twitter.com/LMWeatherford

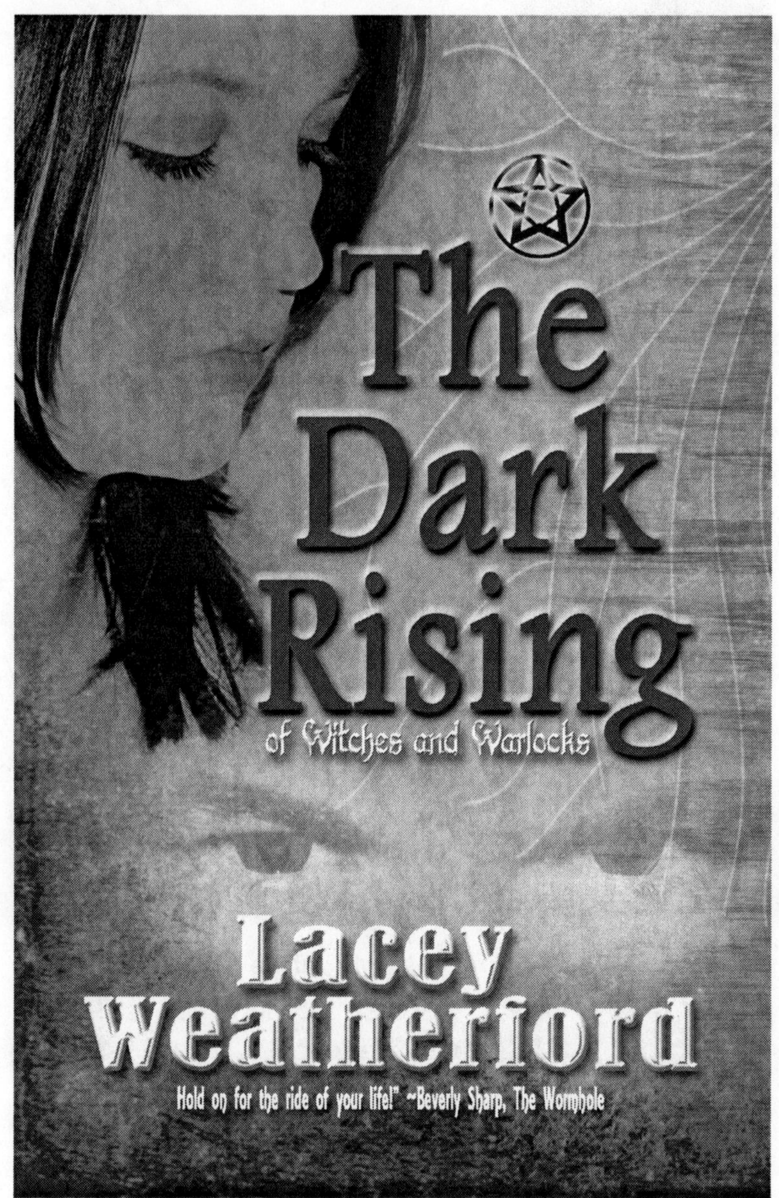
The Dark Rising
of Witches and Warlocks
Lacey Weatherford
Hold on for the ride of your life!" ~Beverly Sharp, The Wormhole

When Portia Mullins discovers the love of her life is still alive her heart soars. But reality sets in immediately causing it to plummet when she realizes he doesn't remember his past life with her. Unwilling to give up, she embarks on a loving quest to restore his life to him.

Vance Mangum sees the beautiful girl claiming to be his wife, and while he can't remember her, he can't deny the intense pull he feels between them. Not knowing where else to turn, he agrees to give her the time she's asked for and to assist her in the effort to recover his memories.

The two quickly reconnect, but dark surprises are lurking in the wings when Vance discovers a desperate longing for something he feels he can't withstand. Will he be able to resist? Or will evil raise its head in a new form, leaving Portia as the prey of the very man her heart desires?

Darkness reigns supreme in this haunting tale of love and desperation, Of Witches and Warlocks, The Dark Rising.

Once again, Lacey Weatherford has demonstrated her ability to craft a magnificent tale that is dark and dangerous, but filled with love and hope. Of Witches and Warlocks continues with The Dark Rising and Wow! You are not ready for this one! Hold on for the ride of your life as Portia and Vance continue to battle the darkness. Will their love be enough? Wonderfully written. Couldn't put it down!
~ Beverly Sharp, The Wormhole

CPSIA information can be obtained at www.ICGtesting.com
Printed in the USA
LVOW111721070212

267543LV00001B/90/P